What kind of woman would turn to her ex-lover to find her husband?

It was no dream. There Joanna was in Drew's office, dressed as he'd seen her a thousand times so many years ago. "I'm sorry, Jo, I can't take your case."

Instantly she turned on her heel, but before she could open the door, his hand covered hers. When she jerked away from his touch, he spun her around to face him. He stared into her eyes and held her gaze.

"It won't be easy," he said. "I'll be asking questions you'll hate me for asking. Before I'm finished, I'll know more about your life with Evan than either of us wants me to know."

"Drew, please—" She tugged away from him, but he held her tight.

They were standing face-to-face, so close he could feel her breath on his face, see the streaks of light in her eyes. "If I don't find him, you'll blame me. If I find him dead, you'll blame me...."

"Just find him, Drew." Her voice cracked and for one reckless moment he thought he might kiss her. "I have to know."

At that moment answers were something Drew didn't have. One question occupied his mind—*What kind of fool was I to ever let you go?*

Dear Reader,

You're about to rejoin THE SPENCER BROTHERS—cowboys, brothers, but as different as night and day. Cole is the rough 'n rugged rancher, while Drew is the urban cowboy. Years ago they'd put their differences aside and opened a P.I. agency offering everything from detectives to bodyguards. But then Drew Spencer walked away from it all...until now....

Laura Gordon brings you the stories of two remarkable brothers bound by blood but separated by spirit.

Laura loves to hear from her readers. Write her at P.O. Box 55192, Grand Junction, CO 81505.

Happy reading!

Debra Matteucci
Senior Editor & Editorial Coordinator
Harlequin Books
300 East 42nd Street
New York, NY 10017

Spencer's Bride

Laura Gordon

Harlequin Books

TORONTO • NEW YORK • LONDON
AMSTERDAM • PARIS • SYDNEY • HAMBURG
STOCKHOLM • ATHENS • TOKYO • MILAN
MADRID • WARSAW • BUDAPEST • AUCKLAND

For Connor Matthew Chavez
my newest hero
who, like his father,
gets better looking every day

With appreciation and affection for my editor,
Bonnie Crisalli, for her tireless efforts and
valuable expertise

ISBN 0-373-22396-X

SPENCER'S BRIDE

This edition published by arrangement with Harlequin Books S.A.

Printed in U.S.A.

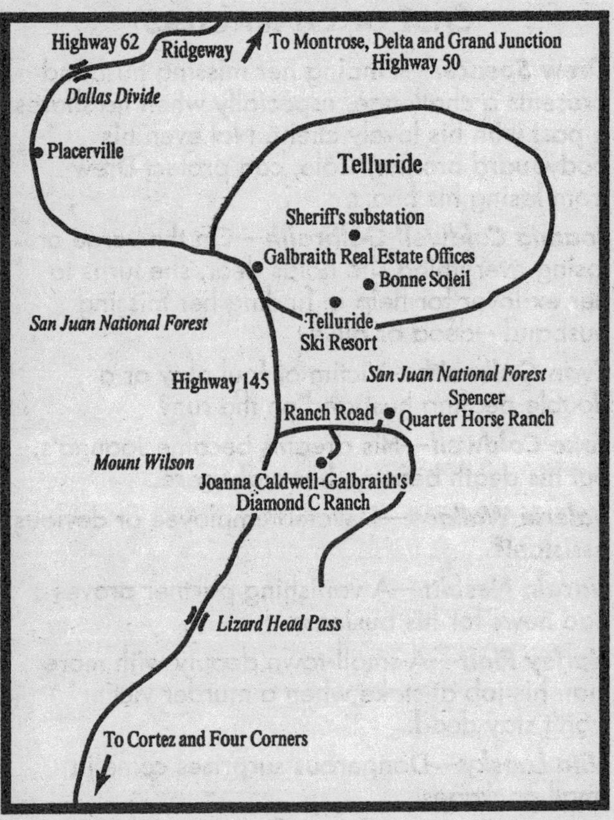
Highway 62
Ridgeway
To Montrose, Delta and Grand Junction
Highway 50
Dallas Divide
Placerville
Telluride
Sheriff's substation
Galbraith Real Estate Offices
Bonne Soleil
Telluride
Ski Resort
San Juan National Forest
Highway 145
San Juan National Forest
Spencer
Quarter Horse Ranch
Ranch Road
Mount Wilson
Joanna Caldwell-Galbraith's
Diamond C Ranch
Lizard Head Pass
To Cortez and Four Corners

CAST OF CHARACTERS

Drew Spencer—Finding her missing husband presents a challenge, especially when he shares a past with his lovely client. Not even his bodyguard brother, Cole, can protect Drew from losing his heart.

Joanna Caldwell-Galbraith—On the verge of losing everything she holds dear, she turns to her ex-lover for help in finding her missing husband—dead or alive.

Evan Galbraith—Victim of foul play or a double-dealing husband on the run?

Jake Caldwell—His dreams became Joanna's, but his death became her nightmare.

Valerie Wallace—Devoted employee or devious assistant?

Lincoln Nesbitt—A vanishing partner proves bad news for his business.

Harley Platt—A small-town deputy with more than his job at stake when a murder victim won't stay dead.

Nita Lansky—Dangerous surprises come in small packages.

Calder Johannsen—A name that means many things to many people, and murder could be one of them.

Prologue

The strains of Pachelbel's Canon in D faded as the bridesmaid, dressed in a simple gown the color of a cloudless Rocky Mountain sky, took her place at the altar. After a second of silence, the organist signaled the guests to rise with the first chord of the familiar processional.

Here comes the bride...

At the sight of her, framed by the arched doorway at the back of the chapel, murmurs of subdued approval rippled down both sides of the aisle. Drew didn't make a sound, and he couldn't take his eyes off her as she began her steady, graceful journey to the front of the chapel.

She wore ivory. A fitted gown, stunning in its simplicity. Elegant. Classic. Understated. A perfect reflection of the woman who'd chosen it.

In place of a veil or a hat, she wore miniature roses arranged around the chignon at her nape, the creamy length of her neck beautifully revealed.

Drew preferred her hair down, cascading past her shoulders in luminous mahogany curves. Without closing his eyes, he could envision the way her hair looked fanned across his pillow in silky disarray.

The thought of her in his bed made his mouth go dry.

From where he stood, he could see the sparks of excitement in her dark eyes and the blush of anticipation on her high, sculpted cheeks. What was she thinking?

As she moved closer, Drew found himself struck anew by her grace. Whether in two-inch heels or in a pair of dusty boots, the woman carried herself with the poise of a dancer.

He tried to remember not knowing her, but his memory didn't reach back that far. From grammar school to college, she'd always been there. Friends, lovers, even rivals, once.

Remembering that scrawny twelve-year-old in lopsided pigtails and a mouthful of braces, he smiled inside, thinking of how small and vulnerable she'd looked riding into the show ring. That day, he'd tried to ignore her. After all, at the advanced age of thirteen and a half, he'd had more important preoccupations, until he found himself in the unenviable position of having to compete head-to-head with her in the open class. From that day on, she'd commanded his complete attention.

Even then, everyone knew Joanna Caldwell was special. On horseback, the awkward girl disappeared and the confident young woman took over. She rode with complete control, with a seemingly effortless ease that even now made Drew itch with envy. With a velvet touch on the reins and leg cues all but invisible to even the most experienced judges' eyes, she won the blue ribbon and Drew's grudging respect that day.

Three years later, she'd won his heart.

Someone behind him coughed, dragging his attention to the present. His eyes shifted for the first time to the silver-haired man at Joanna's side.

Jake, he wanted to shout. *Old friend, am I dreaming?*

When his gaze shifted to hers, their eyes met for a heart-stopping moment before she blinked and looked away, seeming as startled as if someone across the room had shouted an obscenity.

I can't go through with this. What the hell had made him think he could? *Jake, tell me this isn't happening!*

Remarkably, she seemed completely composed. Only someone who knew her smile the way Drew did would have noticed the change, the almost imperceptible tremor at the corner of her mouth.

At the altar, the late summer sunlight spilled through the high, arched windows behind the pulpit, bathing the bride in a warm gold light. Drew felt his breath hitch in his chest when Jake kissed her cheek and gave her hand to the man with the pale pink rosebud in his lapel. The man with the too-easy smile. The man standing beside Joanna Caldwell at the altar. The wrong man.

Chapter One

Joanna had never seen Harley Platt looking more somber than he did this morning, standing in her doorway, his pale brown eyes downcast and his tan San Miguel County sheriff's hat in his hand. From that first night, when she'd been forced to realize that Evan wasn't coming home, she'd dreaded this moment. Dreaded seeing this expression on any officer's face.

"Come in, Harley," she said and pushed the screen door open. At five-ten or eleven, the deputy wasn't an especially big man, and yet the shadow he cast this morning seemed to drive a chill into every corner of the small, usually bright and cheerful living room.

Joanna stood with her arms wrapped around herself and her stomach churning. She didn't think to offer him a chair. "What is it, Harley?" she asked, unable to bear the suspense any longer. "Have they found... something?"

He shook his head. "No."

She exhaled the breath she'd been holding, wishing she could feel relieved, but knowing by the dark look on the deputy's face that there was more. The knot of anxiety that swelled in her chest pushed against her heart like a fist, and the muscles in her neck and shoulders burned with a tension that had been steadily building for weeks.

"I wish there was some way to make this easier," he began tentatively.

Would anything ever be easy again? "Just tell me, Harley, please..." She knew he meant well, but his timidity was pure torture. "You just said they haven't found... anything—" they both knew she meant Evan's body "—so how bad can it be?"

"The decision has been made to suspend the search."

"What!" If he'd told her Evan was outside on the porch, she couldn't have been more shocked. "But this is crazy! They can't!" But then, hadn't this possibility already occurred to her? Hadn't she considered, at least in some distant corner of her mind, that it might come to this eventually? *Eventually!* But not now! Not when she alone knew just how high the stakes had risen.

"I can't believe you're just giving up on him." She sank down into one of the winged chairs beside the native stone fireplace—the chair she still considered Jake's—and gripped the armrest in an attempt to still the dizziness that swarmed over her.

"No one's giving up," Harley assured her, his voice low and firm, as though he thought he could somehow calm her.

"But to just call off the search... I could understand if the weather had turned, if a storm or a blizzard forced this—" She glared at him. "For God's sakes, Harley, it's the middle of summer! Warm. Dry. You'll never have better conditions. You have to tell them to keep looking. They can't do this!" But the fact was, they had, and that only meant one thing, that they'd given up on finding Evan alive.

"It isn't what you're thinking..." It was as though he'd heard her thoughts.

"Oh? Then what is it? Explain it to me, Harley. Because nothing you've told me makes any sense."

A sigh slipped out of him, and the dark shadows around his eyes showed it had been too long since he'd had a full night's sleep. Despite her growing irritation with the agency he represented, Joanna couldn't help feeling compassion for Harley's situation.

"The case is still open," he said. "We're still hoping to find Evan. But we just don't have the resources to keep up the all-out effort that's been going on day and night for the past month."

She opened her mouth to tell him it had only been three weeks, but he didn't give her the chance.

"In the meantime, we have other emergencies to deal with, other people in trouble who need our help and the help of all the other people and agencies who have been working to find Evan. Like the Civil Air Patrol," he added pointedly, immediately triggering in Joanna's mind the image of the photographs she'd seen on the news last night of the family whose single-engine plane had crashed somewhere in the mountains between Telluride and Aspen.

Joanna felt sick when she remembered the faces in the picture. The young pilot, his wife and their two freckle-faced sons had been all smiles. "Has anyone made it to the crash site yet?"

He shook his head, and Joanna felt a deep helplessness filling her. She had to fight back the tears that seemed to come far too easily these days. "I shouldn't have blown up at you, Harley. I'm sorry."

"It's all right. We're all under a lot of stress. Just remember that we're not giving up on finding Evan."

She could only nod, feeling suddenly more bone-tired and heavyhearted than she'd ever imagined a healthy woman of not quite thirty-one could feel. "It's all just...so frustrating. The not knowing—"

He put his hand on her arm and his expression softened, reminding her that he'd been a family friend for as long as she could remember. "All the information about Evan, his picture and the description of his car is still out there," he said. "Every law enforcement agency from here to California has been alerted, and the FBI's computer system is the link between all of them. Trust me, Joanna, if any lead comes in from any direction, we'll be on top of it."

She tried to feel heartened by his assurances, but the trouble was, there hadn't been any leads since that first night, when the leather jacket Evan had been wearing the evening he'd left his office in Telluride had been found in the ditch along the highway just south of Ridgeway. That night, everyone involved in the search assumed the jacket would be the beginning and that, as more evidence began to surface, it would be only a matter of time before Evan was located.

Unfortunately, no more evidence had been found. Day after day, the search had continued without another clue. Evan seemed to have vanished without a trace.

"So what happens now?"

"Well, for starters, Sheriff Miller wants more samples." His expression said he hated asking.

"Of course. You can take anything you need." It wasn't the first time they'd asked for some of Evan's belongings. In addition to the jacket found along the highway, they'd used other articles of clothing and even a bottle of Evan's cologne to help the search dogs become more keenly aware of his scent.

This morning, it was hair samples for the lab.

With Harley behind her, Joanna moved woodenly down the hallway to the bedroom she and Evan had shared as man and wife for a little less than ten months.

"His brush and comb are in there." She pointed to the bathroom. "The drawer on the right was...is his." She waited in the bedroom while Harley gathered what he needed from the vanity.

When he emerged a few minutes later, she noticed the edge of a Ziploc bag protruding from his jacket pocket, and she suppressed a shudder.

At the door, Harley said, "Just remember, if there's anything, anything at all..."

She offered him a smile that had become almost automatic in response to the outpouring of kindness that had never stopped coming from her friends—Nita, Valerie, Peggy and Doc Anderson, and especially from her closest neighbor, Bess Spencer.

Bess had called every day without fail, just "checking in," as she phrased it. That checking in had also included food—casseroles and pies every other day or so, and on the day the search had been concentrated around the house, a twenty-five-pound turkey with all the trimmings to help feed the hungry volunteers. And whether it had been Bess's idea or their own, from the day Evan had been declared a missing person, the hired men from the Spencer ranch, Seth James and Pete Hawthorn, had, without her asking and without any mention of pay, swung by every evening to take over the chores on the Diamond C.

"Thanks, Harley. Everyone has already done so much. You've been especially kind, making trips all the way out here to keep me informed."

"I could help a lot more, if you'd let me. I've managed to stash away a little here and there, from time to time. All you have to do is say the word, Joanna...."

Embarrassed for both of them, she shook her head. It wasn't the first time he'd tried to offer her money. A close-knit community could be a blessing in times of crisis, but hiding one's dirty laundry could prove nearly impossible.

"Thanks for the offer, Harley. But as I've said before, I'm fine." Trying for her most hopeful tone, she added, "My practice is keeping me busy, and I haven't had to rob the poor box yet."

His grim expression said her attempt at levity had failed. "I don't like the idea of you staying out here all alone, either."

"Harley, are you forgetting how long I took care of this place alone when it was just Jake and I and he had that long hospital stay?"

Grudgingly, he remembered. "But with no family, not even in-laws..."

Like Joanna, Evan had no real family. His parents had both been in their late forties when they'd adopted him at the age of eleven. Ill health claimed his father while Evan was still in college, and a couple of years ago, his adopted mother suffered a massive and deadly stroke. If Evan knew, or was at all interested, in his birth parents, he'd never confided as much to Joanna. His lack of curiosity astounded her. She remembered nagging Jake from the time she could form questions about the details of her absentee parents.

"It just doesn't seem fair," Harley muttered, "what with you losing Jake such a short while ago."

Five months and three days, to be exact. And if he'd given her a couple more minutes, she could have narrowed it down to the number of hours since that awful afternoon she'd found Jake on the floor in the garage beside his workbench. No one had heard the shot, but the gun he'd been cleaning was still in his hand, the gun that had accidentally discharged, taking his life, and taking from Joanna not only her grandfather but her dearest friend and only family.

She let the screen door swing closed and walked with him across the porch and out to where the cruiser was parked in the circle driveway. "I appreciate you coming out, Harley. Be talking to you soon."

"Are you sure there's no one you want me to call?"

She shook her head. "No. But thanks for asking. I'm doing just fine. Really." But even as she spoke them, her words seemed to ring hollow. There was someone. Someone she'd been thinking of calling, longing to talk to since this nightmare began, since it had become clear to everyone that something terribly, terribly wrong had happened. Someone she'd longed to turn to when she'd discovered that Evan had disappeared, leaving behind a leather jacket in a ditch and a quagmire of financial misdealings that, unless Joanna acted quickly, would probably cost her everything—the ranch Jake had taught her to love so deeply, the meager savings he'd insisted she maintain even after she'd married, the only home she'd ever known. Everything.

In a way, it felt like losing Jake twice.

"Call if you need anything," Harley reminded her unnecessarily before he left.

"Thanks. I will." She watched the cruiser pull away and returned his wave, telling herself she could never call on Harley for real support, not in the way he meant, anyway. He'd been a good friend throughout this ordeal, but a woman could sense when a man wanted more than friendship, and she had no intention of misleading Harley Platt by allowing him to foster any misconceptions about a possible relationship.

Aside from the fact that she felt no attraction to Harley, she *was* still a married woman, after all.

Standing there alone, watching the deputy's car kick up dust on the winding ranch road, she heard his promise to call with new leads ringing through her mind. Deep in her heart, she held out little hope for any new leads. In almost a month of intensive searching and investigating, there hadn't been a single sighting. What chance could there be of finding a lead now that the search for Evan had been officially suspended?

Her eyes drifted from the road, and she gazed absently at the peaks in the distance. Summer was already half-over, and the time had come to face the hard reality of her situation. Evan might never be found. Whether he'd left of his own accord or been the victim of foul play, she might never know. He might even be dead.

"It's the uncertainty," she'd said last night when Bess Spencer had called. "The not knowing." Remembering her words allowed the wave of guilt she'd been warding off for weeks to engulf her. *What kind of wife considers not knowing if her husband is dead worse than knowing that he is? A wife in name only. A wife betrayed,* she reminded herself quickly as she strode to her pickup and climbed in to begin her rounds. A wife who'd learned the hard way that she couldn't trust her husband any further than she could toss him.

Shoving the keys into the ignition switch and gunning the engine to life, she remembered how Jake had tried to warn her. Unfortunately, she'd been too stubborn and too ashamed to admit she'd made a mistake. With stinging irony, she remembered how, in a way, it had been for Jake's sake that she'd finally agreed to marry Evan—not that she'd ever let on to either of them.

And not that it did any good to dwell on that now, she told herself as she negotiated the road. "Well, what should I do now, Jake?" she murmured, blinking back the hot tears that welled in her eyes and made the gravel road in front of her a swirling ribbon of chalky brown.

She swiped at her eyes and glanced back to the road just in time to see a cow and a newborn calf standing squarely in her path.

Slamming on the brakes hard enough to send a jolt of pain through her ankle, Joanna narrowly avoided slamming into the pair. She didn't, however, manage to avoid smacking her forehead on the rearview mirror. The pain brought fresh tears to her eyes.

She sat behind the wheel, shaking. Her tears were instantly replaced with dry-eyed anger. For a full minute, she let fly a string of swear words that would have made even Jake blush.

By the time she finished turning the air blue, the cows had wandered into the meadow and her heart was hammering so hard she could feel it in her ears.

"Damn it, Jo," she scolded herself, putting the truck in gear. "Enough is enough." Although she hadn't been going fast enough to do anything more than bruise the mother, she knew that if she'd hit the small white-faced calf, she'd have probably killed it. The close call and her burst of emotion seemed to have provided the jolt she needed to make the decision.

That's it, she thought as she put the truck in gear. *You've wallowed in your misery long enough, Joanna Caldwell! It's time to stop crying and take the situation in hand and deal with it.*

As she drove, she called Doc Anderson on the car phone and asked him to cover for her while she was gone. She took a minute to fill him in on the filly whose leg she'd splinted yesterday and the Jessups' aging collie she'd admitted to the animal hospital in Ridgeway last night. "Lady should be all right," she told the veterinarian, who had gone into semiretirement and shifted most of his caseload to Joanna over a year ago. "Just be sure to keep the wound clean and dry."

Next, she called Frank Jessup to inform him that Al Anderson would be checking on Lady in her absence. While she had Frank on the phone, she asked him to keep an eye on the Diamond C. As she made the rest of her calls, leaving a message for Harley, canceling appointments and informing her answering service that she'd be out of touch for a couple of days, she thought about calling Drew Spencer.

But by the time she reached the highway, she'd changed her mind. If he was going to refuse to help her, he'd have to do it face-to-face, she decided—not that seeing her would stop him. After all, it wasn't like he hadn't turned her down before.

DREW HELD THE PHONE between his ear and his shoulder as he scribbled notes on the legal pad in front of him. "Well, what do you think, Cole? We both know it's not our kind of case, but if you think we should consider it, I'm game." He dropped his pen and swiveled in his chair to stare out the large, octagon-shaped window behind his desk as he listened to his brother tick off the pros and cons of the case they'd been considering all week.

Downtown Denver rush hour was moving at an unusually smooth pace and seemed lighter than most days. But then, it *was* Friday, and anyone who could had probably taken off early to get a jump on the weekend. Which was exactly what Drew had intended to do, but he'd promised the prospective client an answer, and the decision about this particular case had to be made before he could leave.

"According to our client, he never even met the woman," Cole replied. "Now, all we have to do is prove it."

"But I'm not sure we can." Drew had skimmed the lab report earlier in the day. "Or that we want to even try."

"My thoughts exactly."

"So we decline this one?"

"That's my vote."

"I'll let him know." Drew heard his sister-in-law's voice in the background. "Something tells me I'm cutting in on family time."

Cole's deep laughter came over the line. "Anne says to tell you this branch of the Spencer Agency is closed for the day, but the bar is open and there's a T-bone with your name on it, if you'd like to drop by on your way home."

It was tempting. He'd been hard at it the entire day—most of it behind his desk—and he still had a stack of paperwork to attend to before he could leave. "I have a few loose ends to tie up before I leave."

"I envy you," Cole said. "Not the paperwork, of course. But I wouldn't mind spending a day or two with a fly rod in my hand."

"I appreciate you holding down the fort, buddy," Drew told him.

"You've earned it. And besides, in a couple of weeks I'll be asking you to return the favor."

"No problem. I'll throw the biggest ones back to give you an even chance." If he closed his eyes, he could see the secluded trout stream where he intended to spend the next seventy-two hours in sweet oblivion, listening to nothing more complicated than the hiss of a fly line over water so crystal-clear you could see the streambed with equal clarity in three inches or three feet of water.

"What about that steak?" Cole asked.

"I'll take a rain check, but tell Anne thanks anyway."

Before he hung up, Drew thanked his brother again for taking over the responsibility for the agency they shared in equal partnership. He hung up the phone and turned his attention to the stack of work still waiting for him.

With a sigh, he opened the first file and made his closing notes on a thorny custody case that had demanded his attention for the past five months. The highly emotional case had sapped him of more energy than he cared to admit.

If he'd had more time, he'd have preferred to spend this impromptu vacation at his family's ranch in southwestern Colorado, just outside Telluride. But with Cole now back at the agency, business had never been better, and Drew didn't feel he could justify the time away from work the long drive to the Spencer ranch would take.

It was the drive and the time restraints, he argued with an inner voice, and not the fear of running into Joanna that kept him from going home. She was someone else's wife, and that was all there was to it. He'd accepted it, finally. And the fact that he'd only been home once since her wedding had nothing to do with anything but the volume of his business.

"No more calls tonight, Francine," he said, pressing the button on his phone that allowed him to talk to his secretary in the outer office. "And as soon as you've finished proofing the final report for the Preston case, why don't you call it a night?"

"I've already finished that file," Francine's pleasant voice came back. "And I've been clearing my desk of a few other things. It shouldn't take me much longer. Want me to lock up when I leave?"

"No. Sid Preston might be dropping by to settle his account," he said. "I want him to be able to get in."

He reached out to disconnect them, but before he could, she added "Hey, Drew, have a nice vacation, okay? Forget about this place for a while. Believe it or not, we'll survive a day or two without you, and I'll see to it that Cole stays out of trouble while you're gone."

"Not an easy task." He laughed. "But if anyone can do it..."

For the next hour, Drew immersed himself in the paperwork he was determined to finish before leaving town. When he heard his office door open, he didn't look up. "All finished?" He glanced up to see the woman he'd mistaken for his secretary and the words, "Have a nice weekend," froze in his throat.

"Hello, Drew."

He stared at her, disbelieving, imagining for one crazy moment that he might have dozed off and dreamed her. Her hair hung in soft waves past her shoulders. She was dressed as he'd seen her a thousand times, in blue jeans and a white cotton blouse and brown boots. But for some reason, he was struck anew by her natural beauty. He couldn't seem to take his eyes off her.

"May I come in?"

"Of course." He rose and started toward her. She met him halfway, and as natural as it might have been for them to embrace, neither made a move into the other's arms.

"How are you?"

She blinked. "Then you really haven't heard." It might have been a question, but she didn't give him time to respond. "I thought Bess might have called you."

Her complexion was still flawless, but the healthy glow he remembered had dimmed and she seemed pale, almost wan. He noticed faint shadows beneath her eyes, and he remembered they only appeared when she'd been crying.

His heart contracted at the thought of her in tears. He'd known her long enough to know she didn't shed them without good reason.

"Sit down, Joanna," he said and, taking her elbow, ushered her into one of the two matching leather chairs opposite his desk.

He stood facing her, leaning against the desk with his arms crossed. "Can I get you something?"

"A glass of water, if it's no trouble."

He brought her bottled water and a glass with ice from the wet bar across the room. She thanked him. Polite, distant, composed. If only more of his clients handled trouble with such grace. He watched her drink, and despite the picture she presented, he detected an uncharacteristic vulnerability that seemed to penetrate her cool reserve.

"I was surprised to find you here this late."

"Did you just get in?"

She nodded. "I drove straight through."

"Alone?"

"Yes."

If I were her husband, she damn sure wouldn't go visiting her former lover alone. Oh, Joanna, a voice from his heart whispered. *What kind of fool would ever let you go?*

When she lifted her gaze to meet his, he saw his own reflection in her eyes.

Chapter Two

To Joanna, it seemed she'd been talking nonstop for an hour. "And that's where it stands now," she said finally. "No one has seen or heard from Evan. His car hasn't been found. We have no clues as to where he went or why, and Harley Platt told me this morning that the search for him has been suspended." The recounting of events since the night of Evan's mysterious disappearance seemed to tap the final reserves of her physical and emotional energy.

"Harley insists the sheriff's department hasn't given up, but I know nothing will happen now without convincing evidence that Evan can be found." *Alive,* she added silently, although the look on Drew's face said he'd heard her unspoken fear.

Somehow she'd always felt he knew what she wanted to say before she said it, and this evening was no exception. Unable to stand even his perceived intrusion into her private thoughts, she rose and walked to the window, then gazed at the city beyond the glass.

"I have to know where he is, what's happened to him," she said without turning. "And I'm hoping you'll help me."

For a few minutes, they allowed each other the silence needed for introspection. But even as Joanna watched dusk enfolding the city, she felt Drew's eyes on her. Though she tried to ignore it, the sensation evoked strong feelings of the last time they'd been alone together, just after Jake's funeral.

That night, desperate for the privacy of the darkness in which to confront her seemingly boundless grief, Joanna managed to slip away from the crowd of friends and neighbors gathered in the living room. Outside, assuming she was sheltered by the night and the shadows of a towering pine, she'd allowed her tears to run unchecked for the first time since Jake's death.

Too late, she'd sensed him moving up behind her, and the next thing she knew, she was in his arms.

Never, before or since, had she felt so tempted to damn the consequences and beg Drew to give their love a second chance. But, fortunately, before her pride and her marriage could be sacrificed, a woman stepped onto the porch looking for Drew. At the sound of the stranger's voice, Joanna swallowed the confession that might have irrevocably changed her future.

Something about that voice—the tone or the inflection or the way Drew's expression changed when he heard it—had told Joanna everything.

In a moment of excruciating awareness, she'd known, without him saying a word, that he and the woman were lovers.

The memory of that scrape with emotional disaster renewed Joanna's resolve to keep her dealings with Drew and the Spencer Agency strictly business.

"I need your help," she said simply, turning to face him, her reserve and her confidence partially restored. "I want to hire you to investigate my husband's disappearance."

He opened his mouth to say something, but before he could she cut him off. "I can't pay a retainer, but my practice is growing, and I'm good for monthly payments."

She despised the sympathy she saw soften his expression. "You needn't feel sorry for me, Drew. Believe me, if

I knew anyone else who did the sort of work you do, I'd have called them. But I don't." She moved to the chair, sat down and reached for the water glass to give her something else to look at besides the pair of intense blue eyes that sparked so many dangerous memories. "So, will you take the case or not?"

His smile was sardonic. "How could I refuse such a gracious offer?"

Touché, she thought, but wasn't about to apologize.

"You never were one to pull a punch," he said.

If he was trying to make her squirm, he was doing a great job of it. "I think if this arrangement has a chance of working, we should avoid discussions about the past." *How could I have thought this was a good idea? What kind of woman would turn to her ex-lover to find her husband?*

A desperate woman, an inner voice replied. *A woman on the verge of losing everything. A woman with few options and less time.*

"According to what you've told me," Drew began, tugging her out of her thoughts, "half the law enforcement agencies in the state, including the CBI and the FBI, have been looking for Evan day and night for almost a month. What makes you think I can accomplish what they haven't been able to do?"

She battled against a sinking sense of defeat. "I don't know. I guess I thought private investigators had more latitude in these kinds of things."

"Latitude? What are you implying, Jo? That I break the law?" One dark brow arched and one of the set of matching dimples showed itself in his left cheek.

She glared at him, but in truth she was more angry with herself for noticing how attractive the man was, how sensual and incredibly seductive he was, even more than she'd remembered. "I'm not implying anything," she replied tartly. "So educate me. What do you call it when you delve into someone's affairs without a court order?"

"With a wife's permission, I call it legal, and so would a judge."

"Are you saying you'll do it? You'll take the case?"

He frowned and dropped his pen onto the yellow pad in front of him. He seemed lost in thought for a moment before he said, "No. I can't take your case. But I will give you a referral for someone who will."

"Don't bother." She rose and stalked toward the door. "Sorry to have wasted your time, Drew. Send me a bill. You know my address."

How he managed to close the distance between them so quickly she'd never know, but before she could open the door, his hand was covering hers on the knob. When she jerked away from his touch, he caught her hand and spun her to face him.

He stared into her eyes and held her with his gaze more firmly than with his hand. She felt warm, suddenly too warm, in a way that had nothing to do with the temperature in the air-conditioned room.

"It won't be easy," he said, his voice edged with cold steel that cut straight through her. "I'll be asking questions you'll hate me for asking."

Her hand felt lost in his grip, and her thoughts swirled in a dozen dangerous and forbidden directions. *I am still a married woman,* she reminded herself, and no one knew better than she the pain of broken vows.

"Drew, please—" She tried to tug away from him, but he ignored her halfhearted struggle and held her tight. Despite her resolve not to, she remembered how he'd always seemed to excite and infuriate her, often at the same maddening time.

"Before I'm finished, I'll know more about your life with Evan than either of us wants me to know," he warned.

They were standing face-to-face, so close she could feel his breath on her cheek and watch the tiny streaks of silver sparking in the depths of his blue eyes.

"If I don't find him, you'll blame me. If I find him dead, you'll blame me. If I find—"

"Just find him, Drew. Dead or alive. I told you, I have to know. Can you understand that? I have to know—" When her voice cracked, he released her hand, and for one reckless moment she thought he might kiss her. What's more, she knew if he did, she'd damn well kiss him back.

"Joanna—"

"I need your help, Drew," she cut in quietly. "Will you help me or not?" She vowed not to ask him again.

His eyes bored into hers, and his jaw was set as if in granite. Joanna felt light-headed from the intensity of his stare.

When he finally spoke, she almost jumped. "I need to call Cole," he said, walking to his desk and reaching for the phone. "He'll have to cover for me while I'm gone."

"Then you'll do it? You'll come back with me to Telluride?"

"Yes."

"When?"

"I'll be ready to leave in an hour."

THE CALDWELL RANCH HOUSE seemed smaller than Drew remembered, but he thought perhaps his impression had something to do with his inevitable comparisons to the ranch house where he'd grown up just a few short miles over the ridge of foothills that separated the two properties.

"Nothing much has changed," she said, switching on lights as they walked through the house. "This room," she said, pushing open the door to the bedroom he remembered as hers, "is now the ranch office."

She flipped on an overhead light to reveal a desk and a couple of filing cabinets. The twin bed and straight-backed rocker on the opposite wall indicated that the room also served as a guest room. She stepped into the room and picked up a stack of mail. Her expression grew somber. "If you're trying to get a feel for the situation Evan left behind, you might want to start in here."

"Strange you should put it that way."

"What?" Her dark eyes were wide, and she seemed genuinely unaware of what she'd said.

"You said 'the situation Evan left behind,' implying that Evan might have left of his own volition."

She didn't seem shocked. "To be honest, it's something I've had to consider, and I know the authorities have, too."

"Based on what evidence?"

She thought a minute before saying, "For now, I think I'll let you draw your own conclusions about that—which I'm sure you will when you start going through all this." She made a sweeping gesture with her hand to indicate the stacks of files and what looked like bills piled on the desk and filing cabinets.

"Give me a hint," he said, leaning one hip against the desk and crossing his arms over his chest.

"To begin with, the Diamond C has been in financial trouble for the past couple of years. Beef prices are down, and Jake made a couple of dicey investments that didn't pan out. Evan came up with some...strategies he thought might solve the problem, and it seemed, for a while, at least, we had a solution. But now—" She stopped short.

"But I thought Evan was some sort of genius."

"A financial wizard?"

He nodded.

"Frankly, so did I, and so did Jake. But in the last couple of weeks I've begun to wonder." Until tonight, he'd never heard a note of bitterness in her voice, and it saddened him to hear it now.

"What changed your mind?" Or was that something he'd have to find out on his own, as well?

"It started even before our wedding, but since then..."

"Go on," he prodded, eager to get past the image of Joanna's wedding day.

"Last month Lincoln Nesbitt, Evan's partner in the development, showed up, and I really had my eyes opened."

"What development?"

"Vista Grande."

"Never heard of it."

"Neither has anyone else. That's the problem." She sighed. "Do you really want all the gory details tonight?"

"Is it a long story?"

She released a dry laugh. "Very long. And I'm afraid it doesn't look like there'll be a happy ending."

"Then perhaps we'd better let it ride until tomorrow."

"I agree." She dropped the files on the desk and started for the door. "You know, I think whoever it was that said bad news can wait must have been a rancher."

"I'm sure he was," he agreed even as he made a mental note to carve out some time tomorrow to ask detailed questions about Evan's so-called development scheme and his partner. If it turned out that Evan had met with foul play, Joanna would need all the help she could get in settling her husband's business affairs—affairs that, according to what little she'd told him, seemed extremely complex.

In the hallway, he said, "Jo, I know it's late, but I have to know. Do you think Evan would run out on you?"

"I—I..." she began. "No," she said finally, but not as firmly as he sensed she would have liked. "I don't want to believe Evan could...would do something like that to me." As she spoke she ran a hand over her hair in a gesture Drew found startlingly familiar. She'd never been vain. In fact, she'd always seemed quite unaware of her natural beauty. She'd never been one to primp, either, and she only resorted to toying with her hair when she felt nervous or unsure.

Obviously his question had upset her. "It's beginning," he told her.

"What?"

"The part I told you about before we left Denver, the part where I start digging into your life and you start resenting it."

Her hands went to work again, pulling her hair over one shoulder and absently twisting it into a long, loose braid. "I don't resent anything," she said, but he sensed she did, and it gave him the perfect opening to lay down his most important rule—that he expected nothing less than total honesty from all his clients.

"All I want is for this entire ordeal to be over," she said. The weariness in her voice and the shadows around her eyes had deepened, and he decided that his lecture could wait. It was almost three in the morning, and the face that had seemed a little pale in Denver was now almost chalky white.

"Joanna, are you feeling all right?"

"Why?" She seemed almost angry that he'd asked.

"It's just that you're so pale and—"

"I'm fine, Drew," she said, adjusting her tone to one noticeably more reasonable. "It's just that the past month has been an incredible strain."

"I understand." And he really did. A little over a year ago, he'd had a similar experience when he'd thought Cole and Anne were missing. Although his ordeal had only lasted for one long, winter night, the worry and strain had taken a toll.

"It's been a long day for both of us," he said. "And I want to get an early start in the morning. I'll have to talk to Harley first. Afterward, I'd like to take a look at Evan's office in town. Do you think you could arrange that?"

She nodded. "Of course. Do you want me to pick you up, or should we meet somewhere in Telluride?"

She was throwing him out, he realized. When he'd followed her here in his own car, he'd assumed he'd be staying at the Diamond C. Well, he'd assumed wrong. But what had he expected? She *was* a married woman, after all, and it wouldn't do for her ex-lover to spend the night, despite the fact that half the county probably thought her husband had either deserted her or had met with the kind of foul play that meant he was never coming back.

He scooped his jacket off the chair where he'd dropped it on the way in and followed her to the front door. He'd be lucky if he didn't give Aunt Bess heart failure when he turned up on her doorstep at what she would call "this ungodly hour." But after the shock, he was sure she'd be thoroughly delighted by his surprise visit.

"We'll meet in town," he said. "Is Evan's office still in the Greenwood building?"

She nodded.

"Will eleven be too early?" He wanted to give her a chance to sleep, though he doubted she would.

"I'll be there."

"Afterward, we'll come back here and you can fill me in on all the details." Such as identifying the skeletons he suspected rattled around in Joanna Caldwell-Galbraith's closet.

She said good-night, and he was in his car before he realized he'd left his keys in Evan's office. He'd crossed the yard and was about to step onto the porch when he heard her calling him back, her voice just this side of a scream.

"JOANNA!" he yelled. "Where are you?"

"Back here," came the unsteady reply. "In the bedroom. Hurry!"

He followed her voice to her bedroom, and when he saw the state of it, he understood her panic. The room looked like a twister had blown through the middle of it. The dresser drawers were open, clothes spilling out of every one. The mattress had been pulled off the bed, and the closets had obviously been rifled. The matching nightstands had been similarly violated, and a freestanding mirror lay on its side with the glass shattered.

Joanna stood in the middle of the room, silent and trembling. Her eyes were wide and disbelieving and glistened with angry tears.

"Stay here and don't touch anything," he ordered, and with his hand curled around the small-caliber handgun in his jacket pocket, he left her to make a quick search of each room. When he was certain the intruder wasn't hiding somewhere in the house, he found a flashlight in the kitchen and searched outside.

The darkness afforded him no perspective on when the break-in might have occurred. But since they hadn't encountered another vehicle on the ranch road when they'd driven in, he concluded the intruder had come and gone much earlier.

As soon as he stepped inside the house, he heard Joanna being sick in the bathroom. The sounds coming from the other side of the door caused every protective instinct Drew possessed to reach out to her.

He stood in the hallway, respecting her privacy. After a few minutes, he heard water running, and then silence. He tapped on the door. "Jo, are you all right? Is there anything I can do?"

He heard water running again, and, then a moment later, she opened the door.

"I—I'm all right," she said, but her ashen face said otherwise.

He reached for the terry-cloth robe hanging on the back of the door, draped it around her shoulders and put his arm around her. Slowly he led her down the hall to the living room.

She sank down on the couch and willingly lifted her feet so he could pull her boots off. "Lean back," he ordered gently.

Without argument, she did as he instructed, letting her head fall back against the cushion. Her eyes seemed impossibly sunken, and she was shivering as though it was the middle of January instead of July. He pulled a multicolored afghan off the back of the couch and tucked it around her. When he saw her glance toward the hallway, he was glad he'd thought to close the bedroom door.

"I searched the house and the yard. Whoever did this is gone."

She nodded and closed her eyes, obviously fighting another bout of nausea.

With aspen logs and kindling from the box beside the fireplace, Drew built a fire, and in a few minutes, the room was filled with the glow of yellow flames dancing in the hearth.

By the time he returned from the kitchen with a cup of hot tea, the small room felt cozy and warm. Joanna had stopped shaking, and a bit of color had come into her cheeks. He didn't have the heart to tell her that while he was in the kitchen, he'd discovered the lock on the back door jimmied. Tomorrow he'd call a locksmith, but the chair he'd wedged under the doorknob would suffice for what was left of the night.

"I guess I should call Harley," she said, her voice thin.

"It can wait, at least until daylight. You've been through enough for one night. Right now, I think you need to get some rest."

Remembering there was a linen closet in the hallway, he gathered a pillow and a blanket and brought them into the living room.

"Thank you, Drew," she said softly, handing him her empty cup. "I'm glad you decided to come back with me." That simple statement warmed him in a way that the heat pouring out of the hearth never could.

"I'm glad, too. Now, get some sleep, Jo." He stood in front of the fire, studying the flames for a long time, wondering why someone had taken the time and trouble to break in and had then stopped with one room. Did the break-in have anything to do with Evan's disappearance? Or were the two events coincidental?

He stopped to think about what might have happened if Joanna had been alone when the intruder struck. He shuddered and vowed to make the Diamond C his headquarters while his investigation proceeded. People could think what they wanted. Joanna's safety far outweighed the risk presented by idle gossip. Her visceral reaction tonight worried him. Despite her outward display of strength, the strain caused by weeks of worry was obviously wearing her down.

He turned to study her while she slept and felt his heart going out to the woman who'd once been such a vital part of his life. They'd been good together. So good that all his subsequent relationships had seemed to be only hollow imitations of the real thing.

With the last breakup, he'd had to admit he was the kind of man who could only give his heart once. Immersing himself in work and limiting his socializing to family and friends had helped him if not to forget Joanna, at least to find a balance whereby he could accept and learn to live with his loss. After all, she hadn't given him much choice when she'd made the decision to marry another man.

Joanna, he thought as he settled into Jake's chair to keep vigil while she slept, *my sweet Joanna.*

But she isn't yours any longer, a bitter, inner voice reminded. *She belongs to someone else now.* And whether Evan Galbraith was dead or alive, Drew could not afford to let himself forget Evan was the man Joanna had chosen.

HE AWOKE with a start with the sun in his eyes and his back aching as though he'd slept standing at attention. When his eyes shifted to the blanket folded neatly at one end of the empty couch, his brain immediately cleared and the events of the night came back in a rush of fragmented and disturbing images.

"Joanna!" he called, his voice hoarse from sleep.

"In here," came a quick reply from the kitchen.

He couldn't remember coffee ever smelling better than it did as he walked into the kitchen to find her standing over the stove, attending to a skillet full of scrambled eggs. Her skin glowed with a fresh-from-the-shower scent that almost made him forget the coffee.

When she saw him, her brow furrowed. "You look awful," she said.

"Thank you. I wish I could return the compliment, but you seem to have experienced a miraculous recovery." In fact, she looked quite beautiful.

"It's amazing what a new day and a hot shower can do for a person." Her eyes were bright and clear, and her hair shone like polished mahogany. It pleased him to see that she had dressed in the soft yellow blouse and blue jeans he'd gathered from the bedroom last night after she'd fallen asleep. He hadn't wanted her to face the mess in her bedroom upon waking this morning.

"Go wash up," she said. "Your breakfast is almost ready."

He did as she'd instructed after making a quick trip to his car to grab the athletic bag he'd packed last night before leaving Denver.

Ten minutes later, after a quick bracing shower, a shave and a change of clothes, he felt almost human again. Joanna and his breakfast were in the small, sun-drenched nook Jake had added to the kitchen's south end a few years ago.

The room, enclosed on three sides by glass, offered a view of the mountains that was no less than postcard perfect. "I remember thinking that someday I'd climb every one of them," he admitted. "Now, I'm content just to look out at them a couple of times a year."

"I know what you mean. I try to spend at least a few minutes a day out here. I find it puts things in perspective for me, you know what I mean?"

He did. But if gazing at the mountains offered perspective, the sight of Joanna Caldwell-Galbraith sitting across from him, looking as radiant as the new day, scattered it hopelessly.

When their eyes met and held, he could almost feel her growing discomfort. "I've got to get going," she said as she rose. "While you were in the shower, my service called, and I've got a busy morning."

"Anything serious?"

"Could be. One of Bill Peterson's mares sliced her leg on barbed wire, but it doesn't seem too bad. Don't worry. I'll still make our meeting." She rinsed her cup and set it in the sink. "I called Harley a few minutes ago. Would you mind waiting for him? I expect he'll be here soon." Over her shoulder she said, "Eat your eggs before they get cold," and then she was gone, and Drew found himself already longing to see her again.

"DREW, you son of a gun! How the heck are you?" Harley strode across the yard to meet Drew on the porch.

"Can't complain. How's business with San Miguel's finest?"

Harley shook his head and frowned. "Brisk, to say the least. This here is Inspector Godwin, with the CBI. He came down here to help us out finding Evan. He's going back to Denver this afternoon, but when Joanna called, I thought I might just as well bring him along."

The tall, blond officer, dressed in a blue suit, white shirt and red tie, looked like he'd just stepped from a church pulpit. When he moved to shake Drew's hand, he practically beamed. "I've heard a lot about you, Mr. Spencer."

"It's Drew, and don't believe a word of what this guy tells you."

The younger man nodded. "Yes, sir. But it wasn't from Officer Platt that I heard about you. You see, I did my field training in Denver when you and your brother broke the Lewellyn murder case."

The assistant D.A.'s murder had been in all the newspapers and covered extensively on TV. The case, which had nearly cost Cole and Anne their lives, led to major arrests, including a prominent member of the judicial staff in the juvenile probation department.

"Mrs. Galbraith is lucky to have you working for her."

Drew stared at him a moment, nearly uncomprehending. Somehow hearing Joanna referred to by her married name for the first time jolted him. "She's an old friend," he explained, and turned and walked toward the bedroom with the two men following him.

Half an hour later, when Harley and Inspector Godwin finished examining Joanna's bedroom and dusting the furniture for fingerprints, Drew asked, "Well, what do you think? Could this break-in be related to Evan's disappearance?"

Harley pulled his hat off and ran a hand over the hair that had earned him the nickname Sandy as a kid. "Lots of newcomers in the area. Mostly good people, I guess. But with lots of growth and money, there's also room for crime."

"So I noticed." Drew glanced over his shoulder at the mess left by the intruder.

"I think we lifted a couple of pretty clear prints. It could turn out they belong to the Galbraiths, but we'll run them through the system, and who knows, we might get lucky," the CBI agent said.

Harley concurred. "We could use a little luck in this case," he muttered as the three men walked to the sheriff's cruiser.

"Will you be in town later?" Drew asked Harley. "I need to be brought up to speed on this case. I'm also interested in what you know about Lincoln Nesbitt, Evan's partner." *Good job,* a sardonic inner voice announced, *you've managed to say her husband's name without sneering.*

"I'll be taking Godwin to the airport," Harley explained, "but this afternoon I'll gladly give you the rundown. Check in at the substation, and if I'm not there, they'll call me in."

After they'd gone, Drew turned to the house. Inside, he stood for a moment in the doorway of Joanna and Evan's bedroom. Something deep inside him ached at the thought of them together on the mattress, which at the moment, was still laying askew on the floor. Fighting images that, if he let them, would quickly drive him insane, he began the task of restoring order to the room.

He worked for a solid hour, and when he was finished, he stood surveying his accomplishment. He'd enjoyed doing this for her, and for one unguarded moment he let himself imagine what it would be like if this was his and Joanna's room. He thought about how it had been making love to her.

Excited and tortured at the same time, he vowed to avoid, at all costs, any more dangerous flights of imagination.

She'd hired him to do a job, he reminded himself. Not just any job, but the job of finding her husband and bringing him back to her. Despite the pain of their past, Joanna had sought him out, which meant she still trusted him on some level. She trusted him and, in a way, still considered him a friend, someone to whom she could turn for help. He had an obligation to her, as a client and as a friend, to respect that trust and keep his professional distance, to give her the kind of help she needed and deserved.

The lady wanted her husband back, he told himself as he closed the bedroom door. And one way or another, he'd get the job done before he left her again for what, in all probability, would be the last time.

Chapter Three

It was just a little past noon when Joanna drove into town, but she felt as though she'd already put in a full day. To begin with, the injuries to Bill Peterson's mare turned out to be more serious than he'd described over the phone. Reacting to the pain and the presence of a stranger, the young mare, Kia, had acted anything but angelic, presenting a challenge to Joanna's considerable horse-handling ability.

Even with Bill holding Kia's halter firmly with both hands, the horse had pawed and snorted and fidgeted the entire time. Under normal circumstances, Joanna would have calmed the animal with a sedative. But because Kia was due to deliver her first foal any day, sedation was not an option Joanna felt comfortable taking.

Finally, after a long and exhausting battle of wills with the overwrought animal, Joanna had managed to expertly stitch and bandage the wound. She'd been on her way out of the stall when she'd caught a too-late glimpse of the powerful hind leg coming straight at her. With a single stunning blow, the bulging-bellied palomino had found a way to have the last word.

Twenty minutes later, her hip aching where Kia's hoof had connected and her jeans torn at the knee from her fall, Joanna pulled her truck up beside Drew's car in front of Evan's office.

On the sidewalk, she couldn't help noticing the glaring contrast between their vehicles. A contrast that, in a strange way, illustrated the differences between herself and Drew. Her faded red pickup was battered from miles of hard duty, but as dependable as a pack mule. Jake had bought the white topper that covered the bed and protected her medical equipment from the elements and sometimes served as a mobile emergency animal hospital. And, in exactly the same way her truck reflected her life-style, Drew's low-slung, late-model sports car, with its gleaming chrome trim and custom wheels, spoke no less loudly of his.

With a twinge of deep regret, she thought back to the time when they'd naively believed their differences wouldn't matter, that somehow, despite their differing goals and directions, they'd find a way to share a future together. That love was enough.

As difficult as it was for her to comprehend now, she'd once believed their relationship could survive his leaving Telluride to pursue his career in law. Just as she knew Drew believed her decision to return to the western slope to care for her ailing grandfather represented no more than a temporary inconvenience to their future plans.

How careless they'd been, she thought sadly. How foolish and arrogant, taking for granted what they'd shared, their most precious possession—their young, starry-eyed love.

If only they'd known, she thought.

But unfortunately, by the time a more mature understanding had finally dawned, they'd disappointed and hurt each other in a dozen different ways, and their dream for the future—a dream that had once seemed so easily transformed into reality—had become unattainable.

With a sigh, she pulled herself to the present and prepared to walk into the Greenwood building. At the entrance, her eyes flicked to the patrol car parked at the corner. It was a San Miguel sheriff's cruiser, which meant Harley would be waiting inside, as well.

Automatically every nerve in her body tensed. Would she ever be able to see a cop car again, she wondered, without reliving the ongoing nightmare that had taken over her day-to-day life?

Thoughts of Drew and Harley waiting for her in Evan's office shouldn't have seemed daunting. She'd known them both for years, and both of them were trying their best to help her. Why then, she asked herself, was the prospect of facing them so frightening? Without any more thought, the answer came to her.

Going through Evan's business records with the police had been bad enough. But now, not only the authorities, but Harley, a family friend, and Drew, the man who'd once been her lover, would begin to believe what everyone else in town already suspected, that Evan's disappearance might be directly linked to his financial problems, the problems he'd seemed to think he could solve by marrying Jake Caldwell's granddaughter and exploiting the Diamond C.

Almost too ashamed to admit it even to herself, Joanna realized her pride was about to take another beating.

At the door, she took a second to smooth her hair and dust off her jeans. At least she was still in one piece, a remarkable achievement, she thought, considering that she'd just done battle with a seven-hundred-pound pregnant equine with an attitude.

A glance at her reflection, and then she reached for the door. "Ready or not," she murmured, "it's round two." Compared to dealing with the police and her former lover, the episode with the touchy mare suddenly seemed like a mere warm-up.

Inside the office, Joanna was confronted by Evan's secretary, a neat well-dressed woman whose flawless skin, light brown hair and trim figure gave no clue to her age. Based on what she knew of the woman's family, however, Joanna assumed Nita Lansky had to be somewhere in her mid-forties or early fifties.

"Joanna," Nita said, coming around the desk to greet her. "My goodness, how *are* you, you *poor* dear?" It wasn't something she'd ever admitted to Evan, but sometimes Joanna found Nita's effusive nature a bit overwhelming and even irritating.

Like now, when she reached for Joanna's hand and squeezed it a little too hard and a little too long. "Honey, you *just* look exhausted—pretty as ever, of course," she amended with a big, reassuring smile, "but *so* tired. I can just imagine what you're going through."

Joanna felt an almost irresistible urge to ask Nita how she could *possibly* know what it felt like to have her husband missing for almost a month, but she checked that impulse, saying instead, "I'm fine, Nita. Really." As gracefully as she could, she extracted her hand from Nita's intense grip.

"They only just got here," Nita said, inclining her head toward the door to Evan's office. "When I took coffee into them a few minutes ago, they hardly noticed I was in the room. You know," she said, lowering her voice, "is it just me, or do those two have a personality conflict of some kind?"

Nita was a born snoop, as Joanna well knew. "I'm sure I wouldn't know." It was a lie, but if Nita noticed or took any offense to Joanna's evasion, she didn't allow it to show.

"Well, the air in there seemed pretty icy to me." She rolled her big blue eyes. "Harley's all puffed up like a toad, and your attorney looked like his back was made of steel."

"He's not my attorney," Joanna corrected, regretting it when Nita's brows rose.

"Oh? I'm just sure Harley said Mr. Spencer was a lawyer."

"He is a lawyer, but he's also a private investigator."

Nita's eyes widened. "An investigator! Oh, my! Just like 'Unsolved Mysteries!' "

Joanna didn't respond. She'd been around Nita long enough to know that sometimes the best way to get out of these inquisitions was to be quiet and let the woman assume the worst.

"Is Valerie around?" she asked. Galbraith Realty only had two agents, Evan and Valerie Wallace. Evan listed all kinds of property, business and commercial, while Valerie restricted herself to single-family homes and Telluride's burgeoning condo market.

Nita frowned. "Now that, I wouldn't know," she said. "These days, I *never* know *what* Valerie is doing. Before she left the office on Friday, she said something about an open house this weekend. But you know Valerie. She could be just about anywhere."

Too bad, Joanna thought. "When you see her, could you ask her to call me? Better yet, I'll leave her a message." On the extra message pad lying beside the phone, Joanna scribbled a note, all the while thinking that today, of all days, she could really use Valerie's levelheaded presence in helping explain to Drew the details of the floundering Vista Grande development.

Thoughts of introducing Valerie to Drew, however, sent a ripple of discomfort through her. A feeling as disturbing as it was unexpected.

Joanna truly liked Valerie, she had to remind herself, and until this moment the fact that Valerie was a single woman with a face to match her fashion-model figure had never altered or colored Joanna's perception of her. The sudden edgy feeling seemed to have come out of nowhere, resembling jealousy too closely for Joanna to dignify it with further thought.

Vowing to get a handle on the feeling and send it to whatever distant corner of her mind it had crawled out of, Joanna finished the message and slipped it into the plastic message box attached to Valerie's door.

"Would you like to take a cup of coffee in to your meeting?" Nita asked.

"No, thanks. But if there's soda..." With Evan's approval, Nita kept a refrigerator and a small pantry in the back room well-stocked. The last time she'd looked, Joanna had noticed a couple of bottles of wine, a cabernet sauvignon, the same vintage as the case Evan had special ordered last Christmas.

"What will it be? Cola, diet or lemon lime?"

The lemon lime sounded good, maybe even the perfect remedy for the latest bout of nervous stomach that had struck Joanna again without notice.

"Thanks. But I'll get it," she said. "I'm sure you have work to do."

"Well, not really," Nita admitted, falling in beside Joanna as she walked down the hall. "In fact, I was wondering..." Her voice faded and she hung back in the doorway while Joanna fetched her soda.

"What?"

"Well, I was thinking that maybe I should start looking...that is, maybe I need to think about finding..." Again her voice tapered off.

"A new job?" Joanna finished for her. "Is that what you're trying to say?" she asked, popping the top on the cold aluminum can.

The secretary seemed suddenly unable to look Joanna in the eye. "Well...yes. I mean, I know that sounds just terrible of me. So disloyal."

"It's all right," Joanna assured her as they headed to the reception area together. "I'd be asking the same thing if I were in your position."

Nita blew out a relieved breath. "I knew you'd understand. Thanks, Joanna. You don't know how I've dreaded bringing this up...but with Michael starting college this fall and Debbie making the cheerleader squad again, well, we just need two incomes. Raising a family these days takes so much. I just don't know how anyone does it alone, do you?"

"No, I really don't," Joanna said and meant it. "I'm sorry you've been put in this position, Nita. I know if Evan were here, he'd beg you to stay. You've given so much to the business. Unfortunately, I can't guarantee how much longer Galbraith Realty will be in business."

Nita sighed and her brows drew together. Clearly something else was bothering her, but she couldn't seem to bring herself to reveal it. In a flash of insight, Joanna took her best guess. "Forgive me, Nita, but I just this minute realized that you've been working for the past month without a paycheck. How much do we owe you, anyway?"

Her frank question seemed to embarrass the woman. "Oh, Joanna, I'm so sorry. I guess I just couldn't bring myself to ask." Her gaze dipped away from Joanna's again. "I don't want to add to your troubles, believe me."

Reaching for her purse, Joanna sat in the chair opposite Nita's desk, then withdrew her checkbook. "I don't know if I can cover the entire amount," she said, leaning over so she could use the corner of Nita's desk to write the check. "All right. How much does he—do *we*—owe you?"

Nita sat on the steno chair behind her desk and withdrew a small spiral pad from the top drawer. "Are you sure you really want to know?"

No! Joanna wanted to shout. *I don't want to know any of this! All I want to know is where my husband is and what the hell I'm going to do if he never comes back!* But instead, she nodded.

Nita slid the notebook across the desk, and Joanna almost gasped when she saw the figures Nita had recorded in long neat columns. "But Nita! This is just awful! I had no idea." If what Evan's secretary had written was accurate—and Joanna had no reason to believe it wasn't—he hadn't paid his secretary since March. "But why didn't you say something sooner?"

Nita sighed. "I guess I just haven't had the heart. Evan kept promising he'd make it up to me if I could just hold on a little longer. He said once they closed the deal on Vista Grande... And then when he disappeared..."

"Please, don't say any more, Nita." Ashamed that she'd been irritated with this woman who had tried so hard to be a friend, Joanna felt she'd burst into tears if she heard any more.

How she was going to deal with her anger when the situation her husband had left behind grew worse every day? And how was she to conquer the guilt that anger triggered? she wondered.

She wrote quickly, making the check out for the full amount and wondering, even as she filled in the numbers, if she'd have time to get to the bank this afternoon to deposit the check Bill Peterson had given her this morning. Even with that, she knew she'd need to get an advance on her credit card to cover the amount. Going through the mental calculations made her feel dizzy, and by the time she got to the signature line, her hand was shaking so bad she wondered if the bank would question whether the scrawled handwriting was hers.

She tore the check out of the pad. "I hate to ask you to do this, Nita, but if you could wait until tomorrow to cash this, I would appreciate it."

"Of course."

But when Joanna held the check out to her, she found it intercepted from behind, and she jerked around to see Drew standing behind her with the check in his hand. "What do you think you're doing? Give that back to me!" Joanna snapped.

He smiled a humorless smile at the astonished secretary, reached for Joanna's hand and urged her gently but firmly to her feet. "Excuse us a moment, won't you, Ms. Lansky?"

Nita nodded, her eyes wide and questioning.

When Joanna pulled her hand out of his grasp, he said, "Joanna, please. Just come with me a minute." He took her hand again and pulled her into the hallway.

The door to Evan's office was open, but Joanna was too distracted by Drew's strange behavior to notice Harley inside.

"Would you please tell me what the heck you think you're doing?" She reached for the check, but he pulled it away again before she could grab it. "And will you please give me that check!"

"No. Not until we've had a chance to talk."

"Talk? About what? This has nothing to do with you!" She glared at him, so angry she could spit.

"Oh, but that's where you're wrong."

Joanna stared at him before understanding slowly dawned. She hadn't paid Drew a dime for his services. Nor, come to think of it, had they bothered to discuss his fee, and if he'd spent any time discussing Evan's situation with Harley, he had to know the desperate financial straits she was facing. Seeing her writing a check this size to Nita had probably made him wince. He would realize there'd be nothing left to pay his fee.

Choking back her anger as well as strange nagging disappointment, Joanna told herself that Drew was in business, after all, and he had every right to expect to be paid. So, with that in mind, why did she resent him so much for thinking of money at a time when her entire life was being destroyed right before his eyes?

"You'll get your money, Spencer," she managed to whisper between clenched teeth. "Every penny. Even if I have to work the rest of my life to pay you off!"

They were standing so close that Joanna was sure neither Nita nor Harley could see or hear what was going on between them. But unfortunately, although it protected her privacy, that intimate proximity also afforded Joanna a close-up view of Drew's expression when it turned from shock to red-hot anger.

"Is that what you think I brought you back here to say...that you owed me money?" His face was inches from hers. She could feel his breath on her face and the warmth radiating off his body in angry waves.

The look on his face grew stormier by the second, especially when she snatched the check from his hand. "Well, isn't it?"

He backed up a step. His mouth was set in a grim line, and his deep blue eyes had turned icy. "Go in and talk to Harley," he ordered in a low, barely controlled voice. "He's been waiting for you and he says he doesn't have much time."

"But what about Nita?" she asked, knowing that the secretary had to be straining to hear what was going on in the hall. "She deserves to be paid."

"I intend to take care of that right now."

"Now?"

"Yes. Now, give me that check, and go deal with Harley, will you?"

Joanna glanced over her shoulder to see the deputy pacing the floor in front of Evan's huge oak desk. "Okay. But when this is all over we have to talk about this."

He nodded. "Yeah. Okay. Whatever you say. When it's over..."

He headed toward Nita's desk, and Joanna took a deep breath and steadied herself to deal with Harley.

"Hey, Harley," she said in a voice that told her she was having only limited success pretending she wasn't upset. "Drew said you wanted to talk to me."

"Yeah." He peered past her, and she knew he was dying to see what was going on in the outer office, just as he wanted to know, but wouldn't ask, what had just transpired between her and Drew in the hallway.

"Well?"

His gaze moved to her face. "Oh, yeah, well, I just wanted you to know that we managed to lift a couple of real clear prints off your dresser. We're running them through the system right now. And with luck, we might have a match by tonight or tomorrow."

"Harley, do you think last night had anything to do with Evan's disappearance?"

He shrugged. "At this point, we just don't know. Maybe those prints will give us an answer. But no matter how it turns out, I'll let you know."

Questions without answers, combined with a frustrating waiting game, seemed to be the maddening pattern of her life these days. "Thanks for coming by, Harley," she said as she walked with him to the door of Evan's office. "Would you mind telling Nita I said she could call it a day? Remind her to turn the sign around on her way out, as well."

Harley said he'd be glad to relay the message, and when he left, he closed the office door behind him.

Left alone for a few minutes with her thoughts, Joanna sank like a rag doll into one of the chairs opposite Evan's desk. Her stomach rolled, and she remembered her soda was still on Nita's desk.

When the door opened, she sat up straight. Drew walked toward her and handed her her soda, then stood looking at her when she took a sip.

"Nita's gone home. She said if you need her to call." He gazed intently at her, not allowing her own gaze to slip in any direction. "I gave her a check to cover her wages for the past and through the end of the week." He let the news settle before he added, "I don't want to get into a lengthy discussion of finance right now. We'll settle up when it's time, but for now, we need to move on to more important matters. Like finding Evan." For once, she found herself unable to argue with his logic. She needed to make a number of pressing decisions, including whether or not to close down Galbraith Realty until further notice. Arguing about a check that was probably close to what Drew earned in a week was just not worth the energy. She had to start prioritizing, she told herself, before her inner resources were totally tapped.

But for some reason, the fact that she was alone again with Drew took over every other thought, and all she could think about was putting a safe distance between her and the blue eyes that had always been able to see what she'd just as soon they didn't.

To that end, she stood and moved to the closest of two tall filing cabinets behind Evan's desk. Pulling a drawer open, she asked, "Where do you want to begin?"

"Where would you suggest?"

She thought a moment. "Well, just about anything you want to know about Evan's financial situation is in here. I guess where we start depends on what we're trying to prove."

"Exactly." He crossed to Evan's desk and leaned against it, facing her. "If we're trying to prove Evan met with foul play, we'd be looking for someone who might have had a motive for harming him. But if we suspect Evan might have simply taken off, we'd be looking for a reason—a damn good reason—for him to go to such an extreme."

"But couldn't the same circumstance have motivated either scenario?"

He folded his arms and smiled, driving those wonderful dimples into each side of his face and causing extremely appealing laugh lines to wing out from the corners of his eyes. "You always did have a logical mind, Jo. It was one of the things I always found fascinating about you."

Why his unexpected compliment warmed her to the degree it did, Joanna didn't even want to guess. "I guess I have to blame my training for that. Medicine involves a lot of investigating. Whether trying to pin down a diagnosis or piece together the events that caused an accident or a particular injury, it seems doctors and vets are always on the trail for clues." As she spoke, she focused her attention on Evan's files, doing whatever she could to suppress the old emotions that being around Drew brought to the surface. "Was Harley able to answer some of your questions?"

"Some. But I got the feeling he's still angry that you went to our senior prom with me instead of him."

She couldn't help smiling. "I doubt he even remembers." She certainly hadn't remembered Harley asking. Back then, being on the arm of Drew Spencer would have made accepting any other boy's offer completely out of the question.

"I think you might be surprised how much Harley remembers. He mentioned a high school game when he thought a ref cheated him out of a touchdown."

Joanna shook her head and sighed. "Poor Harley. Still reliving those glory days." She turned to the files again to escape the burning yesterdays she saw in his eyes...and the feelings of guilt that swarmed over her. "So what did Harley tell you about Evan's situation and the development of Diamond C?"

"He gave me some sketchy details, but after talking to him, I'm more convinced than ever that you're the only one who can tell me what was really going on in Evan's life in the weeks and months prior to his disappearance."

"I wouldn't be so sure," she said without thinking.

"What do you mean?"

She hesitated before allowing herself to explain, to take that first real step across the thin line that divided loyalty from betrayal. "Evan spent a lot of time away from home these past few months. He was working very hard on the Vista Grande development."

"What about you? Were you involved in the planning of the development?"

In trying to decide whether her relationship with her husband was relevant to Drew's understanding of this complex financial situation, she had to remind herself again that she'd hired Drew to do a job. The fact that he had once been such an important part of her life would make it harder to keep that perspective, but she had to try.

Drew had agreed to take on the task of finding Evan, yet she wasn't prepared to let him have all the information he needed to do that. And that just didn't make sense. But hadn't he predicted exactly what would happen before they'd left Denver? Damn! She had always hated it when it turned out he was right.

If only there was some way she could start thinking of him as a professional—like a cop or a minister—it might be easier to stop thinking about their shared past and move forward.

But every time she thought back to last night, how he'd put his arms around her and reassured her with his touch, she knew it was hopeless to imagine she could ever think of Drew without remembering what he had been to her—her first love. The man who'd held her heart and her future in his hands. The man who could so easily reclaim her heart if she didn't constantly stand guard.

Chapter Four

She pushed the file drawer closed and faced him squarely. "Evan and I had been extremely involved in our respective professions," she admitted. "Some might even say we'd lost touch with each other, drifted. Ever since Jake's death, Evan had been immersed in getting the Vista Grande development up and running. And with Doc Anderson retiring, my practice was just getting started."

His eyes never left hers. "What are you trying to tell me, Jo?"

She moved away from the cabinet to stand at the window that looked out onto the main thoroughfare through town. "Some might say Evan and I don't have what you'd call... the best marriage. Especially lately."

"Is that what *you'd* say?"

When she answered yes, it was in a voice just above a whisper and with the sinking feeling that she'd just delivered another blow to the foundations of her already shaky marriage. It wasn't going to be easy to admit, especially to Drew, that the pretty young secretary—Helen something—at the closing company next door would probably know more about Evan's state of mind than his own wife. Or for that matter, Nita or Valerie might be able to discuss Evan's hopes and dreams with more understanding. When she thought about their life together, she felt like a failure.

"Let's start with the development," Drew suggested, drawing her back to the business at hand. "What did you call it? Vista something?"

"Vista Grande," she replied, eager to turn the conversation from her personal life.

"Tell me what you know about Evan's partnership with Lincoln Nesbitt."

"What do you want to know?"

"I guess a good place to start would be an explanation of how a chunk of Diamond C land ended up zoned for development." His frown reflected his disdain, and Joanna couldn't help comparing Drew's reaction to Jake's when Evan had first presented the idea.

"I know. I never thought I'd live to see the day, either. But when Jake finally agreed, Evan didn't waste any time." To expedite the process, he'd hand-delivered the paperwork whenever possible. At times, Joanna wondered if Evan hadn't been operating under the constant fear that Jake might change his mind.

"But how could Jake have agreed to something that would put the ranch at such risk?"

"I'm sure he wouldn't have, if the Diamond C hadn't already been in deep financial trouble. I assure you, it wasn't easy for Jake to admit he could no longer make a go of it. The Diamond C meant more to him than almost anything. He'd poured all his energies and resources into the place for so long, it had become a part of him. But with beef prices falling and taxes getting higher every year, he was fighting a losing battle. By the time Evan approached him with the development scheme, we'd sold off as many animals and pieces of machinery as we could without selling ourselves out of business. In the end, there was nothing left but a few head of cattle and the land itself."

Drew's expression had become somber. "I knew from conversations with my aunt that some of the independent ranchers in this area were having a real struggle surviving, but I had no idea things were that bad for the Diamond C. I'm sorry, Jo," he said quietly. "I wish I'd known Jake needed help. Maybe I could have done something."

She accepted his concern with a heartfelt sigh. "There was no way you could have known."

"I guess since my family's operation is limited almost exclusively to horses, they haven't felt the same crunch as cattle ranchers." His dark lashes dipped his tanned cheeks, and he toyed with a pen on the desk, obviously trying to avoid facing her.

He'd never been entirely comfortable with his family's success, playing down their prosperity with a genuine modesty she found deeply admirable and charming. Although he'd be hard-pressed to admit it, she knew that the quarter horses bred and trained on the Spencer ranch had long been considered a standard of excellence against which breeders across the nation were judged.

"Go on, Joanna," he prodded. "How did your grandfather manage to hang on until Evan came up with this scheme?"

"Well, you know Jake. He always said he'd try anything—once. And he did. Odd jobs, mostly. Small repairs, patching leaky roofs, that sort of thing. He even worked at a convenience store on the highway for a while. When my practice began making a small profit, I added what I could. Unfortunately, by then, it was a case of too little, too late." She sighed and ran a hand through her hair. "You can't imagine how hard it was to get Jake to accept my help."

One side of his mouth quirked into a wry smile. "Oh, I don't know about that. I've always considered myself something of an expert on the depth and breadth of the infamous Caldwell pride."

She felt a warmth traveling to her cheeks again, and this time she was the one who tried to avoid his eyes and the old memories she saw flickering in them. "Jake first met Evan when he called the real estate office looking for an appraiser to give him the figures he needed to obtain another mortgage on the Diamond C. One thing led to another, and before Evan and I had been introduced, he had a pretty good idea of just how desperate things were with the Diamond C. It wasn't long before he came up with his plan." She remember him referring to it as a win-win prospect, a venture with almost no risk, using half the ranch—five hundred acres—to support the rest.

"At first, Jake was dead set against any kind of compromise that included development."

"I'm sure my folks, along with most of the other ranchers in the county, would have reacted the same way. As far as they're concerned, development is a dirty word."

"Exactly. But eventually Evan managed to convince Jake that he only had three options—sell the ranch outright, hold out and hope a miracle occurred to forestall inevitable foreclosure, or try to find a way to successfully develop those acres to generate enough income to pay his property taxes and maintain a working cattle ranch."

"Sounds like pretty good advice, under the circumstances."

"That's what we thought, Jake and I. But a development like the one Evan envisioned—two- to three-acre lots, custom homes, water districts, roads, sewers, sidewalks, greenbelts—you're talking a lot of money just to get it off the ground. And cash was one thing we were always short of."

She sensed him listening intently as she went on to explain how once Evan won Jake's approval, he put things in motion with amazing speed.

"The low-interest consolidation loan he arranged at the bank took the immediate pressure off. Jake was so relieved, he didn't ask a lot of questions about where the money for the loan came from. By then, the stress had already taken a severe toll on Jake's health." She felt guilty, knowing that so much of Jake's battle to keep the ranch solvent came from his desire to leave her the Diamond C debt-free. "How ironic that it wasn't his heart condition but a freak accident that finally killed him."

The sadness on Drew's face reflected Joanna's emotions. She missed Jake every day, and sometimes she wondered if the ache would stop.

"Anyway," she said, after clearing her throat, "Evan secured that loan and then everything seemed to fall into place." *Everything,* included the whirlwind courtship and brief engagement. When he'd invested some of his own money to make some badly needed improvements in the ranch house, Evan had finally convinced her that his interest in the Diamond C was genuine.

"When Evan and I came back from—" she hesitated, disturbed that for some reason she couldn't bring herself to say the word *honeymoon* "—he offered to take over the chore of keeping the books for the ranch. I have to admit, I relinquished the job gladly. Since Jake's first heart attack, I'd been struggling to keep up with that particular chore." In fact, she'd been thinking about asking Evan to take over the business aspect of her practice—the aspect she'd need to focus on even more now that the possibility of losing the Diamond C was imminent.

No more letting accounts ride, she told herself, which would come as a severe blow to those patients who had grown accustomed to Doc Stewart's oh-so-easy payment plans.

"Within a couple of months," she continued, "Evan had lined up a potential capital investor who expressed a desire to come in as a full partner on the development. The investor had no problem with giving Evan all the on-site authority to make decisions, hire construction crews and oversee purchasing of materials. He even seemed amenable to supplying the front money the bank required—money to be held in escrow—so that, in the event the lots didn't sell immediately, there would be an account to start making payments when the note came due."

She walked over to the long wall opposite Evan's desk, where a detailed map of the proposed development still hung.

"Vista Grande," she said, staring at the drawing wistfully. "An appropriate name, don't you think?" With an unsurpassed view of the rugged San Jauns in one direction and a verdant valley in the other, the sites provided the most gorgeous settings this side of heaven. "Did you know that some of those sites were appraised as high as two to three hundred thousand dollars? Can you imagine such a thing?"

Drew smiled. "Do you remember when we used to ride like wild Indians through those hills? We could ride all the way to the base of the ski area without ever crossing blacktop, remember?"

After an answering smile, she said, "Well, our personal playground has become a haven for a whole new generation of residents, Drew, and some of them are very rich. Vista Grande would have attracted the most wealthy, with a golf course, a four-star restaurant, pro shop and, of course, a top-notch indoor-outdoor tennis facility. It would have been one of the most exclusive areas on the western slope, if not in the country. Add in the accessibility to world-class skiing, and Vista Grande had it all."

"Sounds too good to be true," Drew noted.

"And you know what they say about that—if it sounds too good to be true, it isn't. Well, that's what I thought. But when Evan and Lincoln Nesbitt began hammering out the details, I got as excited as anyone. In January, Evan flew to California to finalize the deal. Before his trip, he spent endless days preparing the presentation." And countless nights, she added silently, when his work had kept him from coming home. Eventually, she'd become accustomed to the calls, the apologies and the occasional bouquets of roses that had been Evan's way of making amends for a birthday dinner or some other special occasion missed. Joanna had grown accustomed to being alone, living alone and sleeping alone.

"I think he would have gone to any length to ensure the deal, and in the end, Nesbitt obviously appreciated Evan's efforts, because he agreed to put up the money the bank required to approve the loan."

"It must have been a healthy chunk of cash."

"Almost a million," Joanna said. "Cold cash. It doesn't get much healthier than that, does it?"

When she turned from the map to face him, she saw that he had settled into a chair where he sat with his fingers steepled in front of him, watching her. His clear blue eyes, so intelligent and assessing, looked right at her, as they always had, missing nothing. No detail or implication escaped his astute mind.

To distract herself, Joanna continued. "You should have seen how excited Jake was the day Evan flew back from California. The deal wasn't official, but it was so close."

"But?"

"What do you mean?"

"I sense a very big disclaimer coming."

Go ahead, she told herself. *Just get it over with.* For Drew to help, he had to know the facts. "I know Evan tried to make it work. I really believe—" she *had* to believe "—that it's just a case of him getting in way over his head."

One dark eyebrow arched as Drew waited for her to go on.

"After Jake died..." She sank into the chair behind Evan's desk. "With Nesbitt's down payment, the bank approved a very large line of credit."

She gripped the padded leather arms of Evan's chair. This wasn't disloyal. Drew had to know. Evan had created this mess, if not by malicious intent, then by gross mismanagement. Either way, his mysterious disappearance had cast the situation in the worst possible light. And now, left to her own devices, Joanna had to do whatever she could do to find a way out.

"A few days after Evan's disappearance, a loan officer from the bank called to tell me that Vista Grande's account was... overdrawn." Just saying the words made her feel almost as heartsick as she had that morning.

"It was just awful," she admitted. "I don't think I'll ever forget how the people at the bank stared at me when I walked in to meet with the loan officers."

Unable to sit and wait for his reaction, she stood and walked to the wall map again. "All sorts of crazy thoughts went through my mind. I was even afraid they might arrest me." When her voice cracked, she cursed her lack of courage.

She heard him coming up behind her, but she couldn't bring herself to face him. "I was just so shocked. I didn't know what to say...what to do. I guess maybe I still don't."

His hands were on her shoulders, but still she didn't turn.

"How much?"

"Almost the exact amount of Nesbitt's escrowed funds. Nearly a million." Her mouth went dry, and she couldn't swallow. "Not all of the checks have cleared yet, but of the ones that had, many were simply made out to cash, endorsed by Evan."

"Oh, Joanna, I don't know what to say. I'm so sorry." The hands on her shoulders gently turned her around. She saw that his eyes were filled with deep sympathy. His brows drew together in an almost agonized expression.

He took both of her hands in his. She might have felt self-conscious, and she supposed she should feel ashamed. But she didn't.

With her hands cradled in his, the wild spinning of her personal world seemed to somehow slow for the first time in weeks. And the almost bearable speed felt safe.

A noise from the other room, however, caused her to quickly slide her hands out of his. With everything else that was happening, she couldn't chance someone bursting in on what might appear to be a compromising situation.

"Lincoln Nesbitt had flown in a few days earlier to check on the progress of the development. The morning the loan officer and the president of the bank escorted Lincoln and me into a conference room, I thought Lincoln would die right on the spot. As they went over all the details, I thought for a moment that I might faint. Can you imagine that? Me? Joanna Caldwell, as tough on horseback as any kid in the county, ready to keel over like some hothouse flower exposed to the frost."

He gave her a smile, which faded when he asked, "What about Nesbitt?"

"Lincoln went ballistic. I'd still be spitting suds if Jake had ever heard me use half the words that man started screaming." When his fist had come down on the table, every nerve in Joanna's body had felt the jolt.

"Who else had access to that account?" Drew asked from across the room.

"Just Evan, Lincoln..." she paused, wishing she didn't have to tell him how foolish she'd been. "And me. Evan and Lincoln convinced me to allow them to list me as an officer of their corporation merely as a formality, a convenience so they wouldn't have to bring an outsider in on the deal."

She remembered feeling reservations about having legal responsibility for something she knew so little about. But Evan was her husband, after all. And if you couldn't trust your husband...

"When Lincoln and Evan explained how Jake would have wanted me to step into his role as the third partner in Vista Grande, I agreed."

Drew's expression grew murderous. "I can't believe he did this to you. His own wife!"

Immediately, she felt obliged to defend Evan. "Drew, please...don't jump to conclusions. It's been hard enough dealing with the suspicions of outsiders."

He didn't answer immediately, but finally he released a long sigh and said, "All right, so with the account drained dry, Lincoln's money must be frozen. He can't touch a dime, can he?"

"Right." She wasn't so immersed in her own tangled misery that she couldn't appreciate Drew's immediate grasp of the situation. "Although the first payments on the note weren't due to begin until sometime next fall, with the account already in the red—without so much as an inch of ground broken on the development—the bank had every legal right to seize those funds."

"But that money only covers half the account. What about the rest? And what about you, Jo? Where do you stand? Have you spoken to an attorney?"

She could only offer him a sheepish smile. "Not until now."

His expression relaxed and he gave a short, dry laugh. "I see. Okay. Well, I'm no expert in business law, but with a little research I can at least tell you what your options are. It seems Lincoln has the most to lose, and I imagine the five hundred acres that were rezoned for development will be forfeited to foreclosure."

She sat in the chair he'd vacated, trying to hide the awful truth that shuddered through her. But one look at his face told her he'd already guessed the other shoe was about to drop.

"HE DID WHAT?" he exploded.

"You heard right," she said sadly. "He put up the whole ranch, not just the five hundred acres."

Drew swore for half a minute before he stopped, punched his right hand in his left palm and said, "Sorry. I just can't believe anyone could have convinced Jake to risk the Diamond C that way. Weren't you aware it was being held as collateral? Or was this another one of Evan's brilliant no-risk plans?" The sarcasm in his voice was undisguised.

"Please, Drew. Don't." If he launched into a tirade against Evan, she might feel honor-bound to defend him, and right now, she wasn't sure she had the strength or the heart to do so.

He glared at the map, his mouth clamped shut, his eyes fixed. A tiny muscle flexed rapidly in his jaw. Finally, he turned, pulled a chair around in front of hers and sat down. Their knees almost touched, and when he leaned over and reached for her hands, she almost let loose the tears that had gathered in her eyes.

"I'm just glad Jake isn't here to see this," she said, amazed she'd found her voice and that it didn't crack. He gave her hands a quick squeeze and then released them, rose and walked to the desk where he picked up a yellow pad and made a couple of quick notes.

"All right. Let's go through all the facts one at a time. After we get it all down, we'll see what options are left, if any."

His matter-of-fact approach buoyed her, and when she looked at him, drawing a grid on the paper, she didn't see Drew Spencer, investigator and lawyer. She saw, instead, Drew Spencer, her oldest and dearest friend.

"I just keep thinking Evan will come breezing through that door with a logical explanation for all of this," she admitted.

"Well, for your sake, I guess I hope that happens." His expression, however, said he didn't think she should hold her breath. "In the meantime, let's get to work."

"It isn't easy to accept the fact that the man I married might be an embezzler." It had to be said.

"And like you said, we don't know yet that he is." He dropped the pad on the desk and came to her. "We'll get you through this, Jo. I promise. We'll find a way. It's bad, but it could be worse. You've got to believe that."

Joanna longed to believe, but she knew that if something in her present situation didn't change drastically, and soon, it would mean the loss of everything she'd ever thought of as hers, starting the day she'd been abandoned on her grandfather's doorstep by a mother too weak and irresponsible to live up to her obligations.

Jake had waited to tell her the truth until she was almost eleven. Joanna still remembered every detail of the night he'd come into her room to tell her that her mother was dead. Later, she heard from a close family friend that it had been an overdose. Suicide. Accidental or intended, no one would ever know. It had been difficult for her to accept that she'd been brought into this world by a woman she'd never know.

But even more than her own loss, Joanna resented her mother for the pain she'd inflicted upon Jake. His daughter's death had affected him like no other incident Joanna could ever remember. That night, she remembered hearing him cry. It was the first and last time she ever saw or heard her grandfather shed a tear.

It was also the last time she ever heard him utter his daughter's name.

When Jake had his first heart attack, in the summer of Joanna's eighth-grade year, there had been some talk of trying to find her father. When Jake recovered, the subject had been dropped, never to be mentioned again.

Still, even though she never asked Jake, she couldn't help wondering if her father knew of her existence. If he did, he wasn't without blame, and for many years, Joanna had spent a lot of energy hating both her parents.

She couldn't remember exactly when she'd stopped caring, but it seemed to her it had been right around the time she fell in love with Drew that the pain of her childhood had begun to slowly melt away.

In an adolescent rage, she'd torn every picture of her mother from the photo albums. A reaction she'd only recently begun to regret. The one faded picture of the man her grandfather said she favored she'd kept, for some unknown reason, in the family Bible in the living room. She hadn't looked at that picture for years. But now . . . well, perhaps someday soon she'd want to take another look.

Today, however, she couldn't waste time looking back. The present was all that mattered. At this point, she just had to hope Evan would be found. And soon. One way or the other. Dead or alive. In the meantime, she had to find a way to honor his commitments—the commitments that, as his wife, she felt obligated to bear.

Though she never remembered spending one day of her life with her mother, the woman had taught her more by example about how a wife and mother ought to behave than the woman could ever have imagined.

Bitter lessons well learned, the most important being that a wife didn't run out on her husband. She didn't desert her children. Even in the most desperate times.

Deep down, Joanna wondered how much worse this awful time could get for her. For Evan. For their future. Would this battering tide recede or had the wave of disaster just begun to break?

Chapter Five

"Wait a minute! You can't go in there!" At the sound of Nita shouting at someone, Drew bolted for the door. Joanna followed hot on his heels.

In the outer office, Drew realized it wasn't the diminutive secretary who needed protecting, but the man she had backed up against the door.

He loomed a good eighteen inches over her, yet Nita continued to yell at him as though she was scolding a defiant child. "How dare you come in here, anyway? Huh? You've got some nerve, you know that?"

The slender man had to be in his late fifties or early sixties. His short brown hair was losing a battle with the gray, and he possessed that well-groomed, well-dressed look of money. His skin bore what looked like a year-round tan, but despite the glow, something about him suggested that perhaps he was either recovering from or about to embark on a bout with ill-health.

At the sight of Drew and Joanna, the man moved toward them, seemingly oblivious to Nita's continuing tirade.

"What's going on here?" Joanna asked.

"I tried to tell him," the harried secretary blurted. Her hair was standing out from her head as though she'd run a fifty-yard dash in a gale, and her face was flushed a pinkish-red color that reminded Drew of a ripe watermelon.

"I was stopped at the light down by the Quick-Way when I saw him," Nita said, still breathless. "But by the time I could get turned around and drive back, it was too late." She glared at the subject of her remarks with disdain. "He was already here."

"It's all right, Nita," Joanna said evenly. "I'll take care of this."

Drew stayed close but took her at her word. Never had he seen Joanna more coolly in control.

The man's gaze flicked between the three of them before it stopped on Joanna. "I'm sorry if I've disturbed you. I should have called. But for the life of me, I can't imagine why your secretary feels she has to protect you from me." It struck Drew that the man was telling the truth, that he hadn't come to do anyone any harm. There was a softness about his dark brown eyes.

Before Joanna could respond, Nita stepped forward. "You want a reason? How about this? No one has seen Evan since the day the two of you had that big blowout in his office. Try explaining that, Mr. Nesbitt!"

So this was Lincoln Nesbitt, Drew thought. The guy with all the money at stake. Whether he deserved the abuse Nita was heaping on him, Drew didn't know. But the man possessed patience, Drew had to give him that. In the face of her not so thinly veiled accusation, he hadn't flinched.

"What do you want, Lincoln?" Joanna asked.

When Nesbitt took a step closer, Drew insinuated himself between them. First impressions and instincts were often wrong.

"Please," Nesbitt began. "All this drama really isn't necessary. I know I reacted badly the last time I was here—"

"Badly!" Nita scoffed, her small hands curled into fists and planted firmly on her hips. "Punching a hole in a wall, is that what you call *badly?* What do you do for an encore, Nesbitt, kick the door in?"

Now it was Lincoln's face that flushed crimson. "I have already apologized for that and offered to pay for all damages. I admit I acted like an idiot, and again, I'm sorry." His apology was directed to Joanna. "But we have to talk." It seemed as though he might emphasize his appeal by touching Joanna, but a sideways glance at Drew seemed to make him reconsider.

"As you said, you should have called. I could have saved you the trouble of coming down here. I don't know enough about Vista Grande to do either of us any good. I'm a veterinarian, Mr. Nesbitt. My husband was the businessman."

"But your name is on our agreements. You took over your grandfather's role as third partner."

At the mention of Jake, Joanna's bravado seemed to crumble, and Drew intervened. "Look, why don't the three of us go into Evan's office, sit down and sort this out." Drew realized that if he wanted to get the entire story behind Vista Grande, he'd never have a better chance.

"There's nothing to sort out," Joanna said flatly. "Mr. Nesbitt has made it clear what he intends to do."

"Joanna, a lot of money is missing," Lincoln said. "Money that was supposed to have been spent for construction crews, surveying, building permits... We can't just ignore this situation. Can't we discuss what needs to be done next?"

Drew thought it a reasonable request.

"I can't tell you what to do," Joanna said, her voice hoarse. "But my main concern is finding out what happened to my husband. Believe me, if I could help you recover your money, if I knew where Evan was or what he'd done..." Her voice cracked.

Nesbitt's face reflected compassion. "Believe me, Joanna, I couldn't be more sorry about all of this."

"Why should she believe you?" Nita snapped. "How do we know what you might have done when you found out what Evan—"

Joanna shot Nita a look that said, "Enough."

"I don't know what you people are trying to do or imply, but whether you choose to believe it or not, I was as baffled by Evan's disappearance as anyone. Maybe even more so under the circumstances."

"And just what's that supposed to mean?" Nita shot back.

Lincoln sighed. "This is getting us nowhere." He focused his attention on Joanna again, obviously fighting to ignore the antagonism coming off Nita in waves. "I apologize if I've upset you, Joanna. Obviously, no one has had a more difficult few weeks than you. I guess we're all operating under a great deal of pressure."

Drew was struck by the man's graciousness in light of the reception Nita, and even Joanna, had given him. If Lincoln Nesbitt was lying, he was better at it than anyone Drew had ever seen or heard. "Drew Spencer," he said, extending his hand. "I work for Ms. Caldwell... Galbraith," he corrected quickly. "I'm her attorney and I'm also engaged in some investigative activities, which we hope will lead to finding Evan."

He accepted Drew's hand. "Lincoln Nesbitt. I've just placed a notice in the local paper offering a cash reward for information about Evan's disappearance. I'm sure the sheriff will keep you apprised of any leads that come in."

Nita made a disgusted sound with her tongue.

When he turned his attention to Joanna, Drew knew she was bristling. "I'd like a chance to talk to Mr. Nesbitt," he told her. "He may have information that could help me put the events of the last day Evan was seen in sequence."

"I'd be happy to answer any questions," Lincoln said. "Joanna, I know this has been a horrendous ordeal for you, and I've tried to respect your situation. But unfortunately, my own circumstances are making demands that I cannot ignore much longer. I've got to go back to California soon, and before I leave, I really think we need to discuss how our mutual business concerns can be resolved."

"Your money is lost and my ranch will be foreclosed upon. That's the resolution, Lincoln, like it or not."

Drew had seen Joanna dig her heels in, but he'd never seen her be so downright unreasonable. Obviously, if she felt this strongly about not talking to Lincoln Nesbitt, she had to have a good reason. For most of her life, her stubbornness had served her well, in every area from winning competitions in the show ring to working her way through a very difficult course of study at the university.

But like anyone else, Joanna's strengths tended to also be her weaknesses. And in this situation, Drew sensed she was setting her jaw at the wrong time.

"Joanna, if you don't mind, I'd like to hear what Mr. Nesbitt has to say." The look she shot him could have cooled Hades, but he persisted. "Between the two of you, I believe there's a very real chance we could finally shed light on what might have happened to Evan."

Lincoln seized the opportunity. "How about tonight?"

Joanna opened her mouth, but Drew interrupted her protest. "Joanna has had a long day, so let's make it early, say seven, out at the ranch?"

Lincoln nodded, his demeanor still completely agreeable and gentlemanly when he turned to go. At the door, he said, "I really am sorry for what you're going through, Joanna. If there's anything at all you need . . ."

Joanna shook her head but didn't speak. Drew couldn't help staring at her. Had she always been this tough, this unyielding? He couldn't wait to get her alone and hear the rest of the Vista Grande story.

And, judging by the way she'd looked when she came out of Evan's office to see Lincoln standing there, it would be a story he wouldn't soon forget.

DREW'S HOPES of having another private conversation with Joanna evaporated when she said, "I have a patient to see at the other end of town. Since you've set up a meeting, I guess I'll see you later this evening."

She turned to Nita, dismissing him with an icy anger that chilled the air despite the warm afternoon breeze that slid through the door she held open. "If you need me, you have my pager number." And with that, she stalked out, leaving Drew staring at a closed door.

He spent a few minutes gathering his notes from Evan's office, long enough so he assumed Joanna would be gone, attending to the appointment she mentioned.

When he left, Nita was behind her desk again, going through some files. She seemed less angry, but she barely acknowledged his leaving. Clearly, his conciliatory attitude toward Lincoln Nesbitt marked him the enemy.

To his surprise, when he stepped onto the sidewalk, he saw that Joanna was sitting behind the wheel of her pickup, obviously deep in thought.

Drew walked over, leaned his arms on the ledge of the open window and said, "Want to tell me what that was all about?"

She shook her head. "Not really."

"You know, I've never thought I was a perfect judge of character, but he seems sincerely eager to work things out with you. Don't you think we ought to at least hear him out?"

"Oh, he's eager, all right," Joanna said bitterly. "Just ask the county clerk's office how eager he is."

"How would they know?"

She faced him, dry-eyed and pale. "They would know because he was there getting a full legal description of the Diamond C just two days after Evan disappeared."

"Isn't that a matter of public record?"

"Yes."

"But how—"

"How did I find out?"

He nodded.

"Valerie Wallace was in the county clerk's office that afternoon, filing some papers for a property she'd sold. She recognized him, of course, and couldn't help overhearing."

"Valerie Wallace?"

"She's a Realtor who works for Evan. She deals mainly with single-family homes, condos. Evan handles the larger properties, businesses and so on."

"Did she ask Lincoln why he wanted that information about the ranch?"

"I don't think so. But as soon as she got back to the office, she called me. Think about it a minute, Drew. Why would Lincoln need information about the Diamond C?"

"I suppose he could have had a number of valid reasons, but I get the feeling you think he had only one."

"Right."

"You think he's got his eye on acquiring the entire property."

"When the bank forecloses, he could pick it up for a song. Isn't that right?"

"Look, I don't know what Lincoln Nesbitt has in mind, Jo. But I do know it isn't a crime to be interested in buying real estate. Why don't we at least give him the chance to explain?"

"You already gave him that chance, remember? Tonight at seven."

He pushed back a strand of hair that had blown across her cheek and gazed into her defiant eyes. "You know, I've got to tell you, I never knew you could be so closed minded about something, or should I say, about *someone?*"

She tipped her chin. "There are people in this town who believe Lincoln is the prime suspect in Evan's disappearance. I know the authorities haven't ruled him out. As a matter of fact, for the first two weeks after Evan's disappearance, they specifically asked him not to leave town."

Drew wondered what evidence Harley and his department had based their suspicion upon, and he made a mental note to find out.

"Anyway," she sighed. "I really do have an appointment." She shoved the key in the ignition, but didn't turn it.

"Where's your office? Or is this vehicle self-contained?"

"Actually, it is, but I do have an office, or at least access to one. Doc Stewart retired, and until I can afford something else, I'm using his office."

She glanced at her watch. "I've got to go. I'm due in a few minutes to vaccinate a puppy. When I'm finished there, I have to swing by the bank—" She stopped herself from telling him why. "Afterward, I'll check in with my service, and if I don't have any more patients to see, I'll head home. Harley may call with information about those prints, and I want to be there to hear what he has to say."

"I'll be right behind you. Oh, and while you're at the bank, see if they'll issue you copies of all the canceled checks written on the Vista Grande account."

She stared into his eyes so intently it almost felt like a touch. "That could take some time, and even longer to go through them all."

"You know the old adage, follow the money?"

"Sure. Started with Watergate, right?"

"Yeah. But I've found it works just as well in a lot of cases this side of the Oval Office."

"Okay. I'm sure I won't have a problem getting copies. It might take me a bit longer to get home, though."

"Well, I guess maybe I'll need a key," he said.

"Will you be staying?" He knew she meant overnight.

"Yes." He didn't leave any room for argument, and she didn't seem to want to offer one. It was just as well, since she couldn't have won. After what had happened last night, he had no intention of allowing her to stay alone on the ranch for even a day.

"I'll be going home to see my aunt, but I promise I'll make it back to the Diamond C before Lincoln Nesbitt shows up at seven."

She reached for her leather purse, and after searching for a moment, handed him a key. "It fits the back door. We may be coming and going at different times. If you have your own key, it will make things easier."

When he took the key from her, their fingers met in a way that shouldn't have caused any reaction in either of them—just a brief brushing of flesh. But something happened. He felt it, and the look on her face told him she'd felt it, too.

He found his voice tight when he started to speak. "Is there anything—" he cleared his throat and shoved the key in the front pocket of his jean's "—anything in Evan's office we might need to reference when we talk to Lincoln? Files, documents, things I can ask Nita to help me find?"

She shook her head. Worry had taken the place of any lingering spark their unintentional touch had ignited. "We've been asked not to remove any files or records from the office. Someone from the D.A.'s office dropped by shortly after Evan disappeared."

"The D.A.?"

"It just goes from bad to worse, doesn't it?"

"Jo, what in the hell..."

"I wish I knew. I'm sorry." She glanced at her watch again. "I'm not trying to avoid your questions, but I really do have a patient waiting."

"You're something, Joanna Caldwell-Galbraith," he said. *You always were.*

She gave him a tired smile. "In light of what you've just learned, I'm not sure that's a compliment."

"Oh, it is. Believe me." He couldn't resist reaching over and tucking back the strand of dark hair the breeze had rearranged again. "Your husband has been missing for almost a month, last night someone broke into your home, you had a terrible night and by the looks of your clothes, less than a banner morning..." He stopped short of saying *And your former lover has just taken up residence in your guest room.* "And with all of that weighing you down, you're worried about distemper shots for somebody's mongrel."

"I'll have you know, Brandy's a purebred," she corrected with a playful smile.

"My mistake."

"Thanks for the vote of confidence. But if I do make it through all of this, the credit goes to Jake. He taught me early in life that you don't just walk away from commitments because things get a little tough."

She held his gaze for a long minute, and he knew she was giving him an important message, one he'd already suspected. She was married to Evan Galbraith. Committed to her marriage. Missing or not, sinner or saint, Evan was still her husband. If he'd incurred debts, engaged in shady business practices, gotten himself killed or merely flown the coop, she would not desert him. Not now and not until the game was officially declared over.

Drew allowed his eyes to soak up every lovely feature of Evan Galbraith's wife, and he couldn't help wondering if the man knew how lucky he was to be loved by such a woman.

"Take care, Jo," he said when she turned the key and the old engine grumbled to life.

"Always," she replied with a weak smile.

Despite her attempt to make them both feel better, Drew saw the stress around her eyes and the strain in her smile, and he couldn't have felt more touched by her sadness if she'd been sobbing.

He stood watching her until she made a right at the corner. He'd just climbed into his own car when the sight of

Nita Lansky emerging from the office caught his eye. For a minute he'd almost forgotten she was still in there.

But it wasn't Nita that intrigued him, but the stylish black-and-white tote bag she carried, which appeared to be stuffed to capacity. The bag piqued his interest when she set it beside her to free her hands to lock the door and it tipped over, exposing the manila file folders inside.

With the door finally secured, Nita scooped up the bag and looked around as if to assure herself that no one had been watching. Before her gaze moved his way, Drew slumped down in the seat and remained there until she drove away.

Joanna had said the D.A. had ordered that no documents be taken from the office. Surely Nita would have known about that order. He thought about her unexpected reappearance in the office while he and Joanna had been in Evan's office. Nita said she'd come back because she'd seen Lincoln Nesbitt heading that way, but had she had a different motive?

A dozen plausible reasons for Evan's secretary taking work home flashed through Drew's mind as he watched her drive away. And before he was finished with this investigation, he vowed, he'd check into every one.

AFTER STOPPING at the grocery store to pick up steaks and vegetables for the dinner he planned to fix Joanna before their meeting with Lincoln Nesbitt, Drew packed the groceries in a small cooler in the trunk and drove out to the Spencer ranch to see his aunt.

As always, Bess's simple wisdom and clear perspective helped him ground his thoughts. "I hate that she's being put through this," he told Bess as they sat together an hour later on the redwood deck that stretched along the back of the Spencer ranch house. The afternoon sun felt warm on his face, and the pine-scented breeze brought back fond memories of those long summer days in the high country. So many of those days spent with Joanna by his side.

"I don't think I've ever seen her looking so afraid as she looked last night. And yet today, when she confronted Lincoln Nesbitt in Evan's office, she seemed capable of bending steel."

Bess sipped her lemonade and gazed out at the mountains for a moment before she replied. "When I spoke to her last week, I heard the strain in her voice. But little wonder. This last month has been a nightmare for her." She shook her head. "Not knowing from one day to the next what will happen, whether Evan will be found, and if he is, in what condition." She released a sigh. "I can't imagine living with that constant uncertainty."

Drew couldn't, either. He'd been involved with Joanna's case for less than a day, and already he was growing impatient with all the unanswered questions.

"Did you know Evan?"

Her expression grew thoughtful. "You know, that's a good question. In a way, I don't think anyone knew Evan Galbraith very well. He only let you see what he wanted you to see—like most people, I guess. But with him, it seemed even more so. When I'd go over to visit Jake or Joanna, he was hardly ever there. And when he was, I always got the impression he was just itching to leave."

"You think he disliked being there, living in the country?"

"Oh, I hardly knew him well enough to guess. I don't know if it had to do with living on the Diamond C or just that he was the nervous type, you know? Edgy. Like a spooked colt, always ready to bolt and run."

"Do you think that's what he finally did?"

Bess thought a moment. "I wouldn't even want to guess, but there are a lot of folks who wouldn't be surprised." She frowned. "When something like this happens in a small town, there are always so many rumors. Lucy Sanders—

you remember Lucy, don't you? Down at the post office?"

He nodded.

"She said Evan was in there the day before he disappeared and that he was acting even more agitated than usual. Said he was worrying over a couple of packages like a cat over her kittens. He asked her all kinds of questions, and when she didn't answer them quick enough, she said he liked to have bit her head off."

"What kind of questions? Did Lucy say?"

Bess shot him an indignant look. "Why, Drew! I'm surprised at you. Lucy holds a position of trust. She can't just go blabbing to everyone what folks send and who they send it to. You know better than that."

He accepted her reprimand graciously, and when she finished, he leaned close and dropped his voice to a conspiratorial whisper. "Okay. So who'd he send those packages to? Do you remember the name?"

The twinkle in his aunt's soft brown eyes said she knew, all right, and that she couldn't wait to tell him.

Chapter Six

It was almost six when Joanna pulled up in front of the ranch house to see Drew's car parked in the drive. Why the sight of his car should have produced a flutter of excitement in her chest, she didn't know. But somehow just knowing that in a few minutes they'd be together again lifted her spirits.

Against her will, her thoughts went to all those lazy summer evenings when her heart had raced at the sight of him. Back then, their lives had been so inextricably woven that nothing seemed more important than their time together.

She remembered how after high school it had been difficult each fall when they'd had to leave each other to go back to college—Joanna to her studies in medicine at Colorado State in Fort Collins, and Drew to Denver and DU for law. Even though they'd been separated by less than a hundred miles, the intensity of their course loads had limited their time together.

But at least they'd never been more than a phone call away, and during those calls, summer had been a frequent topic of conversation. For both of them, summer meant freedom, coming home to Telluride and to each other. Back then, Drew had seemed as near as her own heart.

So much like today, she thought guiltily. He'd been with her since the moment she'd opened her eyes to see him sleeping in Jake's chair, and she felt him stirring in her heart now.

All day, whenever she'd let him, he'd crept into her mind and sometimes he'd seemed almost close enough to touch. Even now, when she closed her eyes, she saw his face, and to dispel his image took an act of will.

She reached for the creaking pickup door and glanced at her left hand to see the sun glinting off the diamond solitaire on her finger. Guilt seared her.

What kind of woman was she to be having such thoughts about another man? What right did she have to harbor feelings for Drew when it was Evan's ring she wore, Evan's life that would, no matter how this nightmare ended, be a part of her in a way that not even her deep, obviously undying feelings for Drew could change?

Before she went into the house to face him, she decided to spend a few minutes reorganizing the supplies in the back of the truck in order to steal some time to regain the composure and control she needed to spend another evening with Drew.

Unfortunately, organizing supplies didn't require the kind of intense mental concentration she needed to clear her mind. In fact, when she picked up her stethoscope, a gift from Drew upon her graduation from vet school, her wayward thoughts shifted to him as naturally as breathing.

It had been a long time since their breakup, nearly five years, and yet she'd never forgotten him, never completely erased him from her mind or been able to entirely close off the corner of her heart that would always belong to him.

The stethoscope she held in her hand blurred when the memory of losing him came back with excruciating clarity. Clinging to that pain like a shield, she turned and walked into the house where he was waiting for her.

She could hear him in the kitchen, humming a country song she had heard many times before. He'd always loved music. They both had. In high school, and even through college, every song had a special meaning, and when she heard them now, they still evoked vivid memories.

"Hey. I'm glad you're here," he said when he saw her. "Go wash up. Dinner's almost ready."

After she showered, she returned to the kitchen to find him putting the last of the food on the table. "Thanks."

"For?"

"Putting my room back together. All day long I've been dreading seeing it the way it was last night."

"No problem. But don't blame me if you can't find anything. Sit down. Your steak's getting cold."

From the moment she'd walked through the door, the smell of beef had piqued her appetite, but now the sight of it on her plate repulsed her. The bright tossed salad, however, looked wonderful, and she attacked it with vigor, but not before she forced herself to swallow a couple of small pieces of beef so as not to offend the chef. Unfortunately, he noticed when she nudged her plate a few inches to the side.

"I can throw that steak back on the grill if it's too rare for you. I thought I remembered you liking it pink."

"No. Please, don't bother. There's nothing wrong with the steak," she told him. "It's me. Lately, I haven't had an appetite for much of anything." When he frowned, she added, "But this salad is wonderful. Thanks, Drew. With all the...distractions of the past few weeks, I'd almost forgotten what it feels like to eat a real meal."

He reached for a basket of rolls, offered them to her, then said, "I stopped by to see my aunt this afternoon. She sends her best."

"She's been wonderful throughout all of this. Those peach preserves—" she lifted the tip of her fork to indicate the jar he'd just opened "—are hers. She brought them over, along with enough food to feed a small army, when she found out." There was no need to specify what Bess had *found out*. "And as it turned out, we did have a small army to feed. Volunteers from all over the western slope—Ridgeway, Ouray, Montrose and even Grand Junction—just appeared at the sheriff's substation to aid in the search, combing the hills and back roads for miles in all directions."

"It must have been difficult to go over the details again and again."

"It was. Especially at first. But then friends took over most of the phone calls—Valerie, Nita, even your aunt." They'd put up an invisible wall of love around her. "Such good friends," she said quietly.

"Small communities can be the best at drawing together, rallying the forces for their own."

For a moment, they ate in silence. She couldn't guess what he was thinking, but she was trying to remember what her life had been like before Evan had been declared a missing person.

"Jo," he began finally, "how well do you know Nita Lansky?"

Where had that come from? she wondered, taking another swallow of cold water tinged with the taste of lemon from the slice Drew had added to each of their glasses. "I think pretty well. Evan certainly knows her better than I. Why do you ask?"

He pushed his empty plate aside, rested his forearms on the table and leaned toward her. "Well, to begin with, what do you know about her relationship with Evan? She seems every inch the loyal employee."

"Yes. I'd say that was certainly an accurate assessment." Sometimes even to the point of irritation, like the many times Joanna had thought Nita might have been covering for Evan. Sometimes she'd felt like an outsider when she'd called the office trying to locate Evan. "She's been with him since he opened the agency. Her husband is a builder, and I believe Evan had contacted him about doing some work at Vista Grande."

"So you'd say Nita likes her job?"

"Make that *liked.*"

"Oh?"

"She told me she's been thinking about trying to find another position. I didn't feel I could ask her to reconsider."

"Are you thinking of closing Galbraith Realty?"

"I don't know that I'll have a choice. I don't know the first thing about the business, and unless...something happens soon, I can't see how I can keep it going. I don't know the rules and regulations, but I suspect that a licensed broker has to sign off on any contracts that come in, and until Evan is found..."

"I'll make some calls tomorrow and see where you stand. In the meantime, do you know any reason Nita would be taking work home from the office?" He picked up the cut-glass water pitcher and filled her glass.

"Thanks. What kind of work?"

"After you left today, I saw her leaving with a bag full of files."

"What?" She got up from the table and headed for the phone. "She knows we've been ordered not to take anything out of that office."

Drew was right behind her, and when she picked up the phone, he said, "I'm not sure the direct approach is the best choice in this situation."

"What are you getting at Drew?"

"I don't know what Nita has done, if anything. But if she is up to something, why give her the chance to think up a creative explanation?"

"It's just so hard for me to believe Nita could be capable doing something illegal."

"And Evan?" When she cringed, he immediately regretted his unthinking comeback. "I'm sorry, Jo."

She took in a shaky breath. "No. It's okay. I have to start facing facts."

"Not facts, yet. Just possibilities." He studied her face, seemingly trying to decide whether to go on. "Joanna," he said, and put his hand at her elbow to usher her to the table. "There's a lot of money missing out of that Vista Grande account, and I'm just wondering if someone other than Evan knows where the money went."

Joanna cringed.

He paused as if to give her a minute to absorb the accusation that, until now, he'd refrained from making aloud. When he began again, his voice was softer, gentler, like someone breaking bad news. "I think we need to start considering that if Evan did drain that account, he might not have acted alone."

"But Nita—"

"Maybe not. But I'm just saying we need to be on guard and not overlook anything as obvious as Evan's secretary removing files she's been specifically told not to."

By the D.A., no less, Joanna added to herself. "Well, if I can't call her, then what? How do you think we should confront her?"

"I'm glad you asked. After Lincoln leaves, we'll drive to Telluride and make an unannounced stop at the Lansky home. I can go alone, but it would probably be better if you were there to back me up. Are you game?"

"Of course. If Nita knows anything about that account, then perhaps—" She stopped, unwilling to finish the thought.

Drew, however, had no problem filling in the blanks. "Then maybe she knows something about Evan's disappearance?"

Joanna folded her hands in front of her on the table to keep them from shaking and swallowed the little sob she felt in her throat. "It's just so hard for me to contemplate that someone close to Evan, so close to me since his disappearance, could be capable of such deceit."

"Money, especially that amount of money, can be an extremely strong motivator."

"But to just stand by and watch what I've been going through, all those people who tried to help..." Her voice faded, and Drew reached across the table to cover her hands with his. His touch sent a reassuring warmth that said he'd help her face whatever came next. But when, without thinking, she responded to that warmth by threading her fingers through his, their contact quickly shifted to something more than the comforting touch of a supportive friend.

Joanna stifled a gasp when she realized what she'd done, jerked her hand away from his and shoved her chair back. She rose so quickly she almost tipped the chair over.

Grabbing up their dishes, she said, "You're right. Going to see Nita is a good idea." Gathering their plates and the leftover food gave her something to look at besides him, and it gave a burst of unnerving energy an outlet. "Afterward, we'll swing by Evan's office. I want you to take a closer look at the Vista Grande agreement." She headed to the sink with her hands full. "Since this entire ordeal began, I've felt as though I've been walking around in a daze, unaware or unwilling to face the truth."

He joined her at the sink, took the dishes out of her hands and set them on the counter. "You've had every right to hold on to the hope that a logical explanation would emerge for the missing money. And as for being in a daze, a person's natural defense mechanisms take over in times of great stress. It's only natural, Jo. You shouldn't be too hard on yourself."

She brushed past him to finish clearing the table. "That may be true, but a month has passed and it's time to get on with things, isn't it? Maybe it's time I find out where I stand, legally, at least. If Evan has—" she still couldn't bring herself to accuse him "—well, no matter what he has or hasn't done, I still need to know what my liabilities are, right? My name is on that agreement, putting the ranch my grandfather loved his whole life and worked so hard to preserve at risk. I don't think I could live with myself if I just let it go. Not without putting up a hell of a fight, anyway."

Finished with her diatribe, she focused her attention on rinsing their dishes to conceal the tears that had sprung to her eyes. What was the matter with her, anyway? In all her life, she'd never been so completely at the mercy of her emotions.

Drew put the leftovers in the refrigerator. Such a simple activity, and yet one she had never engaged in with her husband. In fact, they'd never really had a day-to-day life. Other than meals they'd shared in restaurants, she could count on one hand the number of times they'd sat down for a meal together since Jake died.

Evan seemed to always find an excuse for missing dinner, and after a while, Joanna stopped cooking meals. What was the point of cooking only to watch the food dry up before anyone got around to eating it?

Was it her lingering feelings for Drew that made it easier to see just how far she and Evan had drifted? Or had the truth been there all along and she'd just been too blind to see it?

Drew glanced at his watch. "Lincoln is running late. I think I'll call to see if he's still planning to drive out. If he isn't, I'd like to start going through those files you showed me last night. Do you have Lincoln's number?"

"I don't, but he's staying at the Bonne Soleil."

"It doesn't get much better."

"Five star. He insisted on it. When he notified us that he was coming to Telluride, I offered to help Evan make the arrangements. He was very specific about what he required. We even arranged for a second phone line for his computer. But his top priority was a fully equipped kitchen."

Drew rinsed the last dish and placed it in the wire drainer to air dry. "Seems odd for a man traveling alone. Maybe he's a gourmet cook."

Joanna shrugged. "I just figured maybe he didn't like hotel food. Or maybe he's very particular about what he eats and when."

"That suite must be costing him a fortune."

"Since he's been here, I'm sure he's spent a fortune—after all, he's been staying at the Bonne Soleil nearly a month." *Almost since the day Evan had disappeared,* she couldn't help adding to herself. "I don't think money is a consideration for Lincoln Nesbitt the way it is for the rest of us." *Except when his partner runs through every cent of operating cash in less than two months.*

Drew must have been thinking the same thing, because he said, "Even a man with unlimited resources doesn't shrug off a million dollars."

Joanna didn't have the heart to respond. Lately, whenever she'd allowed herself to think about what Evan might have done, that he might have actually embezzled that money, it felt as though the entire amount had been placed squarely on her shoulders. The longer she went without a reasonable explanation as to where that money had gone, the heavier that weight seemed to get.

Drew made the call to the hotel, and when he hung up the phone, he said, "He must be on his way."

She folded the dishcloth, draped it over the metal rod above the sink and tried to steel herself for the arrival of Lincoln Nesbitt by readying a pot of coffee to brew.

"Did Lincoln and Jake ever meet?" Drew asked, leaning against the counter and watching her fill the coffeepot with water and measure the grounds.

"No, but they spoke on the phone a few times. Why do you ask?"

"No particular reason, except that my dad always respected Jake's opinion, and when I got to know Jake, I did, too. When it came to sizing up a man's character, he seemed to have a sixth sense, didn't he?"

If they still shared anything, it was their fond memories of Jake. "He seemed to have a sixth sense about a lot of things." Warmed by thoughts of the enigmatic man who'd raised her, Joanna smiled. It felt good to talk to someone who loved and respected her grandfather and understood the very special relationship they'd shared.

She'd certainly never felt that way with Evan. After they'd married, Evan had always seemed defensive and unsure of himself around Jake. Like a kid trying to walk in the shadow of a hero. Evan, a successful businessman with confidence to spare in almost every other area of his life, just couldn't seem to meet Jake on an adult level.

At first, Joanna put it down to Evan's background. He'd been raised by an aunt, and there were few adult males for him to pattern his behavior after or teach him how to develop friendships with members of his own gender. Later, she'd realized that much of Evan's problem with Jake stemmed from plain old jealousy.

"Surprisingly, Jake liked and trusted Lincoln from their first conversation."

"Why surprising?"

"Well, although he hated to admit it, as Jake got older, he became overly sensitive to anyone who he thought might be trying to cheat him. Sometimes it seemed he distrusted everyone but me."

Jake's distrust had affected Evan deeply. When Jake questioned him on his handling of the development, Evan became peevish and pouting, even insulting, often over something as simple as Jake asking for a clarification. Sometimes it had been Evan's childishness, and at other times, Jake had been to blame. No matter who had been at fault, it seemed to Joanna that, too often, her loyalties had been torn unevenly between the two men.

"Better turn the burner on if you want that coffee to perk." Drew smiled.

She gave him a flustered smile. "Do you think we'll hear from Harley tonight about the prints they lifted from the bedroom?"

"I wouldn't be surprised," Drew said, and Joanna wondered at the wry smile that tugged the corner of his full mouth. "Good old Harley," he said. "He keeps in pretty close touch, doesn't he?"

"Harley has gone out of his way to keep me informed through this entire ordeal. He's been so helpful and kind."

"Yeah, I just bet he has," Drew murmured as he pulled two mugs out of the cupboard and set them down on the counter.

"And just what is that supposed to mean?"

He shrugged.

"Come on, Drew. That's not fair, and you know it. Out with it."

He went to the refrigerator, pulled out cream and set it beside the empty mugs. "Don't pretend you haven't noticed that the poor guy's been crazy about you for twenty years. I think he might qualify with Guinness for the world's longest crush."

Joanna felt the blood rush to her face, and her cheeks burned. "But that's ridiculous. Harley Platt is a good friend. We've known each other since—"

"Since grammar school," he put in, taking a step toward her. "Just like us, except that Harley was held back, remember? At the end of second grade."

"You're awful!"

"And you were always so cute. Remember our first-grade graduation ceremony?"

"All that pomp and circumstance."

"You were the first girl I ever saw in cowboy boots and a party dress."

She smiled. "The dress was Jake's idea."

They both laughed.

"Do you remember how Harley had that cowlick right in the middle of his head? It stood straight up, just like Alfalfa's in *Our Gang*."

"Poor Harley," Drew said, shaking his head and laughing. "No amount of grease could make that thing behave."

Their laughter grew louder until Joanna felt his gaze locked on hers, and then a sudden quiet crackled between them.

"We had some pretty great times, didn't we, Jo?" His voice felt like a satin ribbon around her heart, tugging all those golden memories to the surface.

"Yes," she said, her voice husky with emotion. "Back then, it seemed the good times would never end."

He put his hands on her shoulders, and she tipped her chin, which she'd lowered to avoid the memories simmering in his eyes.

"If we'd really known what we had, do you think we would have been smart enough to savor it?"

Any reply she might have had lodged behind the lump swelling in her throat when he touched her cheekbone as softly as a sigh, then let his gaze follow his finger as it traced a slow, tantalizing line to her mouth. "Joanna," he whispered. "Why did we throw it all away?"

She held her breath, afraid to move, afraid that if she even blinked she'd awaken and discover this moment was only a trick of her imagination, or a dream. Transfixed, she watched his face coming down to meet hers and felt his lips on her cheek. His arms were around her, drawing her body to his. Automatically, her hands slid up his chest and around the back of his neck, urging him closer.

When his lips grazed the corner of her mouth, an involuntary moan of pleasure escaped her, setting off an inner alarm that startled her backward, out of his arms so abruptly she almost stumbled. Shaken by the physical strength of her longing, embarrassed by her blatant lack of self-control, Joanna felt as though she couldn't get enough air.

Drew's expression matched the shock she felt, but neither of them spoke. Somehow it seemed they'd both been struck dumb by what had transpired between them.

But they hadn't gone deaf, and at the sound of someone knocking at the front door, the spell that had entranced them was shattered, and the invisible barrier they'd long ago erected moved back into place.

Chapter Seven

"That must be Lincoln," Drew said, his voice hoarse with the emotions that had almost undone them both. "I'll let him in."

Joanna grasped the precious gift of a few private moments to collect herself and regain her composure. In a month of shocks, the one she'd received just now, courtesy of her own out-of-control emotions and Drew Spencer's lips, ranked right up there with the most unsettling.

She poured a glass of water and took a few swallows, then pressed the glass against her cheek in a futile attempt to cool the heat that lingered from Drew's touch.

At the sound of footsteps in the hall, she turned to see Harley and Drew. How Drew had managed to regain his calm so easily, Joanna couldn't guess. She still felt thoroughly flustered, and the thundering of her heart had yet to subside. She held on to the glass.

"Jo," Drew began, but then seemed to lose track of what he was about to say. His gaze reflected none of its earlier passion, and it was almost as unnerving as the way he continued to stare.

"What is it?" For the first time she noticed the dark expression on Harley's face, and an electric shiver slid up her neck and fanned out into what felt like a thousand needles beneath her scalp. "Harley? What is it? Was it the prints?

Is that it? You know who broke into my bedroom last night?"

"They were your prints, Joanna. Yours and Evan's." There was something wrong with his expression. A disappointing result with fingerprints shouldn't have caused such a hooded and unreadable reaction.

"Drew?" She held the glass between both hands, oblivious to the droplets of condensation on the outside of the glass that slid down the side and seeped between her fingers.

"It isn't the prints, Jo. They've picked up Lincoln Nesbitt for questioning."

Harley took over. "We think he might know something about Evan's . . . disappearance."

She took a step toward Harley, jumping on this welcome information like a drowning person grabbing at a lifeline. "But I thought he'd already been questioned, at length?"

"We questioned him. But now we've come across new information, and we have reason to believe that he's been lying all along."

She'd wondered from day one why the police hadn't pressed Lincoln harder. His outburst in Evan's office had demonstrated his capacity for violence, and the financial loss he'd suffered, ostensibly at Evan's hands, certainly provided a motive.

"We received a call about an hour ago from someone who claimed to have information proving Nesbitt had something to do with Evan's . . . disappearance."

His slight hesitation pulled a knot in the pit of her stomach. "Who called? What did they say?"

"It was a woman. We don't know her identity yet. She refused to give the dispatcher her name, and when he pressed her to give it, she hung up. The readout came back pinpointing it as a Ridgeway number, though, so an officer has been dispatched to the location, and we should have a name soon."

Joanna tried to think who Evan knew in Ridgeway. The small community, about an hour's drive from Telluride, was noted for its sprawling meadows and spectacular mountain views. The area had been a hotbed of real estate activity for the past few years. Although she wasn't involved in the business enough to know what specific properties were under contract, Joanna suspected Galbraith Realty had probably listed a number of Ridgeway properties in the past year. She made a mental note to call Valerie.

"What did the caller say, exactly? Did she say she'd seen Evan? Was he in Ridgeway? And what about Lincoln, did she see them together?" Her brain fired off questions faster than she could ask them. "Is he all right? What did she say about the way Evan looked?"

Harley put his hand up like a crossing guard. "Whoa, whoa! Slow down. You're way ahead of yourself, Joanna. One thing at a time."

"Harley, just tell us what you know," Drew said, not so patiently.

"According to the dispatcher, when the call came in, he thought it might be just another prank. But something convinced him the woman was for real. Not only wouldn't she give her name, she was evasive about how she'd come by the information."

"And Lincoln Nesbitt?" Drew asked. "What's he got to say about this?"

A scowl drove a deep wrinkle across Harley's broad forehead. "As always, he's playing the perfect gentleman. Glad to cooperate, or so he says." Harley sneered. "They're questioning him down at the sheriff's substation."

"Why not the Telluride police?" Drew asked.

"This isn't their jurisdiction. The county and city forces have been working together. Within the area, we try to work together, but when it gets down to making arrests, we've got certain procedures to follow."

"Lincoln has been arrested?" Joanna asked, her heart racing at a staccato beat.

Harley shook his head, his expression sullen. Obviously he was disappointed. "No. It hasn't come to that yet. But believe me, it's only a matter of time before we nail this guy."

"With what?" she asked, even as the worst scenario flashed through her mind. Was it possible? Could Lincoln Nesbitt have murdered Evan?

"We don't know what the charges will be yet. It's too soon and we're still checking out the caller's claims."

Drew jumped on that. "What's the determination so far, Harley? There must be some corroborating evidence, or they wouldn't have hauled Lincoln in so quickly."

"So far, everything she said has checked out."

Drew moved to stand beside Joanna, so close their shoulders almost touched. "What did she say? What about her story has been checked out and substantiated?"

As it turned out, it was a good thing Drew was close, because when Joanna heard Harley's reply, she felt her knees go weak, and for a moment she thought she might faint.

"We found what we think is a weapon," he said soberly. "A hammer with stains that might be blood."

As though possessed by some unseen menace, the glass Joanna had been holding exploded in her left hand, sending angry shards into her palm and a shower of glass and water down the front of her dress.

Feeling strangely detached, she stood shaking, staring at her hand, and only in some vaguely distant way did she realize she was bleeding. In a rush of reality, everything Harley had said slammed into her like a runaway train.

Instinctively, she turned to Drew, and his arms were there waiting for her.

WITH TWEEZERS he found in the bathroom, Drew carefully removed the slivers, one by one, from her hand. Even though he knew it had to be done, he despised hurting her. Though she didn't utter a complaint, he cringed with her every sigh.

Joanna told Harley where he could find iodine and gauze in her pickup, and he rushed out of the house and brought them quickly. "I should call in," he said.

"There's a cordless phone in the living room," Joanna said as Drew continued to tend to her injured hand over the kitchen sink, where the light allowed him to see the smallest slivers.

"I don't know how you do it," he told her as he extracted another small shard.

"What?"

"Working with sick and injured animals. How do you handle seeing them suffer, day after day?"

"Sometimes I don't," she admitted. "But for me, it's always been just knowing that when things do go right, I've helped them survive. At other times, at least I've helped put an end to the pain."

"Well," he said, without taking his eyes off her palm, "I may not have helped you stop hurting yet. But I think all the glass is out, so you can at least begin to heal."

"First the pain, then the healing," she said softly, almost to herself. "It's a process, and there just doesn't seem to be any way around it."

The sadness in her dark eyes caused his heart to constrict. "No. I guess not."

With both hands, he pushed her hair away from her face and let his thumbs linger on her cheeks. "Are you going to be all right? You're very pale. Would you like to lie down?"

She shook her head. "It was just such a shock...a hammer, Drew," she said, her voice raspy with the horrible thought. "I just can't..." Her voice cracked and she swallowed hard, causing another tightening in Drew's chest.

They were silent as he applied iodine and a light dressing to her palm. She'd been lucky. None of the cuts was deep enough to require stitches, and for the amount of glass, there hadn't really been that much blood.

Harley came into the kitchen and stood a few feet away, watching. "You gonna be okay?"

She managed to offer him a weak smile. "Yes. I'm fine. Thanks for helping, Harley."

"No problem. I guess I'd better get going. I haven't talked to Sheriff Miller yet, but I found out they're still holding Nesbitt."

"Harley," Joanna said, swallowing before she could ask. "Where did they find it...the hammer?"

Inside, Drew cringed when she said the word.

"In the trunk of that rental car he's been driving."

"But how did she know...the caller, I mean."

Harley shrugged. "No one knows. And no one cares," he added almost defensively. "That information is the first break we've had since we found his jacket, and for me, it's the big break we need to nail Nesbitt."

Drew hoped Harley's superiors, the people questioning Lincoln, wouldn't disregard the procedures of sound investigation as easily as his old friend had. "I think we'd better all remember that we haven't heard Lincoln's side of this yet."

He sensed Joanna's reaction, her grudging agreement. Harley, on the other hand, seemed personally offended. "Give me a break! The guy is guilty as sin and everyone has known it from the start. Now all we have to do is come up with a charge."

Drew stared at Harley. Was this guy for real? An attitude like Harley's could set the justice system back two hundred years.

"I know what you're thinking," Harley said with a sneer, his voice rising. "That he's innocent until proven guilty."

"Yeah, now that you mention it. That's the way I believe it's supposed to work."

Drew's sarcasm seemed lost on the irritated deputy. "Yeah, well, just because we can't prove something doesn't make a person innocent, you know?"

The deputy's logic escaped Drew.

"You weren't here to see what she went through when she lost Jake, so maybe you should just back off, Spencer."

Under different circumstances, Drew's first response might have been to teach the overwrought deputy some lessons in self-control. But this unexpected reference to Jake shocked him to the point that he almost forgot his anger. "Jake? What has—"

"Look, this is an open-and-shut case as far as I'm concerned," Harley interrupted. "Nesbitt is going down, one way or another. When we find Evan, and if he's still alive, we'll have enough evidence to send that California jerk to jail so fast his fancy head will spin." With that, he shoved his hat on his head and stalked to the door.

"Just talk to Valerie Wallace, why don't you," he grumbled over his shoulder as he went. "She'll tell you how dangerous this character is." He shoved the screen door open, but before he left, he reminded them, "She was there, you know, when he put his fist through the wall." And with that, Harley was gone, leaving Joanna and Drew standing in shocked silence, staring at the screen door rattling on its hinges from the deputy's angry exit.

Drew thought Harley Platt gave new meaning to the term overreacting, and Joanna must have thought the same thing, because when she finally managed to pull her eyes away from the door, she said, "I know he's been desperate for some kind of lead, but I've never known him to be so adamant and so... well, emotional."

"Desperation can make a man abandon reason—a dangerous situation for a law officer."

Joanna shook her head, obviously deeply disturbed by more than Harley's outburst.

Her shoulders sagged, and Drew couldn't remember her ever appearing so defeated. Except maybe when she'd lost Jake, but then she'd been more than defeated, and no matter how anyone had tried, she'd remained inconsolable. Perhaps he should have tried harder to comfort her, but his pride had still been stinging from the shock of her sudden marriage to Evan.

Thinking back, remembering how Evan had seemed unaffected by Jake's passing, Drew regretted that he hadn't tried harder to comfort her. The night after the funeral, when he'd stumbled over Joanna outside alone, he'd thought for a moment that she might allow herself to break down in front of him. But something had changed her mind, and the next day he'd driven to Denver, knowing that somehow the final door between them had closed—at Joanna's bidding.

Her face looked as chalky now as it had that night, and judging by the tightness around her eyes, she was in the throes of a headache.

"Jo, why don't you sit down. You really don't look well. Can I get you an aspirin or something?"

"No, I can't... That is, I'm fine." She drew a deep breath. "A hammer, Drew. How could anyone be capable of such a horrible—" Her words were lost when a deep shudder shook her, and she wrapped her arms around herself.

"Come on," he said, putting his arm around her shoulders as they walked together into the living room and sat on the couch. "Don't torture yourself, Jo," he said as he gently kneaded the back of her neck. "Despite what Harley said, Lincoln might have a perfectly logical explanation for... well, for whatever they found."

She leaned forward, looking at him with wide, hopeful eyes. "Harley *has* been putting in a lot of hours. He seems as stressed by all of this as anyone. Tonight wasn't the first time he's driven all the way out here to give me firsthand information. He's been very kind, Drew. A good friend. I don't think we should be too hard on him."

He couldn't help admiring Joanna's loyalty and her capacity for compassion. On the other hand, he wondered about her objectivity in this situation. For Drew, an assessment of Harley's outburst had to begin with the deputy's personal feelings for Joanna. As she'd just pointed out, until she'd dragged an outside investigator on the scene, Harley had seen himself as her support, her main contact with the case.

Injury had probably been added to insult when that investigator turned out to be none other than a hometown boy who'd flown the coop for the big city. To Harley's way of thinking, that made Drew not only unqualified to meddle in local affairs, but a double threat, as well.

Joanna seemed lost in thought for a moment before she surprised him by saying, "You know, I think we should take Harley's advice and talk to Valerie Wallace. Like he said, she was there, the only witness when Evan and Lincoln had that terrible argument. She's been closer to all of this than anyone. I think you need to hear what she has to say. But not on the phone." She glanced at her bandaged hand. "Would you mind driving?"

"Not at all. And I agree it's important for me to hear Valerie's version of what went on the day Evan disappeared. But are you sure you're up to this?" Her face still hadn't regained all its color, and around her eyes, the smoky circles persisted.

She looked into his eyes intently. "When I drove to Denver and asked you to help me find Evan, for the first time since this all began, I felt as if I had actually taken a step forward, that I was finally doing something that might make a difference. I can't tell you how much better it felt. Now, when it appears that things might even be worse than I'd been trying to prepare myself for, I think it's important for me to keep up that attitude. I can't bear the thought of slipping back into that awful waiting. Can you understand that?" Her eyes pleaded for understanding, which he gave immediately and without reserve.

"Of course." Although even the most stressful times of his life couldn't compare to the ordeal she was going through, he'd never taken a wait-and-see approach to the challenges life had sent him.

And with someone like Joanna, who'd been compelled from an early age to prove her courage, that ability to steer her own course was even more important. It was a trait he'd always admired in her, the way she faced adversity, her surprising bravery.

At the door, she said, "I want to go by the sheriff's sub-station, as well. If they've found anything...more, I need to know."

Drew didn't reply. They both knew what she meant. If they'd found Evan, she had to be there. Dead or alive, she had to know.

A FEW MINUTES LATER, being careful to avoid the deepest ruts on the Diamond C's dirt road, Drew guided his car toward the highway.

"If Lincoln has been released, I still think we should seek him out. I have even more questions now."

Joanna nodded, sitting grim-faced and silent, seemingly lost in her own thoughts. Night had encroached, and the high-country air had turned cool. Within the cozy interior of his sports car, however, the air felt warm, and the clean, sweet scent of Joanna filled Drew's senses.

As he negotiated the rough ranch road, their shoulders touched from time to time. Every time contact was made, he could somehow sense her stiffening. For long minutes she didn't speak, and the silence in the car couldn't have been more complete or more isolating if they'd been traveling in separate vehicles.

He knew she'd been upset by the implications of the hammer found in the back of Lincoln's car. He also knew her well enough to know that she was feeling guilty about the kiss they'd stolen earlier that evening. Remembering the feel of her soft, warm mouth, Drew allowed his thoughts to drift, and he couldn't help wondering if that kiss could have happened had Joanna been deeply involved in a marriage of love, devotion and commitment.

Hadn't she said they'd drifted? But then again, maybe he was just making excuses, hoping for more, eager to make more of her remark than she'd intended.

In his business, he knew better than most how extreme pressure caused people to react in strange ways. And Jo's situation couldn't be more extreme.

So what did that make him for pressing his advantage, for taking liberties with a woman whose husband might have been brutally murdered? Self-loathing welled inside him, and after another minute of silence, Drew felt ready to explode.

God only knew what awaited them in Telluride. If the hammer the authorities had recovered from Lincoln's car was, as Harley suggested, a weapon used to inflict injury on Evan, tonight could be the night the body was found.

With this latest development in the case, Drew foresaw his role shifting from that of Joanna's paid investigator to that of her attorney and friend, someone who could protect her interests—personal and professional—in a tangled legal and emotional jumble. Now was not the time to agonize over a kiss or daydream about some distant romantic reunion.

Besides, he told himself, if the future did hold a chance for the two of them, the hurtful things they'd said and done to each other, the physical and personal obstacles that had kept them apart for five years would have to be resolved. They'd have a lot of ground to cover, not the least of which would be the guilt they'd have to face if they did break down and admit their feelings for each other now.

Drew resolved not to make things worse. He wasn't, however, fool enough to believe it would be easy to maintain his distance. Even now, with her sitting so close, the desire to delve into their past, to grab the opportunity to right past wrongs, was almost irresistible. Five years ago, he'd let pride, distance and stupid ambition keep him from the only woman he'd ever loved.

If he truly suspected he had another chance, if he thought for even one minute that she wanted him, he wouldn't be fool enough to let anything come between them—including his own intense physical longing for her.

But that desire would have to be harnessed, he told himself, even as he inhaled the fresh scent of her and allowed his gaze to linger too long on her delicate profile. For her sake, no matter what the outcome, they needed to be able to work together, and the rapid pace with which events were unfolding didn't leave time for any unspoken feelings to simmer.

One way or another, whether Evan was alive or dead, guilty or innocent, nothing would change how Drew felt about Joanna. He knew that now with a certainty he hadn't possessed five years earlier. Whatever happened in the next few hours, days and weeks, neither of them could deny that something had stirred to life between them tonight. The thought exhilarated him even as it brought shame. There was more at stake here than the revival of an old flame, and this time Drew wasn't prepared to let Joanna walk away a loser.

When they reached the end of the ranch road, Drew brought the car to a stop. It was the opening he needed. Without explaining why, he shut the engine off, doused the headlights and switched to parking lights.

Joanna turned in the seat to face him—the first time she'd really looked at him since they'd left the house. "Why are we stopping? Is something wrong?"

"Yes."

She leaned forward, almost across his lap, to scan the sleek instrument panel. "Is something wrong with the car? Are we out of gas?"

The warmth of her body, so tantalizingly close, tortured him with memories of how her silken skin had felt beneath his touch. "Nothing's wrong with the car," he said, fighting the urge to renew those memories.

"Then what is it?" Her irritation was undisguised. "Drew, come on. It's already after nine, and by the time we see Valerie and Nita and—"

"We have plenty of time."

She sat back in her seat and stared at him. "All right. Obviously, you have something you want to say. Go ahead."

He turned in his seat, resisting the natural urge to put his arm across the back of her seat. He sensed her stiffening at the prospect of his touch.

"You're right. I have a couple of things I want to say to you, and at the rate things are going, if I don't say them now, I might not have another chance."

"All right." She inhaled sharply, her demeanor one of obvious dread.

"I want to apologize, Jo."

"Apologize? For what? The incident today with the check?"

He laughed. "Well, no, but now that you mention it, I am sorry for barging into your business that way." He reached into the pocket of his denim shirt and handed her the folded check she had written. "I paid Nita, just like I told you I would, but not with your money."

She jerked to face him. "You did what?"

"I paid her because right now you can't afford to and I can."

"Darn it, Drew," she said, clearly exasperated. "Sometimes, you can be one presumptuous jerk, you know that?"

"So I've been told." He'd felt the sting of her remark, but found a way to check his temper by reminding himself that Joanna was a Caldwell, after all. And a Caldwell was nothing if not proud. "We've been friends for a long time and I wanted to help—" When she opened her mouth to interrupt he stopped her. "Look, hear me out, will you?" He told himself that the sparks in her eyes wouldn't have seemed so intense, so exciting in the light of day, and that it was the soft glow from the dash lights and the darkness beyond that created that feeling of privacy and intimacy that roused his passions.

"Go on," she said, her eyes still trained on his face and her expression unreadable. "You said you had something else to say."

"I was apologizing," he reminded her. "It was something Harley said that made me realize I'd let you down. That I hadn't been there for you when Jake died."

She lowered her eyes, and he heard her draw a ragged breath.

"I knew, maybe better than anyone, how much he meant to you, and I shouldn't have let our past get in the way of helping you get through a very difficult time."

She didn't respond, merely nodded, and neither of them spoke for a moment—a moment of silence for more than Jake's passing.

"Anyway, I just wanted you to know."

"I'm glad you told me." It wasn't much more than a whisper.

"That isn't my only regret where we're concerned." He hadn't meant to go this far, but at the last minute he found himself longing to speak his heart. "A lot of regrets," he said quietly. "But what happened between us tonight isn't one of them." He paused. "I don't want to be sorry about tonight, Jo. I don't ever want to regret kissing you."

She seemed about to say something, but instead she sighed, leaned back in the seat and closed her eyes. "I'm the one who should be apologizing," she said finally. "I shouldn't have let it happen. It's just..." She hesitated. "It wouldn't be fair of me to let you think it meant... something more than it did."

Her words hit him like a slap, and for a second, he almost couldn't breathe. "I understand," he lied. If that kiss hadn't meant anything to her, Drew told himself, he'd lost every instinct he'd ever possessed for reading her reactions. "It wasn't your fault. You've been under a great deal of pressure. I took advantage." He turned the key and put the car in gear, forcing himself to make each move with slow, calm, deliberate motions, fighting, with every ounce of self-control he possessed, to contain the storm raging inside him. "At least we've cleared the air. I'm glad we understand each other."

But what did he understand? That she loved her husband? A man who'd cheated Jake, embezzled his partner's money, lied and manipulated her out of everything she owned? How could he possibly understand something so inconceivable?

"He's my husband," she said, startling him out of his introspection. "I won't destroy my family for a meaningless fling. You know me well enough to know that I would never do that." Her voice was steady, but the deep sadness he sensed behind every word pierced his heart.

Family. He scoffed, remembering how much a sense of belonging had always meant to her. If only he had a second chance to show her what a real family could be. If he was given that second chance, perhaps he could teach her to love him again.

For now, Drew had no choice but to honor her commitment to a man who didn't appear to deserve her devotion. No matter who Joanna called her husband, she would always be Drew's only love.

HARLEY WAS HALFWAY back to Telluride before he cooled down enough to realize he'd left his hand-held radio on the counter in Joanna's kitchen. It galled him to have to go back and face them—Spencer so damn cocky and smug, and Joanna, her pretty face haggard from grieving for that no-good SOB husband of hers.

But he had to have his radio. So, after turning his cruiser around in the middle of the highway, he sped toward the ranch road. That was one of the benefits he'd always liked best about being a cop, the powerful cars and the unrestricted run of the road. When the turnoff for the Diamond C was only a few hundred feet ahead, he slowed down. And that's when he saw them. The gleam of his headlights cut across Spencer's car. He didn't turn onto the ranch road, but he slowed enough to see them sitting there.

For a moment, after he'd passed them, he considered going back to see if they needed help. But he changed his mind when he glanced in his rearview mirror to see the steady pale orange glow of parking lights instead of the intermittent blink of red hazard lights.

Harley fumed at the thought of them sitting alone in the darkness, even though he hadn't really seen more than their silhouettes inside the car. But he'd seen enough—more than he'd wanted to see—earlier tonight when he'd seen her in Spencer's arms. After that, it had been easy for him to imagine what had gone on before he'd arrived.

Even now the thought burned through his brain, nearly blinding him to the fact that he was racing down the two-lane highway headed in the wrong direction. Cursing and sweating, despite the cool night air rushing in his open window, Harley slowed enough to make a sweeping U-turn without rolling the cruiser. When he was headed in the right direction again, he stomped the accelerator, pushing the speedometer to almost ninety. If they were still sitting there, he didn't intend for them to have the satisfaction of seeing him passing by.

Thinking of them sitting alone in the darkness in that tin can of an import, making out like a couple of teenagers, caused his blood pressure to soar. The bitterness they'd helped to plant in him all those years ago continued to grow. He wondered, sometimes, if his longing for her would someday consume him, especially lately, when it had begun to look as if at last Joanna would be his.

Disappointment followed on the heels of rage, as it always did, bringing him back to cold reality. Be patient, he told himself. Everything was coming together. It wouldn't be much longer, and she'd be his. He'd come so far. Tonight, Drew and Joanna were together, but he'd learned to live with worse—much worse, like seeing her every day with that scum she'd married. He'd even learned to live with the disrespect and the disregard she showed him. But someday...someday all that would change. Someday soon he'd have her. One way or another. Or no one would.

Chapter Eight

Valerie Wallace met them at the door, dressed in black stirrup pants and an elegant white silk tunic that made Joanna feel frumpy in her jeans and Colorado State sweatshirt. As always, not a strand of Valerie's thick strawberry blond hair was out of place. Worn in a sleek geometric cut, it skimmed her jawline and swung freely about her face in animated movements.

"Jo!" she said. "I'm glad it's you. Come in. Come in. My goodness, what have you done to yourself?"

Joanna glanced at her hand. "Just a little accident," she replied, avoiding a more detailed explanation by saying, "I hope we didn't catch you at a bad time." Several pieces of expensive black leather luggage sitting next to the door implied Valerie had either just returned or was about to embark on a trip of some duration. A black-and-white umbrella was standing in the corner, upside-down and open, as if it had been placed there to dry.

"No. No. Not at all. I just got in myself." As always, Valerie's makeup had been applied with a careful hand. But the heavy coat of concealer couldn't hide the shadows beneath her large eyes—green eyes tonight, Joanna noticed idly, wondering how many different sets of tinted contacts Valerie owned.

Something about an open house slipped through Joanna's mind, but before she could remember whether Nita had said this weekend or last, Valerie was ushering them inside.

"You must be Drew Spencer," she said, offering him her hand and a dazzling smile. "Nita told me to expect tall and good-looking."

The three of them moved farther into the living room. Decorated entirely in black and white, Valerie's spacious condo couldn't help but impress. The lack of color, however, had always made Joanna feel a bit chilled.

"Sit down. Sit down," their hostess intoned. Her decor may have lacked warmth, but Valerie seemed to have a knack for making anyone feel comfortable. Joanna remembered Evan once remarking that if science could find a way to bottle Valerie's vitality, there would never be another energy crisis.

"So, what brings you here at this hour, Jo?" Her expression grew immediately serious and she reached for Joanna's arm. "Oh, dear, has something happened? Have they located Evan?"

Located seemed an odd word, but Joanna wrote it off to her own recent and annoying habit of overanalyzing everything anyone said, especially about Evan.

"No, I'm afraid not," she replied. "But Evan is the reason for our coming by tonight." She paused, and with a glance passed the remainder of the explanation to Drew.

"Ms. Wallace," he said as soon as they were all seated on various pieces of very white, very expensive furniture.

"Please, call me Valerie, or Val."

Drew returned her smile and Joanna couldn't help feeling a twinge of envy at the way Valerie seemed to have captured Drew's full attention after only a few seconds of exposure to her incomparable style and undeniable charm. But then, what else should she expect? The woman was in sales, Joanna reminded herself. The success she'd achieved in the short time she'd worked for Evan spoke volumes about her skill in handling people.

"As you may already know," he began, "I'm a private investigator, and Joanna has hired me to find Evan."

Valerie plucked an invisible piece of lint from her sleeve. "Of course, I'll be glad to help in any way I can. Although I've already been interviewed by the police."

"I realize you've already given them your statement. But I was hoping our conversation might be more candid and informal."

Speaking of people skills, Joanna thought, Drew Spencer had a very large corner on that market.

"No matter how insignificant you feel a detail might be," he was saying, "I'd like you to feel free to tell me."

"All right. I think I can do that. Although I still don't think I know enough to be very helpful," Valerie said with a sigh. "But first, can I offer either of you something to drink? I don't know about the two of you, but I've had a very long day." She was on her feet, heading toward a gleaming black-and-white kitchen that seemed to Joanna to have no other purpose than a fancy storage area for Valerie's cappuccino maker and crystal.

"Joanna, what can I offer you?"

"Nothing, thanks. We had a late dinner."

"Oh, come now. Not even one of those tall, cold glasses of milk you seem to be so fond of savoring?"

Joanna smiled, letting Valerie have her fun. Good-natured barbs were just Valerie's way. What was bothering her—unduly, she thought—was the sensation of Drew's eyes on her, constantly studying, boring into her, gazing uninvited into those areas of her heart and her mind where she definitely did not want him prying.

Too often in the past twenty-four hours, she'd felt him reading her in that too-intimate way they'd always had of knowing each other's thoughts. Just to throw him a curve, she said, "You know, I think I might enjoy a glass of wine."

The surprised, almost imperceptible lift of Drew's brow gave Joanna little satisfaction. She might have delivered a mild shock this time, but she knew darn well he wouldn't be thrown off track for long. Just as he wouldn't believe their kiss had meant nothing if she didn't find a way to control her urge to steal glances at him at every opportunity.

Drew settled on coffee, and Valerie acted as though he'd chosen the specialty of the house and invited them to come and sit at the counter while she prepared the brew. After retrieving a wineglass from a black-and-white slotted shelf, she turned to a tall, stylish matching wine rack. Her fingers closed around the neck of a bottle, which she partially withdrew before shoving it back in place and choosing another. She set the glass down in front of Joanna and handed the bottle and a corkscrew to Drew.

Joanna's attention was still focused on the bottle Valerie had decided against. Even from here, she could see the glimmer of the distinctive gold label Evan placed on all his private stock. She remembered the bottles of sauvignon at the office, but couldn't remember seeing the gold labels. At any rate, what did it matter? Evan had obviously given Valerie a bottle of the rare vintage as a reward for a big sale or for some other business reason, and there was probably no more to it than that.

"Valerie, from what I understand, you were there when Lincoln Nesbitt and Evan had a confrontation. Tell me about that."

Listening to him take charge of the interview, Joanna was struck again by the differences in the life-styles she and Drew had chosen. Drew had always been confident, but the keen-edged self-assurance he possessed now she attributed directly to his years in Denver, competing and succeeding in that urban setting, first in law and then in the unique and highly specialized field of investigation.

"After they came back from viewing the property, did you hear Lincoln Nesbitt threatening Evan?"

"No, but when he punched a hole in the wall, the implication seemed pretty clear." Valerie gave Joanna a sympathetic look. "I mean, the man just came unhinged—though I don't suppose I could blame him. Sorry, Joanna, but a million dollars is a lot of cash."

Joanna accepted her apology and dismissed her concern with a shake of her head that said, "No offense taken."

Drew removed the cork from the wine and filled Joanna's glass less than half full.

"Thanks," she murmured and was rewarded with a smile.

"Tell me more about that incident," he said, returning his attention to the interview at hand. "What was Evan's reaction to Lincoln's outburst?"

Valerie thought a moment, arranging Drew's coffee cup and filling a small cut-glass pitcher with cream she'd pulled from the stainless-steel refrigerator. With the door open, Joanna could see that except for a few bottles of imported beer and the carton of cream, Valerie's refrigerator was empty. Not surprising, she supposed, for a single woman living the good life in Telluride, or for someone just returning from a trip.

"Evan reacted badly...sorry, Jo," she said again. "But when he went for Lincoln, I didn't know how far it would go."

"You think they might have exchanged blows?"

Valerie nodded. "If I hadn't been there, I'm not sure what would have happened. When Lincoln grabbed that hammer off the floor—"

Joanna gasped.

"What was a hammer doing in Evan's office?" Drew asked.

"We use it on the properties we list. The ground can be hard as rock sometimes, and we need a hammer to help secure the metal stands that hold our signs. Anyway, when Lincoln reached for the hammer, Evan stopped dead in his tracks. I don't think I've ever seen a man so angry."

Joanna hadn't yet taken a drink of her wine, and it was a good thing, because she felt sure it would be churning in her stomach at the image of a hammer in Lincoln Nesbitt's hands.

Drew asked Valerie a few more questions, mostly details about what time she'd left the office that evening and the last thing she and Evan had discussed.

But for Joanna, no more details were necessary. The mystery was over. The hammer found in Lincoln Nesbitt's rental car and the hammer she could almost picture in his hand the day Evan disappeared formed a gruesome explanation that obliterated all other theories—the hopeful theories she'd been clinging to for a month.

Drew set his coffee cup down and stood. "Well, thank you, Valerie. You've been very helpful. I think we'd better get going. Jo, are you ready?"

Joanna nodded, mumbled her thanks and proceeded Drew to the door.

"If there's anything else..."

"We'll call," Joanna heard Drew saying as she hurried out the door, suddenly desperate for air.

ON THE NARROW SIDEWALK outside Valerie's building, Joanna leaned against Drew's car and gulped fresh air as deeply and as quickly as her thirsty lungs could take it in.

He came up behind her and put his hands on her shoulders. A flood of memories accompanied his touch. In the past, his hands had evoked almost magical responses in her. Tonight, however, it wasn't the magic she craved, but his warmth, his solid support and his understanding. Somehow he seemed to sense all those needs, and with gentle pressure, he urged her into his arms.

"He's dead," she murmured, sagging against his chest. "I didn't want to believe it. All along, I couldn't really bring myself to accept the possibility." She pulled away just far enough for their eyes to meet. "But it's true, isn't it? Lincoln Nesbitt murdered Evan."

Drew started to say something, but he never got the chance. The sound of something skimming across the hood of his car grabbed their attention even before they heard the crack. Instinctively, Drew shoved her to the pavement and sheltered her body with his as he fumbled with the door, then pushed her inside the car. "Stay down!" he shouted and raced around the car, opened the door and slid into his seat behind the wheel.

In seconds, he'd started the car and shoved it into gear, and they were speeding away from the building and onto Telluride's main street, heading for the sheriff's substation. Drew held his car phone in his hand and barked out directions and details of the sniper's attack to the Telluride police.

As they stepped onto the lighted street in front of the sheriff's station, Joanna could hear the scream of a siren in the distance. She hoped it was a police car responding to Drew's call.

"Go inside, Jo," he said, accompanying her as far as the front door. "Stay put until I come back for you."

"But where—"

"Please, just go inside," he said again. "I need to go back and talk to the police, but we also need to know if Lincoln Nesbitt has been released. Tell Harley what's happened," he said over his shoulder as he jogged to his car.

He'd jerked his car door open and was ducking inside when she called out to him. "Drew!"

"Yeah?"

"Nothing. Just be careful." *Please. Just please, come back to me,* she longed to shout, but as another man's wife, how could she?

He stood for a second, staring at her, and then he smiled, that patented Spencer charm penetrating the night and the distance between them, sending a ripple of longing through her.

"I know," he said softly, but loud enough for her to hear. "Now, go inside, Jo. I'll be back. I promise."

TWENTY MINUTES LATER, Joanna glanced at the round-faced clock above the counter that separated the dispatcher from the reception area. It was just past ten, five minutes past the last time she'd checked.

"Are you sure you wouldn't like some coffee, Mrs. Galbraith?" The dispatcher, a gray-haired officer whose name tag read Hoffman, seemed to know Joanna. Unfortunately, she couldn't immediately place him, but then, she'd met so many law enforcement officials over the past month, she supposed there was no way she could be expected to know every one.

"No, thanks. I'm fine."

"I can't imagine what's keeping Deputy Platt," Hoffman said, following her eyes to the clock again. "He called in a few minutes ago. I'm sure he won't be much longer."

"Do you expect Sheriff Miller to be in tonight?"

"Yes ma'am," the dispatcher answered. "As a matter of fact, he's still here. Would you like me to see if he can help you?"

Joanna couldn't hide her surprise that the county sheriff was still in his office at this hour. "Yes. I would like to speak to him, if possible."

When Deputy Hoffman picked up the phone, Joanna took a seat on one of the metal chairs that lined the cinder-block walls. A woman not much older than her sat opposite, absorbed in keeping a squirming toddler interested in a battered storybook.

From time to time, the woman offered an apologetic smile when the youngster squealed or whined. But other than noting the angelic look of the dark-haired baby boy's face, Joanna was still completely distracted by the disturbing events of this long, harrowing evening.

She couldn't stop thinking about the screeching sound of the bullet as it had skidded across the hood of Drew's car. The bone-chilling sound would echo in her mind forever, along with horrifying thoughts of what might have happened had the bullet veered even a few inches off course.

Rising, she wrapped her arms around herself to suppress a shudder as she paced across the room again. She almost stumbled over the toddler, who had crawled after her and sat looking up at her with his chubby little arms outstretched.

"Come on, Nathan, leave the lady alone."

The child ignored his mother, his big brown eyes beseeching. Joanna stooped and gathered the child into her arms.

"He's friendly with everyone," the woman explained. "I'm sorry if he's bothering you, Mrs. Galbraith."

For a moment, it shocked her that the woman knew her name, but quickly she realized that her face—the face of the woman whose husband had been the subject of a month-long search—had been plastered across all the local newspapers.

When the mother reached for Nathan, the little boy smiled and squirmed and wrapped his arms around Joanna's neck, refusing to let go. At that instant, when the child's cheek brushed hers, Joanna felt something deep inside her responding. "He's no bother," she said. "What a darling little boy." Running her hand over his dark curls felt like stroking pure silk. "How old is he?"

"Sixteen months," the woman said with a smile, obviously delighted by Joanna's ready appreciation of her pride and joy.

"What a nice young man you are, Nathan," Joanna told him, for which she received a slobbery grin. "Yes, and my, what a bunch of pretty teeth!" She laughed. Despite the grim circumstances that had brought her to the sheriff's substation tonight, the look on the child's face somehow seemed to make the horrid realities fade, at least momentarily, to the background.

But her respite was short-lived.

"Joanna?"

She spun to face Sheriff Bryan Miller, waiting to usher her into his office. His thick crop of red hair seemed unusually unruly tonight, and the faint red stubble on his chin and cheeks attested to the fact that he'd put in a long day.

"Just a second, Sheriff," she said, turning her attention to the child. "I've got to go now, sweetheart. You take good care of your mommy, hear?"

The child beamed and twisted around in Joanna's arms to reach for his mother.

"Can you give Mrs. Galbraith a hug goodbye?"

The child thought for a moment, curled his hand in a little wave and then lunged forward to bestow an enthusiastic kiss on Joanna's cheek.

"I'm afraid he's still a little confused with the hugs and kisses thing," the woman said as she shifted the child onto her hip.

Joanna turned to join Bryan Miller behind the dispatcher's counter. At the doorway to the sheriff's private office, the woman's voice stopped her.

"Mrs. Galbraith?"

"Yes."

"I...that is...well, I hope you don't mind, but I know about your troubles, and I just wanted to tell you to hang in there." The woman's eyes, so warm and so filled with goodwill, caused a lump to form in Joanna's throat. "I know they're going to find your husband real soon."

"Thanks," Joanna managed to say, and turned to follow Bryan Miller into his office. "Who's that lady waiting for?" she couldn't help asking before she sat in the chair the sheriff pulled out for her. "Is her husband a deputy?"

The look on Bryan's face and the way he sighed and shook his head made her wish she hadn't pried. "I don't think she has a husband. At least, if she does, we've never seen him. Her oldest kid, now, he's another story. We see a lot more of him than we'd like. I don't know for sure, but if I had to guess, I'd say she's here to bail him out again."

Joanna felt her heart sink. Another broken family. Two sons without a father, and a mother struggling to raise them. Not for the first time in her thirty-one years, she thanked her lucky stars for Jake.

"Well, what's going on, Joanna?" Bryan asked her when he'd closed the door. "Hoffman tells me you had some problems this evening."

She leaned forward in her chair, ready to explain, when the door opened and Drew walked in. After introductions, Drew explained to Sheriff Miller what had happened outside Valerie Wallace's condominium. "The Telluride police weren't able to find the slug or determine from what direction the bullet had come."

After discussing a couple of possibilities, including a stray bullet fired inadvertently from someone in a nearby yard or car, Drew asked if Lincoln Nesbitt was still being held.

"We let him go back to his hotel about—" the sheriff consulted his watch "—forty-five minutes ago."

In Joanna's mind, Lincoln Nesbitt was steeped in guilt, but it didn't seem plausible that he could have fired at them tonight.

"I suppose anything's possible," the sheriff said. "But unless he's a superhero, I don't think he could have been the shooter tonight. I could bring him back in tomorrow, if it would make you feel better, Joanna."

"What I can't understand," she said, rising, "is why you released him in the first place. Harley told us about the call and the...hammer." The word almost choked her.

Bryan's expression turned sour, and Joanna sensed that perhaps Harley had spoken out of turn. "We did bring Nesbitt in for another interview," he said. The word *interview* struck Joanna as highly inadequate for the picture of interrogation and assumed guilt Harley had painted.

"We've got a couple of possible leads." Her expression must have reflected the hope he'd ignited, because he reiterated, "Possible leads, Joanna. Nothing concrete. No reason to panic or start swearing out warrants yet."

"But what about the anonymous call?" Drew asked. "How did Lincoln answer the accusations the caller leveled?"

Bryan Miller ran a hand through his thick hair and sighed. "The same way he's answered all our questions from the beginning. He hasn't changed his story one iota."

"But what about the...weapon?" Joanna blurted, her patience stretched to snapping. What would it take before the authorities understood the threat Lincoln Nesbitt presented?

"Joanna, you're jumping to a lot of dangerous conclusions," Drew interjected. "A hammer is not a weapon until it can be proven it was used to intentionally harm someone."

She glared at him and directed her question to the sheriff. "And when will that be proven?" she demanded. "When my husband's body is finally found? And where will Lincoln Nesbitt be by then? He has a lot more money, you know. He could leave the country and we'd never find him."

The sheriff rose and looked at her with his steady green-eyed gaze. "Joanna, you should listen to Mr. Spencer. When we have enough evidence that a crime has been committed, we'll make an arrest. We're working on it. You mustn't lose sight of the fact that we're still trying to find Evan. I promise you. Night and day. No one around here has pulled a normal shift since he disappeared."

His words took her aback, and she swallowed hard. "I'm sorry, Bryan. It's just..."

"I know," he said, coming up beside her and placing a fatherly hand on her shoulder. "We're all tired—sick and tired—of not having any answers. But there's a real danger here of focusing so much in one direction that we stop looking in any other. So long as I'm the officer in charge of this case, there won't be any hasty arrests or mob mentality taking over. Mr. Nesbitt hasn't broken the law, as far as we know. It's not a crime to have a hammer in your trunk. If it were, I'd have to arrest half the people in this county. Now, why don't you go on home and get some rest. I'll call or send Harley out with any news."

Drew put his hand at her elbow and together they walked to the dispatcher's area. "Good night, Mrs. Galbraith," the dispatcher called. "We're all hoping for the best."

Nathan and his mother were still in the waiting area, and the baby squealed when he saw Joanna again. "Goodbye, sweetie," she called to him. "And take care."

They were in the parking lot when Sheriff Miller caught up to them. "Joanna. Drew. I'm glad I caught you before you left. I forgot to mention that I'll be sending a deputy out in the morning to pick up a few...things." The pointed look he gave Drew told her what kind of things. More samples, Joanna thought grimly.

"Of course. Whatever you need," Joanna said.

"Thanks. I know this is a difficult aspect of our investigation, but in order to fully exploit every lead, we have to follow proven procedures."

"What exactly will you need?" Drew asked outright.

When Sheriff Miller replied, "Evan's brush and comb," Joanna was certain they heard her gasp.

Chapter Nine

"But Harley already took hair samples," she told them. "Just yesterday morning."

"Oh. Well, good. Then we've probably got what we need already. I'll check with him in the morning."

"When do you think you'll have the results?" Joanna asked.

"Unfortunately, most of our labwork has to be sent to Denver, but it still shouldn't take that long. Maybe a day or two. I'll be in touch as soon as we have something definite."

Inside the car, Drew asked, "What was that all about? The samples, I mean. Somehow I got the impression that there's more to it than you told Bryan."

She combed her fingers through her hair and released an impatient sigh. "Oh, I don't know. It just seems strange to me that Sheriff Miller wouldn't know Harley had already gathered those samples. In fact, now that I think about it, I distinctly remember Harley telling me Bryan had sent him after them."

He didn't turn the engine on, but turned to her and said, "Jo, the police are constantly gathering evidence, hair and fibers and all kinds of other evidence most people wouldn't even think of. Maybe Harley was just trying to get a leg up on what he knew would come next."

"You? Defending Harley?" she asked, unable to resist the little jab. "Now, that's a switch."

He gave her a good-natured smile. "Yeah. Weird, huh? I guess it just comes from being around law enforcement long enough to see how it works—and sometimes how it doesn't. But even if all Harley was trying to do was impress his boss, you still can't really fault him. The point is, they needed the samples and they've got them."

Feeling mildly placated and a little guilty, Joanna said, "You know, every officer I've encountered through this whole long, awful nightmare has been extremely efficient, especially in light of all the different agencies who have had a hand in this case. I guess one slip-up is nothing to get excited about."

He turned the key in the ignition and gunned the engine to life. "Are you feeling up to stopping by the Lanskys' before we head home? I'd like to ask Nita about those files before she has a chance to do anything with them."

When she hesitated before answering, he asked, "What's wrong, Jo?"

"It's been a long night, Drew. I think we should go back to the Diamond C."

He pulled onto the street and headed the convertible toward the highway. "Of course, you're tired. I'm sorry. I wasn't thinking. It's been a trying twenty-four hours for you."

"The truth is, I just don't want to show up at the Lanskys' at this hour. I know Charlie gets up early, and I don't think it would be fair to intrude, especially since we plan to level accusations at his wife. The situation with Vista Grande will hit the Lanskys hard. Not only is Nita looking for a new job, but Charlie's construction company will no doubt suffer. His crew was awarded the bid for the first spec home."

"I'm glad you mentioned that bid award. It could be that some of those canceled checks you brought home from the bank today are made out to Charlie Lansky. If so, maybe that would explain Nita's scrambling to go through those files."

"I don't understand."

"Well, it wouldn't be the first time kickbacks and payoffs were involved in the awarding of a construction bid."

They rode in silence, Joanna lost in thoughts of motives, stray bullets and construction bids, until Drew turned onto the two-lane highway and headed west for the Diamond C.

"You know," she said, finally breaking the silence, "Nita would have a perfect opportunity to replace those files before anyone knew she took them by just bringing them back with her in the morning. If you don't mind getting up early, we could be there waiting for her. If she hasn't got the files with her, at least we can pin her down with a few questions. If she does have the files, then so much the better. Either way, we've kept the situation away from her home. She has kids, you know."

Drew's hand went behind her seat, and when his fingertips inadvertently brushed her hair, she had to suppress a shiver. "I always knew you were smart. But now I'm beginning to appreciate your investigative skills, as well. Who knows, you might be a born investigator, Jo."

She chuckled. "Right. And flattery will get you nowhere, Spencer."

"Yeah, well. You can't blame a guy for trying." He glanced at her injured hand. "How does it feel?"

"Better," she said. "You're a good nurse."

"Coming from you, Doc, that's a compliment."

"Yes. And something tells me you were born a lawyer."

"Oh? And what brought on that sudden conclusion?"

"Well, for one thing the way you deliberately created that little diversion just now to lighten things up a bit—very tricky, Counselor."

His smile was wide, driving those wonderful dimples into each cheek and making his eyes spark with blue diamond light. "Guilty as charged," he confessed. "But it isn't a tactic I use often."

"No?"

"No. Only for very special clients."

Ah, yes. That was another talent she remembered Drew Spencer possessed—his ability to make her feel as though she was the most special woman alive.

DREW HAD BEEN hunched over the files in the Joanna's spare room-office for only about an hour when he heard her in the doorway and looked up to see her standing there watching him work. She was dressed in a soft, blue robe, and her hair swirled around her shoulders like a wreath. He thought he'd never seen anything prettier than Joanna fresh from the bedroom.

"I thought you were sleeping."

"I guess I was, for a while, at least. I'm not sure what woke me. How about you? It's almost one. You must be exhausted."

He stretched his arms out in front of him and stood up. "I am tired," he admitted. "But for some reason, I haven't felt like sleeping. Must have been that coffee I drank at Valerie's. Maybe it was supercaffeinated, or something."

"Could be. She certainly seems to always have an abundance of energy. How about some hot chocolate? Jake used to make it for me when I couldn't sleep. We might even find a stray marshmallow or two, but no guarantees."

"Sounds good," he said and followed her into the kitchen. "You know, I think we should try to arrange another interview with Valerie. Somehow I think she knows more than she's saying. Is she usually so noncommittal, or did we catch her at a bad time—just getting in from out of town like that? What's she like, normally?"

"You know, that's a tough question. Whenever I've been around her, she's always made me feel welcome. Like she's genuinely glad to see me. I've watched her with others, and she seems to give the same impression of warmth and openness, and yet—" she stopped long enough to find the cocoa in the cupboard while Drew fetched the milk "—yet, when I stop to think about it, she has never revealed very much of herself to me. I've known her for...well, let's see." She thought about it while she combined the ingredients in a saucepan on the stove. "Well, I guess I met her when she went to work for Evan about a year ago. I've seen her on countless occasions, lunches and around the office, and yet I know very little about her personally."

"How about Evan? Are they close?"

"Yes. I believe they are," she said without hesitating. "A couple of months ago they went to Nevada together to look into a property that they were thinking of investing in. Unfortunately, it turned out to be a bad deal, so they didn't make an offer. But I know Evan trusted her judgment and valued her opinion enough to take her along."

As she stirred the hot chocolate, trying to get the cocoa lumps out, she felt Drew's eyes studying her. "Okay, what is it?" she asked without bothering to look up. "I can feel your question from here, Spencer."

"I'm just wondering how you felt about Valerie and Evan going off for the weekend to Nevada."

"What do you mean?"

"Joanna, correct me if I'm wrong, but aren't you the same girl who pitched a fit when I gave Gail Hunter a ride to school because her car was in the shop for a week and she would have had to walk six miles?"

She laughed. "You were a sweetie to do that, given the flack you knew you'd get from me. Back then I could be a real brat, couldn't I? A real green-eyed monster."

"No," he surprised her by saying. "You were smart. And you were right. Gail made a pass at me every day that week."

"What?" She waved her spoon at him playfully. "Why, that little tart!"

"Come on, Jo. I'm serious."

"So am I." The cocoa came close to boiling, so she turned the heat down and kept stirring until it was smooth. "But I've also grown up."

"I guess I just can't imagine any wife being thrilled at the prospect of her husband spending the weekend with a woman like Valerie Wallace. Surely you noticed she's a shameless flirt."

"Oh, you mean the crack about you being good-looking?"

He frowned. "All right, have it your way. Maybe I'm just unenlightened."

She set out two mugs and poured hot chocolate in each. "The marshmallows should be over there." She indicated the cupboard nearest him, and he retrieved the bag and plopped four or five miniatures in both cups and then carried them into the living room, where Joanna curled up in Jake's chair and he lounged on the couch.

"Okay," she said, sipping her drink. "I admit it. Originally, the three of us were supposed to go on that trip. But something came up with somebody's horse—it always happens—and I just wasn't going to make a big deal about them changing their plans. After all, it really was a business trip, to a small town call Goldstrike. There's a motel there—the Vagabond—that was listed in one of those nationwide real estate books. From the picture, it looked like a really nice place, but according to Valerie and Evan, it turned out to be a flea trap. Anyway, they came back pretty disappointed. Evan had been looking for good investment property, especially in California and Nevada."

Now it was Drew's turn to be flip. "But weren't you worried about your husband? I mean, with all Valerie's luggage, a man could hurt himself just trying to be chivalrous."

She laughed. "That is something, isn't it? I don't think I've ever seen black-and-white luggage before."

Their conversation shifted from Valerie and luggage to old times and friends and family. By the time they'd finished the cocoa, Joanna could hardly keep her eyes open, and for the first time in weeks, the accumulation of stinging stress between her shoulders seemed to have vanished.

She stood up and started to take their cups into the kitchen, but he said, "I'll get them, Jo. You're dead on your feet. Go to bed. And this time, stay there."

She gave him a mock salute and a smile. "Thanks, Drew," she said softly, stopping halfway across the room. "It was fun. I mean it. And for little while, I almost forgot about what we're facing tomorrow."

"Good night, Jo," he said and his gaze touched her so lovingly, it could have almost been a kiss.

TWO HOURS LATER, with Joanna sound asleep in her bed, Drew still sat poring over the files in Evan Galbraith's home office. When he thought he heard a rattling sound coming from the back of the house, he prowled through the kitchen to the back door. But by the time he switched on the floodlight to illuminate the backyard, whatever—or whoever—had been responsible for the noise was gone.

It could have been an animal, he told himself. One of the barn cats or a skunk, or even a raccoon or a deer that had wandered up from the creek and was nosing around the back of the house, looking for a midnight snack.

The Diamond C bordered the Spencer ranch on the north and national forest lands on the west, and despite the growth of the area, the land between the ranches and Telluride was still a haven for a large variety of wildlife.

Drew had jury-rigged the lock on the back door and he checked it again to assure himself it hadn't been violated. When he was satisfied, he went back to work, but not before he made a detour down the hall to ease open Joanna's bedroom door to make certain she was okay.

With the light from the hallway falling softly across her face, Drew stood drinking in the sight of her, wishing he could get a closer look—closer touch, maybe. But when she shifted in her sleep, he pulled the door closed and went to the office, feeling lonely and strangely depressed.

The stack of files waiting for him didn't improve his mood. If the D.A. had known how many of Evan's business files he'd kept at home, Drew felt reasonably sure they might have been placed under the same informal order that had been issued in an attempt to protect the files at the Galbarith offices in Telluride.

So far, however, the files he'd waded through hadn't been especially significant. Most were concerned with transactions, but the stack of canceled Vista Grande checks Joanna had brought home from the bank had proved to be very interesting indeed.

Beginning in May, and continuing until a few days prior to his disappearance, Evan had steadily increased the number of checks he'd written, as well as the amounts. It wasn't a clear pattern, but it was something.

As the bankers had explained to Lincoln and Joanna, most of the checks were made out to cash and endorsed by Evan. He'd had to write a lot of checks to siphon off such a large amount of money, especially since an account in the name of a partnership, as this one was, would require two signatures—any combination of Evan's, Lincoln's and Joanna's—for an amount over five thousand dollars.

Of those checks varying between five and ten thousand dollars, most were made out to a company called Calder Johannsen Inc., and both Evan and Joanna's signatures were present on all of them. Drew scratched the company's name at the top of a sheet of yellow legal paper.

Until Aunt Bess had confided in him what her friend at the post office had told her, Drew had never heard of Calder Johannsen, the firm to which Evan had been so concerned about sending packages the week before he disappeared. Drew reasoned that if Calder Johannsen was a consulting or surveying firm, Evan's expenses might have been legitimate.

He remembered Joanna mentioning the expenses involved in setting up a development the size and scope of Vista Grande, expenses that had nothing to do with the actual construction of homes, roads or amenities. Perhaps Evan hadn't misappropriated funds, after all. For Joanna's sake, Drew hoped, despite what he felt intuitively, that this Calder Johannsen Inc. turned out to be a bona fide firm. Perhaps they somehow assisted in preparing a property for development or rezoning. If that was the case, the aspersions being cast upon Evan's name would all be unjustified, and together Drew and Joanna could probably work with Lincoln Nesbitt to dig her out of this financial grave. If the expenses were legitimate and Evan had not absconded, then that led to the grim conclusion that Joanna's husband had met with foul play. Neither conclusion foreshadowed a happy ending, as Joanna had so rightly predicted.

Rocking back in the swivel chair, Drew rubbed his eyes and stretched his aching muscles, trying to decide if he could face another hour.

The sheer volume of paperwork in the room was daunting, not to mention the many implications of the missing money. Included in Evan's papers were several boxes of receipts, canceled checks and miscellaneous documentation for the Diamond C. Many of the Diamond C boxes bore handwritten labels in either Jake's or Joanna's hand,

and as he flipped through them, Drew felt as though he was prying.

When he stumbled across Jake's death certificate, however, he felt such a deep and personal sadness that he forgave himself for digging into their privates lives. He had a right to be here, he told himself, if for no other reason than by virtue of his feelings for Jake and for his past involvement with Joanna. Yes, he had every right to be here, and until she asked him to go, he intended to fight hard to save Jake's dreams.

Reaching for his fourth cup of coffee in the last hour, Drew's gaze wandered between the next stack of files and the single bed in the corner. Each time he felt tempted to call it a night, he remembered Joanna's face when she'd walked into his office yesterday—God, had it really only been a little over twenty-four hours since he'd agreed to take her case? He groaned and shifted a box of files to the floor, feeling as though he'd already spent half that time in this room full of paper.

After another hour of sorting through documents related to the ranch and the Vista Grande development, Drew's eyes started crossing, and the numbers and names on the checks became an incomprehensible jumble. The last glance at the bed did him in, and the bed won out.

But a few minutes later, stretched out in the darkness, his mind refused to be still. Even with his body near exhaustion, he couldn't stop thinking about her. About her bravery and her honor and how perfect she still felt in his arms. How could anything that felt so right be so wrong?

THE MURKY LIGHT of predawn filled the room when Drew opened his eyes, feeling as though someone had sandpapered the inside of his lids. After sleeping on the too-narrow, too-soft bed, his body felt closer to sixty-two years old than thirty-two.

With a groan, he reminded himself that he and Joanna planned to confront Nita when she opened the office. Early, Jo had said. Well—he glanced at his watch—six was early. At least in his neighborhood.

After padding down the hall to the bathroom and quickly showering and dressing, he pushed open Joanna's door. She didn't even move when the door squeaked. For a few minutes, he stood watching her, as struck by her beauty as he'd been last night, and as moved by his longing for her.

He thought about her last night, about the glass in her hand and the worry and fear that had been etched into her face ever since the bullets had started to fly, and he decided to let her sleep. After all, he knew what he had to ask Nita, and he didn't need to wake Jo to do it.

Ten minutes later, he was ready to go. After making sure he had the key to the house in his jeans pocket, he slipped out the door, locking it behind him, and drove to town.

It wasn't quite seven-thirty when he pulled up in front of Galbraith Realty to see Nita unlocking the front door. The black-and-white tote bag was nowhere to be seen, but he thought the medium-size cardboard box she set down to get the door unlocked might prove just as fruitful

When he came up behind her, she jumped. "Oh! Mr. Spencer! You almost scared the life out of me."

"Sorry, Nita. But I saw you carrying that box and I thought I'd give you a hand."

The concern on her face was immediate. "Oh, it's no bother. Really." She grabbed it off the sidewalk. "It isn't heavy. See?"

"Please—" he took it out of her hands "—I insist."

Frowning, she relented, shoving the door open and holding it for him while he stepped inside. "Just set it down over there," she instructed none too gently. "Thanks."

After flipping on the lights, she put her purse in the bottom drawer of her desk and took up her position behind it.

Drew stood in the middle of the room, watching.

"Mr. Spencer," she said. "I don't mean to be rude, but is there something you wanted?"

"Me? Oh, no. Not really. I just thought I'd drop by early so we could have a little chat before Joanna and I resumed our investigation into her husband's files." He emphasized the word files and received exactly the reaction he'd anticipated.

"Well . . . sure, sure, of course. Wh-whatever you want to know, I'd be glad to answer. But first—" she jumped up as though she'd been shocked out of her seat "—I'll put on some coffee. Would you like a cup?"

"Why, yes. Thanks. Actually, I haven't even had my breakfast."

"Hmm. Too bad." But the expression on her face seemed decidedly unsympathetic. "Now, you just go on into Mr. Galbraith's office and get started," she told him. "I'll put the coffee on, and when it's ready, I'll bring us both a cup and we'll have that, uh, chat."

"Fine. Fine. I look forward to it, Nita."

She nodded and hurried away from him down the hall as if she was a passenger on the *Titanic* and the last lifeboat was about to be launched.

JOANNA DIDN'T KNOW what woke her, but she sat up quickly, instantly alert and listening. "Drew?" she called out, but received no answer.

She grabbed her soft terry robe from the foot of the bed, shrugged into it and tied it around her waist before emerging into the hallway just in time to see the bathroom door closing. Hearing the water running in the shower, she tapped on the door and called out loud enough to be heard over the water, "I'm putting coffee on."

The garbled sound of a mouth full of toothpaste made an incomprehensible noise that she took to mean okay. She smiled and padded into the kitchen. Peering into the refrigerator, she pulled out ingredients for a western omelet, cheered that for once her stomach wasn't churning.

For the first time in weeks, she actually felt hungry for breakfast. Perhaps Drew's positive influence was taking effect, or more likely, it just felt good to have someone near enough to touch who was as focused as she was on finding Evan and sorting out the tangle that had become her life. Even if keeping that someone from slipping back into her heart was taking an all-out effort, perhaps the benefits were worth the struggle.

She heard him in the hallway. "Breakfast will be ready in a few minutes," she said. "I'm sorry I overslept. We still may be able to intercept her, though. It's only a little after eight and—"

The sound of the screen door slamming interrupted her sentence. "Drew?" She headed through the house toward the front door. It was standing open, and when she peered beyond the screen she saw that his car was gone. Strange for him to just leave like that, without a word. The sound of an engine roaring in the distance and dust on the road were his only goodbye. Odd. She could have sworn he'd parked his car out front last night.

Slowly, feeling more confused by the second, she walked to the kitchen and set the skillet aside. With one whiff, the smell of frying eggs seemed to make a wake-up call to her stomach, and the queasy feeling she'd learned to live with for the past few weeks came back with a vengeance.

After a shower, Joanna dressed in blue jeans and a T-shirt and checked in with her service. They hadn't received any emergency calls overnight, and the only appointment she had was for later this morning. As soon as she hung up the phone, it occurred to her to call Drew at Evan's office, but just as quickly the idea died. The last thing she wanted to do was interrupt him in the middle of his questioning Nita.

Her stomach turned over again, doing its now familiar roll at the mere thought of what might develop today. She went into the kitchen for a glass of water, thinking that if she left now, she might still catch Drew at Evan's office. Somehow, just the thought of sharing the situation with Drew seemed to unburden her mind.

Her hand was on the door when the phone rang. Before the second ring, she picked it up and said hello, experiencing a small and unreasonable flutter of disappointment when the man's voice on the other end of the line wasn't Drew's.

"Joanna Galbraith?"

"Yes." As it had from the beginning of her ordeal, the sound of a strange male voice automatically set Joanna thinking that the caller was some kind of law officer and that he was calling with news of Evan. Was this the day? Had he been found? Was he alive?

"Joanna. I know where Evan is."

"What? Who is this? Where is he?"

"I know where he is, Joanna. And you'll be going to the same place if you don't do exactly as I say."

Joanna's breath froze. "Wh-what do you mean? Who is this?"

"He's dead, Joanna. As dead as you'll soon be if you don't do exactly as I say. You owe me. Both of you."

Joanna's knees bent, and she sank onto the chair beside the phone. "Please. If you know something about my husband, for heaven's sake—"

"Heaven has nothing to do with the likes of Evan Galbraith," the caller growled. "Now, pay attention. Evan is gone. You got that? And if you want to go on living and take up where you left off with that boyfriend of yours—"

Suddenly, Joanna could hear no more and she slammed the receiver down hard. Shaken, she sat for a full minute before the dizzying nausea hit like a tidal wave.

Chapter Ten

"Just get over here!" Nita whispered, her hand cupped around the receiver. "He's here now, and I don't know what I'm supposed to say or do. Yes! He helped me carry it in. Now get over—" She obviously heard him behind her, because she spun around and dropped the receiver, leaving it to dangle wildly at the end of the spiral cord connected to the white wall phone.

"Oh, my gosh! You scared me half to death."

With a speed that seemed to surprise her, Drew reached for the phone, put the receiver to his ear and said to her, "Your party seems to have hung up."

He kept his eyes on her as he replaced the receiver.

"Oh, it wasn't important. Just a personal call. I was. . . . finished anyway. I was just about to bring that coffee. Hope I didn't keep you waiting."

Drew smiled. "Oh, I've got all morning, Nita."

She barely suppressed a glare before she turned her back to him, slid the glass pot from the base of the automatic coffee maker and poured them each a steaming mugful.

"Do you always come in this early, Nita? The sign on the door lists hours of ten to five."

Without taking her eyes off the task of stirring powdered creamer and sugar in her cup, she explained, "I like to come in early to catch up on my work before the phone starts ringing."

"Very admirable."

"I love my job, Mr. Spencer," she informed him tersely, and flipped the switch on the coffee maker before she turned and stalked to the front office.

Drew stayed right on her heels. He didn't want to give her time to tamper with the contents of the box she was so obviously concerned about. He was keenly interested in seeing how this played out—in finding out who showed up in response to Nita's call for rescue.

"Can I help you with something?" she asked impatiently. "Because if not, I really need to get to work."

"Oh. Sorry. Please, don't let me distract you. I guess we can wait for Joanna, if you'd like, before we have that little talk. In the meantime, I'll just relax and wait out here for her, if you don't mind. That office can be rather dreary, can't it? I mean, not knowing if he'll ever be back, if he's alive or..."

She made a disgusted sound with her tongue and spun around in her chair to yank open a file drawer.

Drew smiled to himself and sat in a chair just a few feet from her desk. He picked up a magazine on home decor that was lying on a small glass and chrome table and flipped it open. Over the top of the page, he glanced up to see her fuming. Her quick, agitated movements told him his presence was doing more than interrupting her daily routine.

When the phone rang, Nita jumped to grab it before the second ring. Her salutation seemed unusually brisk, and Drew almost felt guilty for torturing the woman with his presence.

"It's for you," she said, her forehead creased with worry. "It's Joanna and she sounds real upset."

"THE PHONE COMPANY has promised the caller identification equipment will be delivered by sometime this afternoon."

Bryan Miller sat opposite her with his hands folded in front of him on the kitchen table. Drew stood a few feet away, his back to the countertop, his arms folded.

"In the meantime, let your answering matching pick up your calls. You can monitor them, of course. But if he calls again, don't respond. Let's keep him guessing, at least until we can arm ourselves with a way to track him down."

Joanna nodded. The front door was open, as were the two cross-paned windows in the kitchen, drawing the cool mountain air through the house. But despite the steady flow of sweet morning air, Joanna couldn't seem to get enough.

"Jo, did the voice sound at all familiar?" Drew asked, walking over to the table to sit down.

She shook her head. "No. Not at all. If I've ever spoken to that person before, I have no memory of it. Yet, he did seem to know me. He called me by my first name easily."

Drew's blue eyes seemed to darkened with the deep concern that had been lodged on his face from the moment he walked back into the house.

"For what it's worth, Joanna, we have no reason to believe what he said was true—that anything has really happened to Evan."

"But what about the hammer in Lincoln's car?"

"It does no good for you to keep going back to that," the sheriff said. "We won't have any answers until we hear from the lab. Even then, we'd only be guessing." Bryan turned to Drew. "Will you be here for the rest of the day? I'm not sure I like the idea of Joanna being alone."

"Absolutely. I have no plans to return to Denver until Evan is found."

"Well, I guess that's about all we can do for now," Bryan said and scooted his chair back and stood. "Let us know if the caller contacts you again. I'll be in touch."

Joanna remained seated while Drew showed Bryan out. At the door, she heard him ask if there had been any more calls from the mysterious woman who'd implicated Lincoln Nesbitt in some sort of crime. She heard Bryan's chilling reply, "Okay, Drew. You show me some other way that blood and hair can wind up on a hammer and I'll reconsider."

When Drew came back in the kitchen, he said, "When I walked Bryan out, he told me they'd traced last night's call to a pay phone at a convenience store in Ridgeway. But the phone is outside the store and evidently, the clerk didn't notice anyone. If someone did use the phone, he paid no attention to them. Bryan sent Harley to Ridgeway to track down the local customers who bought gas at that store last night. Hopefully, one of them will remember seeing someone using the phone."

"Sounds like a long shot."

"A lot of investigation seems that way at first, but sometimes we get lucky and that long shot pans out." He sat down in the chair Bryan had just vacated. What a difference having him sit so near, she thought guiltily. She hadn't felt a thing when Bryan had been that close, but with Drew, her heart picked up a beat and her skin felt warm all over.

"Jo, think back. Do you recall anything distinctive about the voice on the phone this morning? An accent? A different kind of speech pattern, maybe? Anything that might help us identify him?"

Joanna shook her head. "I'm sorry. But as I told Sheriff Miller, it was just an ordinary voice. I don't know if I'd recognize it again if I heard it somewhere else, in a different setting or in person rather than on the phone." She slumped in her chair, suddenly tired of fighting the sinking sense of defeat that seemed to meet her on every front.

Drew slid his hands slowly across the table and gathered her uninjured hand between them. She started to pull away, but something in his touch and in his eyes told her he was just being a friend in the best way he knew how.

"It won't always be like this, I promise," he said. "The events of the last couple of days seem to indicate a break in the case. The call from Ridgeway, the mysterious call to you this morning. These things signal a change. If someone truly does know what happened to Evan, it will come out."

Instinctively, she returned his little squeeze of reassurance. "Thank you, Drew. I don't know how I'd be getting through any of this without you. When I heard you leave this morning, I thought for a moment—"

"You heard me leaving? I tried to not wake you. You seemed so exhausted last night, I figured you needed the rest. That's why I decided to go see Nita alone."

"You tried not to wake me?"

He frowned. "Yeah. I really did, but I guess I wasn't as quiet as I thought."

Something didn't make sense. She pulled her hand away from his and sat up straighter. "Wait a minute, Drew. Are you telling me you don't remember me talking to you when you were brushing your teeth? I know you've never been a morning person, but it really wasn't that early."

He stared at her, obviously confused.

"Remember? I called to you outside the bathroom door to tell you I was up and that I was putting coffee on." The look on his face frightened her. "What is it, Drew? Say something. You're scaring me!"

"Joanna, when I left you were in bed." His expression softened when he admitted, "I looked in on you before I left."

If she'd peered over the edge of a forty-story building, her stomach couldn't have dropped any faster. "But if it wasn't you in the bathroom, then who—"

Her heart hammered as a look of absolute shock registered on his face. She didn't have the courage to put into words what must have happened.

"Someone was in the house. Today. While you slept." He was on his feet and charging toward the bathroom without another word. She followed and came up behind him in the doorway where he stood staring. "I don't know what I expected to find," he admitted.

The thought of someone in the house with her oblivious to his or her presence terrified Joanna. "I remember I heard a noise in the hall." Her voice shook. "Then I called your name. Obviously, he had enough warning to duck into the bathroom and pretend he was you."

He turned, pulled her into his arms and hugged her against him with an almost desperate grip. "My God, Jo. Do you realize what could have happened? If he'd hurt you... if anything had happened to you..."

She tipped her face up to look at him and saw so much love in his eyes, it took her breath away. Her heart ached for his touch, for the care and concern that seemed to flow from him so naturally. Nothing had ever felt more natural than to be in his arms again. And nothing had ever felt harder than pulling away.

But she did. She jerked out of his arms before she had a change of heart and a change of mind. She bolted for the door. Even with the house wide open, she needed more air.

Outside, in the warm, bright freshness of a summer day in the San Juans, Joanna almost couldn't believe what had taken place in this seemingly sheltered and peaceful valley. She stood with her hand braced on the wooden porch rail, fighting for emotional equilibrium, staring at the peaks in the distance, taking deep breaths to calm the turmoil that threatened to shake everything that was her world.

She didn't turn when she heard him push the screen door open and step out onto the porch. "I'll call Bryan and tell him about the intruder—although I'm not sure there's much he can do about it now."

"Thank you."

"I still want to find out what Nita's hiding, but I'm not leaving you alone from now until this thing is over. I think you should cancel any appointments, at least for the rest of the day."

What he said made sense. She was in no shape to take on anyone else's problems today. "I'm always on call for emergencies, but I'll ask Doc Anderson to cover the routine cases for the rest of the week." Was it Tuesday or Wednesday? Suddenly, she couldn't remember. Since Evan's disappearance the days seemed to run together in a blur. "Do you think he's dead?" she asked, almost without realizing she'd said it.

He didn't answer immediately. "I don't know." His voice sounded flat, too official, but completely honest. "At first, I thought it was a distinct possibility."

"But now?" She turned, leaned her hips against the rail and crossed her arms.

"Now? Well, now it seems someone is trying too hard to make us believe that he is. But with no more evidence than what's been found, and no car, no real weapon, no witnesses—"

"No body," she added woodenly, her voice not much more than a hoarse whisper.

He nodded, and she saw him swallow before he said, "Right. No body. And to me, that just doesn't add up to murder."

They stood looking at each other, at a loss for words, neither taking a step closer, neither backing away.

Finally, it was Drew who broke the spell. "I'll take a look at the back door and see if I can figure out how the intruder got in. Then I'll call a locksmith. I think it would be a good idea if we had all the locks changed, just as a precaution."

"Yes, of course, you're right." Joanna felt suddenly distanced from him, though she couldn't help admiring his thoroughness as an investigator, and now, it seemed, as a bodyguard, as well.

"I also think we should sit down and try to brainstorm why someone is bent on breaking into your home. Obviously, whatever they were after the other night, they didn't find, and they came back this morning to look again. When they saw my car gone, they probably figured we'd left together."

"I don't really have anything of value in the house," she said. "I keep a little mad money in the kitchen, and there's my grandmother's silver. But other than that..." She glanced at her wedding ring and felt his gaze following hers.

"What about guns?"

She stifled a shudder. Ever since Jake's accident, she'd been skittish on the subject. "Jake had a hunting rifle and—" she swallowed "—his revolver. But I don't know where that is." *I don't want to know,* she added silently. "And I think there's an old shotgun around somewhere. Maybe in the attic. I could check to make sure they're still here."

"Somehow, I don't believe whoever broke in was looking for Jake's old guns, but it wouldn't hurt to check. I tend to think our answers are hidden somewhere in that heap of papers. So, when I finish checking the lock on the back door, I'll get to work in the office, going through more of the canceled checks." He gave her a faint smile and turned to go.

"Wait, Drew," she called. "Before you go..."

He stopped and stood in the doorway, holding the screen door open, waiting. The look of expectation in his eyes stabbed her, and she felt as though she could read his thoughts and feelings as clearly as if he'd spoken them. *What about us, Jo?* he seemed to be saying. *What are we going to do about this love that refuses to die?*

But she had no answers, nothing she could tell him or herself. What could she say about a future that they didn't have and had no right to wish for?

"Joanna?"

"Nothing." She dropped her gaze and turned to step off the porch. "You go on in. I just wanted to tell you that I'm going to take a walk to clear my head."

A flicker of concern sparked in his eyes.

"Don't worry. I won't go far. Just around the barn and the corrals. I feel like it's been a long time since I visited my animals. When I get back, I'll call Doc Anderson and then come in to help you sort through the slush."

MOST OF THE DAY was spent dealing with the locksmith and the phone company. After the technician left, Joanna phoned Bess Spencer and asked her to call and hang up so they could test the caller-identification unit. Bess called back immediately, and the number for the Spencer ranch appeared in glowing red digits the moment Drew's aunt hung up the phone.

Joanna called Bess back to thank her.

"No trouble at all," Bess said. "And, Joanna, please don't hesitate to call if there's anything else I can do to help."

A few minutes later, Joanna walked into the office and handed Drew a glass of iced tea. She'd taken the bandage off her hand, and the cold from her glass felt good against the wound.

"Thanks. Hmm. Mint." He picked up the small leaf and inhaled. "I remember Jake always had a patch of mint in his garden."

"I guess he spoiled me. I just can't seem to enjoy a glass of tea without it."

Drew ran his hand through his hair, tipped back in Evan's chair and took a drink from the frosty glass. "What do you know about a company by the name of Calder Johannsen? Is it a construction firm?"

"Calder Johannsen." Joanna thought, then shook her head. "I don't recall ever hearing of a company by that name. Why?"

"Are you sure?"

"Yes. It's an unusual name. I'm sure I would remember. Why? Should I?"

"I think you would," he said, leaning forward in the chair and setting the glass down in the only clear space on the desk. "You've signed checks to them totaling almost three hundred thousand dollars."

Joanna leaned against the doorjamb for support. She thought she must have heard wrong. "Excuse me, but did you say I signed some checks? That's impossible!"

"Take a look." He held a stack of canceled checks out to her.

Fighting to keep her hands steady, she leafed through the first two or three, then studied the rest harder. Confusion turned to anger, and she slapped the checks down on the desk, almost toppling Drew's tea. He caught the glass just as it started to tip. "What is it? What's the matter?"

"That is not my signature!"

"Are you sure?"

"Of course I'm sure. I did not sign these checks!"

Drew picked up one of the checks and studied the signature line. "It certainly looks like your writing."

"It may look like it, but it isn't. I know my own signature, and what's more, I'd remember signing a check for—" she grabbed the next check "—for twenty thousand dollars! Trust me, I don't do it that often."

Drew let the check slide from his hand to the desk, and for a moment he sat thinking. Joanna stared at the checks again, and for the first time her focus shifted from the forgery of her name to the name on the first signature line—Evan's name.

Whoever had signed her name must have done so with Evan's knowledge. Or even Evan's blessing.

Her anger turned to outrage and then, just as quickly, the temperature inside the room seemed to soar and sweat popped out in clammy beads all over her skin. Before she could make it to the end of the hall, her blouse was soaked and her scalp felt as damp as it she'd just stepped out of a sauna.

A sudden and undeniable wave of nausea hit her halfway down the hall, and she raced to the bathroom, willing herself not to be sick until she closed the bathroom door.

IT TOOK SEVERAL HOURS for the decision to be made as to who would officially take custody of the forged checks—CBI, FBI, the Telluride police department and the county sheriff's department had all been involved in trying to locate Evan. It was the Telluride district attorney's office, however, who finally took jurisdiction.

Once again, Joanna felt heartened to have Drew by her side and involved in the case. Somehow, he seemed the only one with an interest in all aspects, not only in finding Evan and unraveling the intrigue around the missing funds, but in discovering the truth about Lincoln Nesbitt, finding the mysterious intruder and finally—what he seemed to have made his top priority—protecting her.

Outside the D.A.'s office, he turned to her. "How are you feeling?"

"Physically, much better."

He put his hand in the middle of her back as he walked with her down the hall and out to his car. "And emotionally?"

"Totally drained," she admitted, sliding her sunglasses onto her face. "But I'm glad the D.A. has those checks now. Somehow, I think we'll have a better chance of finding the forger close to home."

"Care to explain why you feel that way? Is it just pure instinct, or do you have a suspect in mind?"

She did, but she hated to cast aspersions without evidence. Unfortunately, the man opening her car door was better at reading her thoughts than she was at concealing them.

"Out with it, Jo," he ordered when they were both in the car. "At this point, I'd say your guess would be the most informed."

"But—"

"Don't worry. A suspicion without evidence won't convict anyone. Tell me."

"Nita's loyalty to Evan has been unquestioned from the beginning."

"But forgery? That's above and beyond the call, don't you think? Even for the most dedicated employee."

"You'd have to know Evan."

His look told her he was glad he hadn't had that opportunity.

"Okay," she conceded. "But he can be a real charmer with the ladies. And if he convinced Nita that signing those checks was necessary and even harmless..."

"Well, they did start out small. If I remember right, the first check was only a thousand dollars or so."

Only, she thought, remembering when a thousand dollars would have seemed like a million to her and Jake. What a simple time that had been. A time she longed for, now that millions of dollars—embezzled dollars, no less—had become a part of her everyday reality.

"From a thousand, they seemed to have increased every few weeks to a larger and larger amount."

"And as she got in deeper, it wouldn't be hard to imagine Evan assuring her with each check that I wouldn't ever press the issue." Had he colored Joanna as the unreasonable and reluctant third partner? she wondered. Or had he just stuck with the obvious—portraying her as the cold and uncaring wife? Ironic, she thought. Cold and uncaring was what his deceptions were quickly turning her into. "With my husband as the cosigner," she went on, "whoever signed my name must have thought they would never be confronted. After all, wasn't the development going to benefit all of us in the long run?"

"Including the Lanskys, whose construction company would automatically be awarded the bid in exchange for Nita's devotion."

"Exactly."

"You've built a pretty convincing case, there, Counselor," he said with a wry smile as he pulled the car onto the street. "But Nita still must have known she was committing forgery. A serious crime, especially with the amount of money involved in this case."

"I know. And that's why I don't want to go to the D.A. or the police with any of my suspicions until we have more evidence. An accusation such as this could ruin lives. Regardless of the money pouring in and the way this area is growing, we're still a pretty small town. Everyone knows everyone, at least the old-timers. For heaven's sake, Drew, you played high school football with half the businessmen in this town. Remember?"

"I remember the pretty cheerleaders," he teased. "The ones with the great big—"

She smacked him before he could go further.

"I was going to say megaphones," he finished. "Good grief, Jo! What did you think I was going to say?"

"You're hopeless."

"Not really," he said, his voice suddenly so low and serious it sent a surge of raw desire straight through her.

"Drew, I—"

"I know. I know. You're a married woman. But right now it's looking like that husband of yours has broken every vow in the marriage manual, so spare me. Okay?"

She didn't miss the bitter edge to his voice, and at the moment she couldn't dispute anything he said. Based on what they'd discovered today, he must think her a fool to stay committed to Evan. But Drew didn't know everything, and there was no way she could tell him what else had transpired, what deep bond had been forged between her and her husband. For now, no one could know.

She'd seen the pity on their faces for almost a month now. Even when she'd had a reason to be pitied, it had been difficult for the prideful Joanna to accept that kind of sympathy—the kind extended to a woman who'd married the wrong man.

Now, things had changed. Before long, those who'd suspected Evan of embezzlement, who'd hinted from the beginning that he'd run out on her, would be proven right. Those pitying glances would change, and when the whole truth came out... Well, she just couldn't allow herself to look that far.

For now, she only knew one thing for sure. She'd been through a great deal, thanks to Evan. Endured a kind of pain she hadn't known existed. But to see a look of pity in Drew Spencer's eyes was one thing she didn't have to endure, one thing she didn't think she could bear. Not now. Not ever.

Chapter Eleven

By the time they pulled up in front of the real estate offices, it was almost seven, and it came as no surprise to either of them that Nita had locked up and gone. Once inside, Drew walked immediately to the spot where he'd placed the box he'd carried in for Nita that morning.

"Of course it's gone," Joanna said, dropping her purse on a chair. "I guess we'll never know what was in that box. Whether it contained the files she took home last night, or whether this whole episode is a wild-goose chase."

He hated that she'd been disappointed again. "I wish there was a way to know who she called."

"Her secrets are safe, it seems," Joanna muttered, idly picking up the message pad beside Nita's phone. "This is strange," she said.

He moved over to stand beside her so he could see the message that had captivated her attention.

"This message for Valerie from Nevada. See?" She pointed to the carbon of a message that, according to the notation Nita had made, came in for Valerie a little before noon. "Tony Winston. He's the owner of the Vagabond, the motel I mentioned last night. Remember? The one Evan was considering purchasing in Nevada."

"Yes. But what about the message bothers you?"

"Well, for one thing, neither Evan nor Valerie wanted the place. They turned the owner down flat."

He couldn't see why Joanna was so interested in this obscure piece of information. "Maybe the guy, this Winston, decided to lower the price, or he wants to try again."

"Not possible." The way she said it left no room for doubt.

"You sound pretty sure of that."

"I am. When I was in the office last week, covering the phones for Nita while she went to the dentist, I got a call from Tony Winston's daughter. She called to let Evan know that her father had passed away and that his heirs had decided not to sell."

"Maybe they changed their minds."

"But why leave Winston's name, then? Doesn't that seem strange?"

He took the message pad from her and glanced at it before he set it on Nita's desk. "It seems that everything associated with your husband's business is a bit unusual."

"You'll get no argument from me on that," she said with a sigh.

"Jo, sit down. We need to talk to Nita, anyway. When we confront her, we can ask her about this message, as well. The longer we wait, the more muddled things seem to get. I have a feeling Nita could clear up at least a part of the picture. If we don't confront her, I think Sheriff Miller should." She opened her mouth to protest, but he raised a hand, asking for another chance to state his argument. "Listen, I know how you feel about causing the Lanskys any domestic problems, and I respect you for caring, for being cautious and not wanting to hurl careless accusations. Your integrity is one of the things I always loved best about you." When she started, he said, "It's no surprise I love you, is it, Jo? Surely you remember? I was the one who let you get away."

"Oh, Drew." It came out as a gasp, and she reached over and touched a lock of hair that had fallen onto his forehead, and when her fingers grazed his skin, he felt as though she'd touched his heart.

"Come on." He took her hand and urged her out of her chair. "If Nita is innocent, she has nothing to worry about."

"Nothing to worry about," she muttered as they walked out the door. "I've forgotten what that feels like."

IT TOOK DREW less than ten minutes to drive to the Lansky residence, even though the two-story stone-and-cedar home was outside the city limits. As soon as they pulled into the drive, Joanna sensed no one was home. Nita's car wasn't in the driveway or the garage, and as far as Joanna could tell, Charlie's truck wasn't around, either.

They rang the front bell, and Drew pounded a few times on the door, but no one answered. After a few seconds, Joanna pressed the bell again and thought she heard something inside, but when no one responded, she looked at Drew and shrugged. They walked back to his car in silence.

"Let's go to the office and try again later," Drew said.

Joanna agreed. "There's no sense in going all the way to the ranch, not until we try to reach Nita again," she said. "Do you get the feeling we're running in circles?"

He offered her a consoling smile. "Sometimes."

Twenty minutes later, inside the real estate office, Drew headed for Evan's office, but Joanna lingered around Nita's desk.

"I can't get over this message from Nevada," she said. She picked up the message book and walked into Evan's office to see Drew seated at the conference table, bent over a Vista Grande file. "I'm going to call Valerie and see what she thinks of this."

"That's a good idea." He didn't look up from the papers he was studying. "There could be a very simple explanation."

After six rings, Joanna left a message on Valerie's machine and hung up. She glanced at her watch and saw that it was nearly eight-thirty. "If she doesn't return my call soon, I'll try to reach her again."

Drew leaned back in the chair, leaving the file on the table in front of him. "Jo, how well did Jake understand this agreement? It's so hard for me to believe he would have gone along with risking the Diamond C."

She sighed and dropped into a chair across the table from him. "Using the ranch as collateral was never discussed." At least not in front of her or Jake, she corrected silently. "He wouldn't have approved of the idea. If you remember, Evan sold him the development scheme based on the fact that by developing half the ranch, we could save the other half. If Jake thought there was a chance we could lose it all, I know he would never have gone along with the idea."

"So how did Evan convince him?" He leaned over the document again. "Or you?" He handed her the papers. "This is your signature, isn't it?"

She nodded. "Yes. I'm afraid it is."

"Evan had to have your name on that line before he could put the Diamond C up as collateral, because you were Jake's sole beneficiary and held title to the entire property."

Joanna felt a rush of embarrassed heat move up her neck and spread across her cheeks. "I hate to admit it, but I took Evan's word for what the agreement said. I didn't read every word before I signed the papers. In fact, I read very little of it." She handed the contract to him, leaned back in her chair and rubbed her eyelids with her fingertips. Exhausted, discouraged and feeling nauseous again, she just didn't have the heart to face him. "I feel so stupid," she whispered. "I've made so many mistakes. How could I have let Jake down like this?"

She kept her hands over her eyes, but she heard him get up and come around the table to stand behind her. At the feel of his hands on her shoulders, the tears she'd been holding at bay slipped to the corners of her eyes.

"You trusted your spouse, Jo. If that's a mistake, it's one people make a million times a day."

You should have known, an inner voice accused.

"There's no way you could have foreseen this," Drew said.

She swallowed the lump in her throat and blinked back the emotion that clouded her eyes. "I should have suspected his interest in me and the ranch coincided a bit too conveniently, but I guess I just didn't want to see it . . . him in an unfavorable light. He was so confident, so excited about all these plans." It was time she faced the lie, she told herself, the lie she'd wanted so badly to believe. What she'd felt for Evan had never been love, but gratitude. Deep gratitude for what it seemed he'd been so willing and able to do to help Jake, to help them save the only thing Jake loved as much as he loved her.

How ironic that now she'd not only lost Evan and Jake, but it seemed she would soon lose Jake's beloved ranch, as well.

But perhaps it was only just. After all, she'd had no right to marry Evan without love, and no matter how hard she'd tried to convince herself otherwise, that deep, abiding love a man has the right to expect from his wife just did not exist in her for her husband.

Drew placed a hand on her chair and swiveled it around to face him. "None of this is your fault, Jo. You've got to believe that. You had Jake's best interests in mind. You've been a loyal wife and you've acted honorably through it all."

She could only return his gaze, too overwhelmed by his kindness and his understanding to speak. Taking a deep breath, she told herself that now was not the time to fall apart. "All right," she said. "Where do we go from here?"

He picked up the Vista Grande agreement again. "Well, I'd still like to talk to Lincoln Nesbitt," he said. "If you'd rather not see him, you can stay here and I'll pick you up when I've finished."

The last thing she wanted was to be separated from Drew for even five minutes. But logically, she knew she'd better start getting used to being alone, to not having him around to depend on. "You go ahead. I'll stay here and try to get hold of Valerie again. If you tell me exactly what we're looking for, I'll go through the rest of these files while I'm waiting for you to come back."

"I wish I knew well enough to tell you. At this point, however, we're flying blind. Just keep your eyes out for anything that doesn't jibe with the original idea Evan mapped out for Jake and you. Look for any mention of Calder Johannsen Inc., or any place where money was diverted to Charlie Lanksy's construction company. If it's true that Nita traded your signature for the bid on the first spec home, there could be a paper trail—obscure, probably, but it could be there."

"If she hasn't already destroyed the evidence."

He nodded, his expression grim. "The situation is complex. It would be easy to make a mistake, even for the most careful accomplice. At this point, whoever helped Evan set this up has got to know that we're on to them. Right now, I suspect there's a bit of scrambling going on. And when the pressure is highest, that's when people tend to make stupid mistakes. And that, my dear Joanna, is how criminals usually get caught."

Though he was trying to reassure her, Joanna could only nod. With the personal stakes so high, agreeing with him would be admitting her husband really was a criminal—something she wasn't quite ready to do. Not yet.

"Oh, by the way," Drew added before he left, "I'll give you Cole's number. Give him a call, would you please, and see if he's traced anything on Calder Johannsen. He might have tried to reach us at the ranch."

She told him she would, and after a quick hug for reassurance and a promise that he'd be back soon, he was gone, and Joanna was left alone in Evan's office to face the stack of lies and the reality that her husband, if he was dead, had died trying to cheat her. "Where are you, Evan?" she asked the emptiness. But the silence of the Vista Grande files gave up no answers.

THE BONNE SOLEIL was everything Joanna had described and more. Plush, intimate, five-star. The reserved young woman at the front desk offered Drew a practiced smile and asked him to wait while she called Lincoln's room.

Drew wandered around the well-appointed lobby, taking in the pieces of Western art placed strategically around the room. But the soothing effects of the setting, and even the sounds of the classical music drifting out of the sound system, failed to move him. His thoughts were elsewhere, with the beautiful woman in blue jeans waiting for him at the real estate office across town. Other than losing Jake, he doubted that she'd ever hurt as much as she did now.

Although he had nothing to compare it to, he imagined the pain of betrayal by a spouse ranked right up there with death. The compassion he felt for her, mixed with his renewed love and admiration, welled up inside him, and he realized, with a jolt, that if Evan Galbraith was here now, he could easily wring his neck.

"Drew?"

He'd been so absorbed in thoughts of Joanna, he hadn't heard anyone approaching, and when he turned he saw a subdued and casually dressed Lincoln Nesbitt standing behind him. Lincoln extended his hand and Drew took it, but not without feeling a twinge of guilt. Just making polite social contact with the man possibly involved in betraying Joanna made him cringe inside.

"Is there someplace where we can talk?"

"Of course," Lincoln replied. "We can go up to my suite. Or into the lounge." With a subtle movement of his head, he indicated the direction. "Whichever you prefer."

"The lounge will be fine."

SITTING ALONE in the quiet office, Joanna had to force herself to concentrate on the documents she was supposed to be studying. Composed almost entirely of legal descriptions of the property, the contracts made very dull reading. Even as her eyes followed the words, her mind wandered to Drew.

She thought about his meeting with Lincoln Nesbitt. She worried about his personal safety, then quickly dismissed her fear when she compared his broad-shouldered athletic build and his quick, sharp reactions with the seemingly mild-mannered, lean and almost fragile Lincoln Nesbitt. She had no doubt who would come out the winner in a physical confrontation between the two men. Likewise, she had little doubt that Drew would prove a tough and thorough interrogator.

Thinking about Drew came easy. Over the years, she'd engaged in the activity more frequently than she'd have willingly admitted—even after she'd married. She hadn't always thought of him in the romantic sense, the way people sometimes mourn the loss of a lover. Often she'd just indulged herself with remembering their friendship, the countless hours they'd spent together growing up. It was hard to separate the memories of her young life from memories of Drew and his family. Cole had been almost like a brother to her, as well. Teasing, pesky, just the way she'd always thought a real brother should be. She smiled, remembering the legendary pranks they'd pulled on each other before they'd even reached high school.

She'd spent a lot of time at the Spencer ranch even before her involvement with Drew. Drew's father, Andrew Spencer, had admired her abilities on horseback and had sponsored her for a couple of seasons in the show ring. He had given her a foal to raise as her own when the mare she'd learned to ride on, Starsong, had died.

When it came time for the junior prom, Bess had done the alterations on her dress and Cynthia Spencer, Drew's mom, had helped her with her hair and offered motherly advice on such things as etiquette. She had even offered an impromptu and hilarious dance lesson.

Joanna laughed softly, remembering the look on Drew's face when he'd walked in that afternoon to see his mother and her doing the two-step in the Spencers' living room.

As often as Joanna had thought about their childhood and love affair, she had wondered about Drew's life in Denver. Picturing him as a trial attorney hadn't been difficult, but when she'd heard that he and Cole had embarked on a venture as private investigators and bodyguards, she'd been left with nothing more substantial than images of old television shows. Was he MacGyver, she wondered, or more like the intrepid Remington Steele?

How different their lives would have been had he stayed in Telluride, as she had chosen to do when Jake's health failed.

Drew *had* applied for a position with a firm in Telluride, thinking that perhaps he could make a decent living and build a career where Joanna knew his heart would always reside. Unfortunately, at the time he'd been job shopping, the area had yet to garner the national attention it now enjoyed. The celebrities and superstars hadn't yet flocked to the high country in droves, and the few established law firms in town weren't offering great incentives to entry-level associates. Even the best local offers had come in a poor second to the most modest opportunities Drew could exploit in Denver.

Although she knew he'd thought that situation might change eventually, he'd decided to go to Denver to begin building a career. Joanna remembered well the tears that had accompanied that decision.

The phone rang, yanking Joanna out of her thoughts. Her mind was still reeling with memories when she said hello.

"Hey, Jo. It's Cole." A flood of warmth for her old friend accompanied the sound of his voice.

"Cole, I'm glad you called back."

"We just got in. Anne sends her best. Say, is Drew around?"

"No, but I expect him back shortly. Do you want him to call?"

"I'm afraid that won't be necessary. I haven't got much to tell him. I ran that check he asked me to, on Calder Johannsen Inc., and I'm sorry to tell you I came up with a big fat zero. If that outfit exists anywhere between here and California, I couldn't find it. Today, I concentrated my efforts on the Western states, tomorrow I'll check the other direction. I'll give you a call if I run across anything."

Joanna thanked Cole and spoke to Anne a few minutes before she hung up. She'd only met Cole's wife once, at the couple's wedding, but somehow, something between them had immediately clicked. Secretly, Joanna couldn't help wondering if it was their love of the Spencer brothers that seemed to draw an invisible circle around her and Anne.

When she heard a noise at the front door, she hurried to let Drew in. On his insistence, she'd locked the front door when he'd left, and remembering his admonition, she peered out now before she turned the latch to let him in.

To her surprise, no one was there, but she could see by the swaying branches of the aspen trees across the street that the wind had come up. Perhaps it had only been the wind she'd heard.

Another noise, this one from the back door, brought the hair up on the back of her neck. She was sure it was more than the wind.

DREW WAS half a block away when he saw the dark figure slip into the shadows at the side of the Greenwood building. Pulling over to the curb quickly, he jumped out of his car and ran toward the real estate office. After he banged on the front door a few times, Joanna let him in. He could read in her eyes that something was wrong.

"Drew! I'm so glad it's you. I thought I heard something out back."

"Where?" He edged past her, pulled the front door closed and locked it behind him.

"First it came from the front door and then, just a few minutes ago, at the back. I thought it was the wind..." She seemed to notice the revolver in his hand.

"Get on the phone and call Sheriff Miller. Tell him we've got a prowler behind the building."

"Where are you going?"

"Whoever it is could be long gone before a deputy arrives. Stay here, Jo. And don't open the door unless you're sure it's me."

He was halfway out the front door when she grabbed his sleeve. "Be careful, Drew."

He smiled and planted a quick kiss on her cheek. "Always. Now call Bryan."

Joanna dialed the sheriff's substation and quickly reported their situation. She shut off the lights in the receptionist's area. In the front office, with the large glass windows overlooking the street, she had the eerie feeling of being watched. The lights in Evan's office afforded her enough light to move around in the semidarkness of the front office without stumbling over furniture, and she hoped, without being seen from the street.

Standing to the side of the plate-glass windows, she peered into the shadowy darkness, hoping to catch sight of Drew. But she saw only the undulating shadows of the windswept trees and Drew's car parked at an odd angle at the curb.

Alone in the deserted and dimly lit offices, the sound of her heart hammering against her chest seemed impossibly loud. When the phone rang, she shrieked before she lunged for it.

It was Valerie. "Joanna? Is that you? You sound funny. I just got your message. What's up?"

"Oh, Valerie, I can't talk. I have to call you back. Something's going on outside the building, and I need to get off the phone. I'll call you back."

"What is it? What's wrong? Why are you at the office this time of night? Are you sure you're all right?"

Distracted by the thought of what might be happening outside, Joanna hung up after promising to fill Valerie in on the details later. When the phone rang again almost immediately, Joanna felt irritation explode inside her. "Valerie, please! I just can't talk now."

"Joanna." It was a man's voice, and she recognized it immediately as the voice that had threatened her that morning. But something was different. Somehow she thought the voice sounded vaguely familiar. Was it only because of his earlier call, she wondered, or could this really be someone she knew?

"Who is this?" she demanded, outraged that someone she knew might be putting her through this torture.

"Listen to me, Joanna. And you'd better listen good, because thanks to that fancy gadget on your phone line, I won't be calling you at home anymore. I know where you are, Joanna, and when you're alone. You never know when I might drop by, so don't get any funny ideas about cheating me. Your husband already did that! And we all know what happened to him."

"What do you want?" Joanna pleaded. "Please tell me who you are and what my husband did to you."

"Who I am isn't important. What I need is only what I'm due. Fifty thousand dollars. Unmarked small bills. I'll let you know where and when to deliver it. If you want to stay alive, Joanna, you'd better gather it quickly."

"But I don't—"

"Don't give me that. You've got that whole big ranch. So just shut up and listen! Evan owes me. You can't get away with this. None of you. Fifty thousand." The line went dead, and Joanna hardly had time to catch her breath before a series of loud thumping and thudding noises came from the back of the building and raised an even more desperate alarm inside her.

The pounding continued, and she ran to the back, thinking that maybe it was Drew, in trouble and trying to signal her. She hit the crash bar in the middle of the large metal door, and it swung wide open into the shadow-shrouded alley.

At the sight of the two figures locked in a violent struggle, Joanna felt a bone-deep terror. She immediately recognized Drew, but the other hulking form had his back to her and his face veiled in shadows. There was no way she could tell who it was.

Suddenly, she remembered the exterior lights mounted on each side of the door. Reaching inside, she slapped the wall to flip the switch, and instantly the alley was flooded with light. She saw the glint of a gun at the same time she recognized Harley Platt as the man whose beefy arm was locked around Drew's throat. The struggle for the gun continued. "Harley!" she screamed. "What are you doing?"

At the sound of her voice, Harley spun around and brought his other arm down across Drew's hand. The gun flew into the darkness and discharged when it hit pavement. The sharp retort echoed through the clear, cool night like a scream.

At the sight of blood exploding from Harley's shoulder, Joanna felt as though she'd just been thrown into the deep end of a swimming pool. Down, down she sank, her ears filled with water and her vision blurred. But just before the liquid oblivion swallowed her, a pair of warm arms closed around her, and she realized she'd never hit bottom.

Chapter Twelve

"Joanna." Drew's voice called her back to the light, and she opened her eyes to see his face and knew that she was safely cradled in his arms.

"Wh-what happened?"

"You fainted." She tried to sit up, and the world spun. "Stay still a minute," he said, pulling her gently into his arms again.

She heard the commotion behind them and looked past Drew's shoulder to see two uniformed deputies tending to Harley's arm. He was sitting cross-legged, like a stunned grizzly, and all around them the lights from what seemed like every official vehicle in the county swept the alley with streamers of red and white lights.

Harley finally saw her and said, "I thought he was a burglar."

Even though she felt angry enough to throttle him, she was glad to see that Harley wasn't badly hurt.

Bryan Miller emerged from the crowd of uniformed officers, walked over and knelt beside them. "How are you feeling, Joanna?"

Suddenly self-conscious about her position, half-reclining on the pavement in Drew's arms, she sat up. Drew assisted, keeping his arm around her for support. "I think I'm better now. I—I don't know what happened. I guess when I saw the blood, I must have passed out." She couldn't help a grim chuckle. "Not a great reaction from a doctor, right?" She was the only one even close to smiling. "How's Harley?"

"He'll live," Bryan said.

"Why did the idiot jump me?" Drew demanded. "When I came around the corner, he was all over me."

"He claims that when he drove by the office earlier and saw the lights on, but no car parked in front, he thought someone might have broken in. Then, when he bumped into you in the alley—"

"He panicked," Drew finished for him.

"Probably," Bryan admitted in a lowered voice. "I'll talk to him after they've patched him up. From what I can see, it isn't as bad as it looks. I'd say you were both lucky."

"All three," Drew amended, looking at Joanna. When Bryan left them to return to his men, Drew put his face close to her ear and whispered, "So lucky. When I think about what might have happened, that I might have lost you—"

The possibility that something could have happened to Drew struck her at the same time. She welcomed his hug when he held her even tighter, and she could hear his heart hammering through the soft fabric of his denim shirt.

"He called again," she said weakly.

For a minute he only stared blankly. "Who? You don't mean—"

She nodded.

"Are you sure? What did he say?"

"Let's go inside first, and I'll explain. I feel like an idiot sitting out here." Helping her to her feet, Drew kept his arm around her and shoved the door open far enough for them to edge inside, away from the confusion.

When Drew headed for Evan's office, she put an arm on his sleeve to hold him back. "Please. I don't think I can stand to look at that map tonight." She'd wondered when it would happen, when the anger would begin to take over the fear. It was happening now, and she didn't want to be anywhere near the source of the storm.

"In here," she said, motioning him into the back room.

"Sit down, Jo," he said, pulling out one of the metal chairs situated around a circular metal table.

"Thanks. Before you sit, could you check the refrigerator for a lemon lime?" Her stomach had started to churn again. Nothing like good old-fashioned anger to get the juices flowing, she told herself grimly.

After retrieving the soda, Drew opened a cupboard door. "Need a glass?"

She shook her head. "No. The can will be fine." Behind him on the counter were the bottles of wine Joanna had noticed the other day when she'd walked to the back room with Nita.

"Drew, hand me one of those bottles of wine, will you?"

The look he shot her was openly skeptical. "Jo, are you sure? With lemon lime?"

"I'm not going to drink it. I just want to check the label."

"Hmm. Cabernet sauvignon." He handed her the bottle. "Nice, especially that year."

"Evan thought so, too. I don't even want to tell you what he paid for a case of this stuff—and the funny thing is, I never saw him drink it."

He pulled up a chair and sat down. "What's all this about wine, anyway? I thought we were discussing a phone call."

"We were. And, believe me, right now that's the most pressing issue. It's just that when I saw the wine, it reminded me of the bottle at Valerie's last night. When I asked for wine, she started to give me some from a bottle just like this one. She changed her mind, but I'd seen enough to know—or at least to suspect—that the bottle in her rack had a label just like this one, Evan's label. He ordered these embossed with his initials for his private stock."

"You didn't know he'd given a bottle to Valerie?"

"No, and when I noticed that bottle in her kitchen, I guess I was a bit shocked."

Drew nodded. "I see what you mean. A man who orders personalized labels takes his wine pretty seriously, and you have to be wondering why he'd give her a bottle of his prize vintage."

"Perhaps he took Valerie as seriously as his wine."

"Are you suggesting an affair between them?"

"Actually, you're the one who planted the seed—that trip to Nevada, remember? I guess now that I realize Evan betrayed me on one level, it's easier to believe he could have betrayed me on others." She took several sips of her soda, trying to regain what little composure she had left.

"Not to change the subject, but what did the caller say tonight, Jo?"

She took another swallow of soda, willing it to work its magic on her agitated stomach. "He wanted money. Fifty thousand dollars. In small bills."

"What?" The news propelled him to his feet. "He must be crazy!"

"He said he knew I'd had the caller-identification equipment installed on the phone at the ranch. He said he'd find other...ways to contact me. He said he knew where I was, when I was alone—"

Drew slammed his hand on the countertop. "Damn it. This weirdo is the burglar, Jo. I'd bet money he was the one who ransacked your room." He sat down again, and she saw him clenching his jaw to contain his anger. "We need to get Bryan more actively involved in this. Did the caller say anything else? Anything that might give us a clue as to who he is, why he's calling you?"

"He said Evan owed him, and that if I didn't want to end up...like Evan, I'd better come up with the money."

"When?"

"He said he'd be in contact with me. Soon."

"That son of..." Drew muttered, his blue eyes never more intense, never angrier. "I just hope I'm there when he tries."

Joanna sat staring at her hands, trying to make herself remember what her life had been before, trying to believe that someday she'd find a way back to a normal life—whatever that meant.

"It's going to all work out, Jo." He sealed his promise by reaching across the table to wrap his hands around hers. "Together, we're going to get you through this. I'm not going to let anything hurt you, including your husband's mistakes."

Joanna stared into the eyes of the man she realized she'd never stopped loving. At the moment, she possessed neither the strength nor the will to argue with him, or to remind him that, regardless of Evan's guilt or innocence, she was still his wife, that they'd shared a life together and that putting an end to their relationship might not be as easy as it seemed.

What a difference a few weeks could make, she thought miserably. If only she'd known before. If only she knew now what was right and what was wrong for her, for her family—or what was left of it—and for Drew.

DREW INSISTED Joanna allow the ambulance crew to check her over before the two of them left to return to her ranch for the night. She drew the line, however, when he tried to convince her to go to the emergency room for a doctor's exam. "I only fainted," she reminded him. "You're the one who nearly died of a broken neck, remember?"

An hour later, finally arriving home, Joanna entered the darkened house and felt as if an invisible weight rested between her shoulders. Drew closed the door behind them while she turned on a lamp in the living room and sank down in Jake's chair.

Drew went into the kitchen, and she heard him check the back door. A chill of exhaustion and apprehension shook her, and despite the unusually warm evening, she pulled an afghan around her shoulders.

They hadn't talked much on the way home, and her thoughts still seemed a bit muddled—from the fainting or from the unrelenting strain, she didn't know which. Now, it seemed, all the events of the long evening crowded into her mind at once, and she leaned her head back, closed her eyes and tried to organize her thoughts.

"Drew, we need to talk," she told him after he'd settled himself in the chair opposite her. "But first, I'll give you a quarter if you'll put the kettle on for tea." She didn't know where that had come from, the familiar phrase they used to bat back and forth as kids. She remembered the day it had started, though. She'd been only eight years old, and the older and wiser Drew had conned her into doing his chores for the princely sum of twenty-five cents.

His smile said he remembered, too. "How could I refuse such a generous offer?" Before he left the living room, he came around behind her chair and slid his hands down to rest on each side of her face. Without warning, he bent and kissed the top of her head before walking into the kitchen.

Joanna dragged herself out of the chair to play the messages blinking on her answering machine. The first one was from Valerie, followed by a call from Nita Lansky.

Drew must have heard Nita's voice asking Joanna to call, because he stuck his head around the half wall that divided the two rooms and gave her a quizzical look. "Are you going to call her back?"

She glanced at the cherry wood clock on the mantel. It wasn't all that late, just past eleven. "Yes, I think I will.

Although I can't very well ask her about the forgeries over the phone."

"Of course not. But try to set something up for tomorrow. We need to talk to her, to confront her as soon as possible. Who knows? She may even be involved in the phone calls and the break-in."

With that ominous possibility in mind, Joanna's hands shook as she dialed Nita's number. For some reason, she'd expected Nita to answer, so when her son, Michael, said hello, she found herself momentarily stuck for words.

Recovering quickly, she asked for Nita and waited while Michael put the phone down and went to get his mother. Something about the kid's voice sounded different, she thought. So grown up for eighteen. She remembered Nita telling her how Michael had changed, and yet in many ways how he was still so like the little boy he'd once been.

Joanna's thoughts drifted to the mother and baby she'd encountered last night at the sheriff's substation. Had the woman's other son—the one she'd been there to bail out of trouble again—ever been as sweet, innocent and without guile as his infant brother? Surely, when his mother had held him for the first time, in those fragile first moments of life, she couldn't have dreamed of the troubles to come. And yet, even if she had somehow known, would she have had any choice but to love that little boy even deeper, hold him a little tighter and a little longer, in anticipation of the day she'd have to let him go?

It occurred to Joanna, in a subtle insight, that this was the essence of parenthood. A series of incredible joys and heartaches, laughter and tears, beginnings and endings. And, finally, letting go. With a love that never dies, no matter what the change or the distance between two hearts, each carries a little piece of the other inside forever.

For the first time, she thought of her mother in that way, and a genuine ache lodged in her heart for the young woman she'd never known. Compassion welled in her for the mother who'd lost even more than Joanna had.

When a rustling sound on the other end of the line signaled Nita's arrival, Joanna had to clear her throat to speak. "Nita? Is that you?"

"Sorry, Joanna." She was panting, trying to recover her breath. "I was out in the yard. My...dog got out and I had to chase him to the end of the street. Michael should have told you I'd call you back. Kids!"

Hearing Nita's voice, Joanna had to work to remind herself of the suspicions and conclusions she'd drawn about the woman. Taking a deep breath, she told Nita about the trouble that had occurred in the alley behind the office.

"What a terrible mix-up!" Nita exclaimed. "As if the situation wasn't already bad enough, what with Evan still missing and all."

"Yes," Joanna said. A mix-up. If only it could be that conveniently dismissed. "Well, somehow we'll get through it." She paused to accept the mug of hot tea Drew held out before he sat down on the couch beside her. "Nita, I was wondering, do you think you might have time tomorrow to answer a few questions for Drew and I?"

When Nita wanted to know what kind of questions, Joanna felt utterly at a loss. "Oh, you know. Just some general questions about the business. That sort of thing."

Drew gave her the high sign. *Good thinking,* he mouthed.

After a bit of wrangling to get her to commit, Joanna finally pinned Nita down to two-thirty, and by the time she hung up the phone, she felt as though she'd engaged in a physical contest and won, but only by default.

"Two-thirty," she told Drew. "I swear, the woman sounds almost as suspicious as we are."

"That's okay. If she's on guard, maybe her defensiveness will trip her up."

She picked up the phone again and after a deep sigh, put it back down. "I was going to call Valerie," she explained. "But suddenly, I just don't have any more energy. Talk to me, Drew, before I fall asleep right here."

"Maybe that's what you need to do."

She took another drink of her tea and let the warm, soothing liquid calm her. "No. We need to talk. Oh, before I forget, Cole called while you were at the Bonne Soleil. He said to tell you that he struck out as far as finding anything about Calder Johannsen, but he hasn't given up."

Drew smiled. "Does he ever?"

"Not that I recall. And now it's your turn. Catch me up on your conversation with Lincoln Nesbitt."

Drew ran a hand over his dark hair and sighed. "Well, Jo, I gotta tell you, I just don't think the man's a crook, much less capable of terrible physical violence against another human being. I know he punched that hole in the wall in Evan's office—"

"Can you really blame him?" she interrupted. "Knowing what we know now, I can almost understand how he could have been driven to do that."

"Exactly. Although it must have been a frightening experience for Valerie to have witnessed his outburst, I just can't help feeling that his reaction was just that. The man seems like a quiet, peace-loving soul."

Joanna blew out a long, tired breath. "A quiet, peace-loving soul who had every motive to do in my husband."

Drew had draped his arm along the back of the couch behind her, but now he eased it away and turned slightly to sit staring at her. "You know, I don't think I've ever seen you so dead set against anyone."

She could feel his words causing her to bristle and she worked hard to suppress her irritation. They'd had enough confrontation for one night, and the last thing she wanted to do was fight with him.

"I'm not against anyone, Drew," she tried to explain as patiently as her frazzled nerves would allow. "I'm just trying to find out what happened to Evan, so that I can get on..." She didn't finish her sentence. She didn't have to. The look on his face said he knew how she felt and that no one wanted her to get on with her life more than he did.

JOANNA SLEPT LATE the next morning. Before she went to bed, she left a message with her service to refer all but the most serious emergencies to Doc Anderson until further notice. She had to balance the money she'd lose by taking this time off against her emotional health.

She rolled out of bed at nine feeling more human than she'd felt in at least a week. Her head didn't hurt, her eyes weren't swollen from crying and her stomach seemed as calm as the waters of Lost Lake, where she and Jake used to trail ride when she was a kid.

From the other room, she heard Drew's voice—not a garbled voice this time, but his real voice. From what she could tell, he was talking to someone on the phone. When she appeared in the doorway of the small office, he put his hand over the receiver and said, "Good morning. There's a fresh pot of coffee on the stove, and I kept the water hot in case you'd rather have tea."

She thanked him, but he seemed not to have heard. His face reflected the seriousness of his conversation. Joanna was almost afraid to know who he was talking to and what was being said. Torn between the urge to know and the longing to remain sheltered for just a few minutes more, she went into the kitchen, made herself a cup of herbal tea and took it out onto the front porch.

From the small wooden porch swing, she watched a parade of high wispy clouds move in slow motion across a perfect mid-July sky. The sweet, distinctive smell of someone's fresh-cut alfalfa field rode the friendly breeze, and the soft murmuring of the brook in the near meadow lulled her senses and wrapped her in a web of temporary well-being.

When the screen door creaked open, she patted the space beside her on the swing. Drew walked slowly toward her and sat down. The look on his face was more than grave. It told her that something horrible had happened, that in a month of nightmares, this could be the worst yet.

He started to speak, but she gently pressed her fingers to his lips.

"I know whatever it is isn't good news," she told him. "But, please, just for thirty more seconds, sit here beside me and pretend it never happened."

He looked at her, staring deeply into her eyes. "You're my heroine, Joanna. How did you get to be so special?"

She shook her head and took one last swallow of her tea. "Jake did his best," she said quietly. "Now. Let's go inside and you can tell me." They rose together and he waited while she walked ahead of him through the door.

"Just one thing," she said while he was still in the doorway, "stay with me till it's over, will you, Drew? I know it's not fair, I know you have a life in Denver and a business to run. But I don't think I can get through this without you. And I know I don't want to try."

EVEN AS HE SPOKE the words, Joanna couldn't bring herself to believe them. She watched his mouth moving, but the words—hammer, blood, lab reports, conclusive results—had no meaning to her for one numb moment.

When reality finally did break through, her reaction wasn't the violent internal ripping she'd have thought, but more a quiet shuddering that seemed to start in her toes and vibrate through every nerve ending in her body.

The evidence found in Lincoln Nesbitt's rental car seemed irrefutable. Evan, if not dead, had been seriously injured. He hadn't walked away, but been forced. Violently. The phrase *foul play* took on a very real meaning.

The anonymous caller had been right. Harley had been right. The hammer had been used against Evan. A weapon. From all appearances, the quiet, peace-loving Lincoln Nesbitt was capable of far more than merely putting his fist through a couple of inches of drywall.

"They've brought him in again for questioning," Drew said. "A deputy picked him up, and according to Bryan, the CBI, the Telluride police, and the D.A. are all waiting to take their turns. He said Lincoln would probably be charged this time. Trouble is, since they still haven't found...Evan—" they both knew he'd almost said *the body* "—it isn't clear what the exact charges will be, but Bryan says they're now officially calling it a...murder investigation."

Neither of them spoke while all the awful implications sunk in.

"Lincoln's attorney is coming in from California, and the search has now resumed, centering on the Ridgeway area."

By the time Drew finished giving her the details, or what he knew of them, he was leaning forward in the chair, bent slightly at the waist, as though ready to spring to her rescue should she faint again.

She did not faint, but nodded, serenely, solemnly. "Well," she said. "I suppose this is just the beginning."

"Yes. In a way, I suppose it is."

"Thank you, Drew," she said softly, and even to her own ears, her voice sounded unusually low. The emotion welling inside her seemed contained just below her vocal cords, and she had to fight to keep her voice from cracking. "I'm glad I heard it from you."

She started to get up, but he reached for her hand. "Sit down, Jo."

"Please, Drew—"

"Just a minute. There's one more aspect of this I think we need to discuss."

She relented, still perched on the edge of the chair. She eased her hand out of his, however. Why, suddenly, did it feel so wrong, when for the past few days she'd done nothing but lean on him, depending so heavily on his calming, soothing touch?

Waiting was sheer torture, watching him deciding how best to phrase whatever he had to say.

"I don't think he did it, Jo," he said finally, flatly. Obviously, he'd decided on the direct approach. "I just don't think Lincoln Nesbitt is capable of murder."

Why his simple declaration had the effect it did, she didn't understand, but almost before she knew what was happening, she was on her feet and teetering on the edge of white-hot anger. Fighting for a calm she did not possess, she said, "I need to shower and get dressed." And with that she turned her back on him and strode out of the living room.

By the time she made it to the bathroom, silent tears were streaming down her cheeks and dripping off the end of her chin, soaking the front of her robe.

For the next ten minutes, she stood in the shower crying. For once, she welcomed the sound of the noisy old pipes to mask her sobs. She cried for Evan and for herself, and for what might have been. She cried again for Jake and for her mother, and even for the father she'd never known. Standing beneath the spray, she cried and cried until her shuddering sobs ended and the warm water turned cold.

With all her rage and sadness spent, she turned off the water and reached for a towel, feeling somehow freed. Little by little, she could feel herself letting go of the hurt and the sadness and the rage—or maybe it was letting go of her.

Now all she had to worry about was the future, a future that included, among other events, the day the body was found and the funeral—or perhaps, under the circumstance, merely a memorial of some kind. The day the ranch would be auctioned, and the dreams she and Jake had nurtured for a lifetime would be lost forever. The day Drew would leave, because, despite her blue-eyed ex-lover's promises, that day could not be postponed forever.

And finally, the most important of all days, the day she would give birth to her murdered husband's child.

Chapter Thirteen

Because Drew asked her, Joanna agreed to keep their two-thirty appointment with Nita Lansky. Although her hand felt much better, he insisted on driving, and in a way, Joanna felt grateful. After all, taking two vehicles to town seemed wasteful, especially now, when every dime seemed of monumental importance. Soon she would be looking for a new home and be the sole support of her baby.

"Nita's car isn't there," Joanna said after they turned the corner and she could see the parking spaces in front of the building. "But that's Valerie's Lincoln." Only a year old, the long, luxurious automobile, white with black interior, of course, was difficult to miss. "Pull over, Drew. I want to talk to her. She's established a reputation in this area as a very successful Realtor. Perhaps she'd want to buy the agency."

"Jo, you're not jumping the gun, are you?"

"I hope not. If anything, it feels like I'm running just to catch up."

"Well, it might work out. Even if she isn't interested in becoming the owner, maybe she'd be willing to stay on as manager until..."

She knew he still didn't believe Lincoln had murdered Evan.

"Anyway, no matter how it all turns out, the agency could be a source of income for you."

As desperate as her financial future looked, Joanna wondered if she'd have the stomach to be associated with Galbraith Realty after all that had happened.

"I know you believe foreclosure in inevitable," he said. "But if we could unravel the financial tangle, we might still have a chance to save the Diamond C."

"I wish I could believe that," she said. "I guess for Jake, I should try."

"For Jake *and* for you, Jo. Somehow, I can't imagine you as happy anywhere as you would be at the Diamond C."

No. This time Drew was wrong. Since his return to Telluride, she'd come to believe that anywhere he was she could learn to be happy. But he'd made no offer to take her with him, and when he found out about Evan's baby, that would take care of any illusions he had about their future.

Drew rejecting her would be one thing. It would be like losing him all over again. But to even imagine anyone rejecting her child, well, that pushed every protective instinct she possessed into overdrive—protective instincts she hadn't known she possessed until the reality of her physical situation had finally begun to sink in a few days ago.

WHEN THEY WALKED into the office, Joanna was surprised to see Valerie sitting behind Nita's desk, with the phone to her ear.

"Joanna! Drew!" She replaced the receiver on its cradle, popped up and came around the desk to give Joanna a hug. "I just tried calling you. How *are* you?" Her expression seemed so genuinely sympathetic that Joanna wondered if somehow Valerie had heard about the latest development in the case.

"Lincoln Nesbitt is in custody," Joanna said and then took a deep breath and let Drew take over.

"They've found what they think could be the murder weapon," he said.

Valerie winced. "Oh, my gosh! Oh, Joanna, this is just *horrible.* Poor Evan! Have they found—" She stopped short. Like everyone else, the word *body* seemed to stick in her throat.

Joanna shook her head. "No. They haven't found his body. Not yet."

"Well, at least that's something. Maybe there's still hope." She laid her hand on Joanna's sleeve. "Oh, poor dear. If there's anything I can do... please, just call."

"Thank you, Valerie. I have been thinking a lot about you and how you might be able to help."

"Anything," she said again and reached for Joanna's hand, this time to give it a reassuring squeeze. "Just let me know."

"Where's Nita?" Drew asked.

Valerie's expression immediately hardened. "Now, that's a good question!" She motioned for them to follow her into her office. Neat as always, Joanna thought. Not a paper or a file out of place, the pencils standing at attention in the holder sharpened to perfect points.

"When I came in around ten, the outside lights were still on and the sign hadn't been turned around. I can't tell you how upset I was. Nita promised me Michael would put a couple of signs up for me first thing this morning." She pointed to the metal For Sale signs beside the door. "And there they still sit! I can tell you, the sellers up on Snowbird Lane aren't going to be happy."

Joanna remembered that Evan sometimes paid Michael Lansky to do odd jobs, which often included planting the distinctive blue-and-white Galbraith Realty signs.

"This just isn't like Nita. Evan always said he'd never met anyone so dedicated to her job. According to him, she's always the first to arrive, and often the last to leave," Joanna said.

There was a cynical spark in Valerie's eyes—pale blue today, Joanna noticed in passing. "Yeah. Well, maybe that didn't have so much to do with job dedication as devotion to the boss."

Joanna stifled her shock, but Drew wasn't as polite. "What are you getting at, Valerie? Are you implying that there might have been something going on between Evan and Nita Lansky?"

"Ha!" Valerie's curt, bitter laughter almost stung. "Evan and Nita? Pul-lease. No way. When he's married to her?" She pointed to Joanna and shook her head. "Not that Nita wouldn't have been willing. No offense, Jo, but the woman thought your husband hung the moon." She sighed, and her tone was softer when she added, "Evan Galbraith was a man who enjoyed lovely things. He knew what he had. He wasn't a fool."

Joanna felt a pang of guilt hearing how much Evan cared for her from the woman she'd so recently suspected of perhaps a less than honorable relationship with him.

"Where do you think Nita could be?" Drew asked. "When you made arrangements for her son to place your signs, did Nita say anything about a late lunch or an appointment that might have delayed her?"

Valerie shook her head and glanced at her watch before walking into the reception area. They followed her, and Joanna got the feeling she was ready for them to leave. She didn't take Valerie's actions personally. Everyone knew Valerie Wallace was one of the busiest Realtors in town. Like Evan, Valerie had recently relocated from the northwest, where the real estate market was booming. Joanna had always believed that somehow that background had given both Evan and Valerie an edge in competing in the crowded market in Colorado.

"I don't mean to be rude," Valerie said, glancing at her watch again. "But I have a three o'clock appointment with a new listing, and since it doesn't appear Nita is coming in, I'm going to have to plant those signs myself."

It suddenly dawned on Joanna that she and Drew might be able to help. "Why not let Drew and I worry about the signs?" He flashed her a quizzical look and she explained. "I think we should drive out to Nita's house and check on her, and we can place the signs on the way."

"Oh, could you? That would be an enormous help."

"Sure. No problem," Drew said.

"Here's the addresses." She jotted down the numbers on the back of one of her business cards and handed it to him. "Thanks a million. I really owe you guys."

Drew tucked the card in the front pocket of his Levi's. "Glad to do it. Besides, I like that area, and you never know, I might decide to invest in one of those properties myself."

Valerie beamed, and Joanna wondered if he could possibly be serious. "Go on, Valerie," she said. "Don't keep your client waiting. What I wanted to discuss with you can wait." Joanna didn't want to be the cause of a lost sale, particularly if Valerie did end up managing the business on a percentage basis. "We'll just hang around to see if Michael or Nita shows up. Will you be coming back to the office?"

"No." There was a small hesitation in her voice. "That is, I'd rather not, unless you need me. In fact, I'm leaving tonight, and I'd planned to be out of town for the next couple of days. If you need to contact me, just call my place and leave a message on the machine. I'll be checking in."

Joanna considered bringing up the message from Tony Winston, but when Valerie glanced at her watch again, Joanna decided it could wait. As Drew had pointed out, it might be as simple as the family members changing their minds about selling the motel. Using their deceased father's name still seemed odd to Joanna, but she had to consider that perhaps they'd only used his name as a point of reference for Evan and Valerie.

"Was there something else, Joanna? I really need to get going."

"No. Nothing else. Have a good trip. And good luck with the new listing, as well."

When they were alone, Drew asked her how long she thought they should wait for Nita.

"I don't think we can afford to wait much longer." A possible explanation occurred to her. "Maybe something came up and she tried to call the ranch to change our appointment. I'll call home and check my messages and then we can leave."

When she picked up the receiver from the phone console on Nita's desk, she remembered Valerie saying that she'd just called the ranch. Joanna hit the redial button and watched the readout on the base. When the automatic dialing function dialed an out-of-state area code, she thought she'd hit the wrong button. "Hmm. That's weird."

He came up behind her. "What?"

"I don't know. Maybe nothing." She quickly stabbed the disconnect button and dialed the ranch number manually. "When we walked in, didn't Valerie say she'd just called the ranch?"

"Yes. That's exactly what she said."

"Then something must be wrong with the phone system, because when I hit the redial button, it keyed in a long-distance number."

"How do you know it was long distance?"

"By the area code seven-oh-two."

Joanna listened as her answering machine clicked on and the sound of her recorded voice came over the line. After entering the code that allowed her to hear her messages from another location, she waited for the tape to rewind.

"Do you know what state that area code is?"

"Hang on." Her messages had started playing, and she needed to concentrate to be sure she heard Bryan Miller's message. "It's Bryan," she told Drew, still listening. "He says they've taken Harley's official statement of what happened last night and he's been ordered to give you a formal apology."

Drew's smile was wry. "Oh, that should be good. Straight from the heart. I bet Harley would rather take a bullet in his other arm than have to apologize to me."

The next message came from Cole. "Your brother says...no luck with the Calder Johannsen research, but he's still trying. Don't worry about the office. He's planning to work over the weekend and if you need him, he'll be at the office, or Anne can get a message to him."

"I take it there were no messages from Nita?"

She hung up the phone with a frown. "No, darn it. I'd so hoped she had a good reason for standing us up."

"Well, there still might be some explanation, but after setting up Valerie's signs, I believe we should go directly to the Lansky home."

Joanna couldn't argue. If Nita wouldn't talk to them, they'd have to take their suspicions to the police. Either way, the next few hours were going to be difficult, but postponing the inevitable wouldn't make things any easier.

Drew picked up the signs and Joanna held the door for him. After locking the office, she followed him to the car and waited while he put the signs in the trunk.

When she remembered what they'd forgotten, she felt a shiver of revulsion slide through her. "Drew," she said solemnly when he opened the door. "We forgot something."

"What?"

"A hammer."

DREW EASILY FOUND his way to the first address Valerie had given him. After setting the Galbraith Realty sign in the front yard, he got into the car and drove straight to Nita and Charlie's home. It was almost three-thirty by the time they arrived, and the afternoon had turned cool, with a refreshing breeze swirling down out of the hills.

As they walked to the front door together, the breeze swept Joanna's long dark hair about her shoulders in a silken cape. Even simply dressed as she was in a crisp, white blouse, blue jeans and soft brown boots, Drew found her quite irresistible. Her complexion glowed and her thick dark hair shimmered in long graceful curves. She seemed the picture of health, and yet Drew worried that the strain of the past few weeks was taking its toll physically, as well as emotionally. Her fainting had him especially worried.

"It looks like someone's home," Joanna said at the open front door. "That's Nita's car in the drive."

Through the open doorway, Drew glimpsed a typical, well-lived-in family room. The sound of a television drifted out the doorway, but there was no sign of anyone inside—at least not in the portion of the house they could see.

"Nita?" Joanna called. "Charlie? Anybody home?" She glanced at Drew, one perfect brow arched in a question.

"Could they be out back?"

She shrugged. "Maybe. I don't know about Charlie or Nita, but surely the kids are around. I doubt they would all go off and leave the door open like this."

As they walked across the lawn toward the back, a large golden retriever came bounding up to them. "Hi, boy!" Joanna crooned to the exuberant animal. "This is Arlie," she explained. "Despite his size, he's still just a baby." After accepting a few affectionate strokes, Arlie fell in beside them as they walked past a stand of young aspen trees that divided the front and back yards.

In a small garden plot, Joanna saw Nita bent over working. "Nita!" she called.

Drew would never have recognized Evan's secretary. Dressed in baggy cotton trousers and an oversize denim shirt, with her hair pulled up under a wide-brimmed straw hat, Nita Lansky looked like the quintessential suburban housewife attending to her garden. She dropped her shovel and hurried across the carpet of bluegrass to meet them.

"Hi, Jo," she said, meeting them halfway across the yard. "Good afternoon, Mr. Spencer."

He couldn't see her eyes behind the large sunglasses she wore, but Drew could sense, by the tone of her voice, that she hadn't forgiven him for yesterday.

"Nita, did you forget we had an appointment?" Joanna asked.

Nita's chin dropped, and she tugged off the grass-stained garden gloves as she shook her head. "No," she admitted, her voice somber. "I didn't forget."

Drew and Joanna exchanged glances. "Then why did you stand us up?" he asked.

"Is something wrong, Nita?" Joanna asked, her voice deep with concern.

"I think you'd better come in," Nita said. "Let me wash up and make us some iced tea."

Joanna put her hand on Nita's sleeve as the woman tried to walk past her. "No more stalling, okay? We have to talk." She surprised Drew with her frank assertion. "It's obvious something's wrong, Nita. Please. Just tell me what it is."

Nita's shoulders dropped. "Not out here," she said. "At least let's go into the house."

Joanna nodded, and the three of them walked in through the open back door and through a kitchen where a stack of dirty dishes waited in the sink and the smell of what must have been last night's dinner and popcorn still clung to the air. A slender, blond teenage boy, dressed in ragged cutoff jean shorts and a sloppy white T-shirt, lounged on a well-worn sofa in front of a blaring television. He didn't look up when they walked in. Drew supposed this was Michael, the boy who'd left Valerie in the lurch.

"Michael," Nita yelled. "Turn that thing off and go finish mowing the lawn." The kid on the couch didn't make a move or even acknowledge her command until she shouted, "Now!" He finally rolled, as if in slow motion, to a sitting position and then to his feet and meandered past them out the back door.

"Hi," he said to no one in particular as he left.

"Make yourself at home," Nita said, hurrying into the family room to turn off the TV. "Don't mind the mess. Kids, you know."

Drew chose a straight-back dining-room chair that had obviously been pressed into service for extra seating in the cluttered family room. Nita and Joanna sat down on the couch Michael had just vacated. Nita still didn't take off her sunglasses.

"Nita, why did you ignore our appointment? And why didn't you go in to work today?" Joanna asked. "Are you ill?"

A head shake was the reply.

"But something must be wrong," Drew put in. "You obviously didn't go into the office at all today."

"I told you the other day I was planning to quit," Nita said without looking up.

"Yes, but—"

"Well, I quit. That's all. I've been sitting there day after day, doing nothing but answering phones. No one in the office to talk to, except Valerie—" she almost sneered "—waltzing in and out whenever she pleases, like she owns the place." She paused and shoved her glasses higher up on her nose. "I guess I just couldn't stand it anymore."

They sat waiting for her to continue, but after a long minute of silence, Joanna asked, "Nita, did you take some files home from the office the other day—the day Lincoln Nesbitt came to see me?"

At first, Nita only sat staring at her hands, seemingly fixated by the garden gloves she held in a white-knuckled grip. "Yes," came the almost inaudible reply.

The roar of the lawn mower, sputtering to life and settling into a steady drone filled the momentary silence.

"But why?" Joanna asked. "You know those files were not to be taken off the premises."

"I know," she said, almost in a whisper. "But there were some...things I needed to do. Some things I needed to catch up on before... Anyway, when I decided I was leaving Galbraith Realty, I figured I'd better take the work home in order to get it wrapped up before I put in my last day."

"Which was yesterday?" Drew interrupted.

"Yeah. I guess it was," she said drearily.

"But why?" Joanna asked. "Why leave like this? Without any notice? Nita, are you in some kind of trouble?"

Again, Nita didn't look at them, but sat staring at her hands. "I just have to go, that's all. And I thought it would be easier this way. To just quit."

"That isn't good enough," Joanna said, surprising Drew again. "I think I deserve an explanation for the way you're behaving. Please, Nita," she urged more gently. "Just help me to understand."

Nita finally raised her head and slowly pulled the dark glasses from her face to reveal a deep bruise on her cheekbone that extended to just below her slightly swollen right eye.

Drew heard Joanna's sharp intake of breath before he asked, "What happened, Nita?"

Without taking her eyes off Joanna, she said, "It wasn't his fault...he didn't mean to do it. It's just that he's under so much pressure these days, what with Vista Grande folding and all..."

"Who?" Drew asked.

"Charlie," Joanna answered, her voice harder than he'd ever heard it. "It was him, wasn't it, Nita?"

The woman's shoulders slumped and she put her dark glasses on. "He told me the last time it would never happen again. But last night, he just..." The rest of her sentence was lost when her voice cracked and a tear slid down her injured cheek.

The sound of the lawn mower's engine died, intensifying the difficult silence.

"Where is he now?" Joanna asked.

Nita shrugged. "He left the house early this morning. I'm not sure where he is. His crew was working on a house in Ridgeway, but it's rained up there for two days, so they haven't worked since Monday." At the sound of the back door slamming, Nita jumped. "Michael," she whispered. "I don't want him to hear this."

"Come on," Joanna said, rising. "We're going to put a sign up in front of one of Valerie's new listings. Tell him you're going with us, Nita. We can talk in the car."

Nita nodded and hurried toward the front door.

Drew and Joanna followed.

"What's going on?" Michael asked, stepping into the family room as they were leaving.

Nita didn't answer, but fled quickly out the front door. Drew turned to the young man, whose face glistened with a fine sheen of sweat. "Your mom is going with us to check on some business for Mrs. Galbraith. We'll be back in an hour or so."

The young man nodded, his expression flat and unreadable. He turned to go into the kitchen. Drew couldn't help wondering what the young man thought about his parents' abusive relationship.

Joanna and Nita were waiting for him in his car, and in a few minutes they arrived in front of the property where Valerie asked them to place the second sign. "I'll get it," Drew said, leaving the two women inside the car. With a look, Joanna thanked him for the few minutes alone to talk to Nita.

Like so many of the mountain properties around Telluride, the house was situated halfway up a steep, rocky slope. Not wanting to trespass on the homeowner's carefully manicured lawn, Drew decided to place the sign at end of the driveway.

Unfortunately, the soil there was hard and especially rocky, and when Drew tried to force the metal legs of the sign into the ground, he found the earth completely unyielding.

Anticipating the need to force the sign down by hand, he'd hooked the clawed edge of a hammer into the back pocket of his jeans. He reached for it now, hoping to tap the metal stakes into place. He pounded the right side first with limited success, but when he brought the hammer down on the left side, the sign shifted and he hit his index finger squarely with enough force to draw blood.

Dropping the hammer and the sign, he jumped back, cursing under his breath and sucking on his finger.

A few minutes later, he returned to the car, having decided that if the homeowner wanted the sign planted anywhere other than smack dab in the middle of his lawn, he'd have to move it himself.

"What did you do to yourself?" Joanna asked when he asked her to see if she could find something in her purse or in the glove box that he could wrap around the wound to stop the bleeding.

After searching the glove box, Joanna found a tissue in her purse, folded it in small, lengthwise strips and wrapped it around his finger. He had to fight to keep his eyes from devouring her as she leaned across the seat, tending to the cut. The sun-fresh smell of her hair swept through his senses.

"It isn't deep," she said, "but if you haven't had a tetanus shot in a while, you should probably swing by the walk-in clinic and get one. There's iodine and Band-Aids at the office. Those metal edges are sharp, aren't they?"

"I hate to admit it, but I didn't cut it on the edge," he said.

"Then what?"

With a sheepish smile he admitted, "I smacked it with the hammer." The implication of what he'd just said struck him, and he could see that it occurred to Joanna at the same time. *You show me some other way that blood and hair can wind up on a hammer and I'll reconsider.*

It was the challenge Bryan Miller had posed to Drew just a few short hours ago, and it echoed through Drew's mind now. One look at Joanna's face told him she was thinking the same thing.

"Can you finish your conversation with Nita later?" he asked in a low voice.

Her nod told him she understood that he wanted to talk to Bryan Miller as soon as possible and that Nita's presence would only complicate things.

"Nita, Drew has an appointment. Come with me back to the office," she said when he started the car. "It will be private and quiet there, and we can sit down together and straighten things out."

In the rearview mirror, Drew saw his backseat passenger nod.

Again, his gaze and Joanna's met and held for a meaningful moment. *I can't answer your questions now,* he told her with his eyes. *Please trust me.*

When she drew in a shaky breath and offered him a weak smile, somehow he knew, without her saying a word, that she understood everything completely.

Chapter Fourteen

"Let me get this straight," Bryan Miller said, rising from behind his desk to pace across his office. "You're saying the blood on the hammer found in the trunk of Lincoln Nesbitt's car came from an event that occurred some time before Evan disappeared? That he might have injured himself previously?"

"That's what I think," Drew said.

"Based on . . ."

Drew glanced at his index finger and then at the hammer he'd brought in and laid on Bryan's desk. "Based on what you might call a little accidental experimentation I engaged in this afternoon. If you send that hammer to the lab, you'll understand what I mean." Briefly, he explained to the sheriff what had happened.

"You really think it could have happened that way?"

"I don't know," Drew admitted. "And I'm far from being able to prove it, but the point is, it *could* have happened *precisely* that way."

The sheriff rubbed the back of his neck and released a tired sigh. "Okay. Suppose you're right about the blood. What about the hair? A guy slams his thumb with the hammer, but unless he turns around and hits himself in the head, how does his hair get mixed in?"

Drew hesitated. Leveling an accusation against a law enforcement officer wasn't something he could do carelessly. "I have a few ideas about that, as well. But, unfortunately, even less proof."

Bryan leaned against his desk and folded his thick arms across his chest. "You're not being deposed, Drew."

"But I *am* talking on the record to the county sheriff."

"Okay," Bryan said. "Then let's change the situation to a couple of concerned parties talking theoretically. How do you explain it, Drew? How did Evan Galbraith's hair get on the end of that hammer, unless the hammer made contact with the man's skull, drawing blood and ripping out hair with it?"

"Someone supplied the hair after the fact."

Bryan stood up straighter. "What are you saying exactly?"

Drew matched his stare. "Still one concerned party to another?"

"Yeah."

"Ask your deputy, Bryan. Ask Joanna. At first I thought she was just being paranoid, but now I'm not so sure."

"I'm afraid I'm still missing something."

"Harley Platt. He requested Evan's hair samples before you ordered them. Joanna pointed it out the night before last, when someone fired that shot at us in front of Valerie Wallace's condo. Remember?"

Bryan's expression said he did. "And you're saying Harley planted the hair on the hammer? Which means you must believe he's trying to set Lincoln Nesbitt up for murder."

"I don't know that I would put it that simply, but it's a theory. I've always had a problem with the anonymous caller conveniently knowing the location of such damning evidence. And, frankly, I've just never been convinced that Lincoln had it in him to unleash that kind of violence on anyone. And then there's the matter of Harley trying to choke the life out of me last night. Also the slug we never found after the sniper fired on us. Do I need to go on, or are you finding as many similarities as I have with this picture?"

Bryan walked to his chair, sank down and rubbed his chin, seemingly examining Drew's theory for plausibility. "I am. And, unfortunately, it's creating the same image. For what reason? Why would Harley go to such lengths?"

Drew shrugged. "The motives are usually pretty standard in cases like this, aren't they? Greed. Jealousy." He stood up to leave. "Love or money," he said as he opened the door. "The longer I'm in this business, the more I believe it inevitably comes down to one or the other."

"Or both," Bryan said as he picked up the phone.

"I FEEL BAD about this," Nita admitted, sipping from the coffee mug Joanna handed her. "I haven't had a drink in the middle of the day since the champagne toast at my wedding."

"Your secret's safe with me," Joanna said, smiling. She had to admit she'd experienced a perverse pleasure opening a bottle of Evan's precious sauvignon for the express purpose of soothing Nita's frazzled nerves and loosening her tongue. Her smile faded, however, when Nita pulled her glasses off and Joanna saw that the bruise around her eye had turned a deeper purple.

"Nita, what are you going to do about... Charlie hitting you?"

Nita took another sip of wine and set the mug down before she admitted, "I don't know. We've been together for twenty-two years. We've got two great kids. A life... or at least, we did have a life until..." Her voice faded.

Joanna grabbed a soda out of the refrigerator and sat down in the metal chair facing her. "Do you still love him?"

"Yes, I suppose I do." The tears gathered in shiny pools in her eyes. "Does that make me a fool?"

Joanna reached across the table and patted Nita's hand. "No. Of course it doesn't. Love—real love, anyway—doesn't just stop because you've been hurt. It isn't that easy." She startled herself by realizing that if she'd ever loved Evan, it certainly hadn't been with the same kind of devotion Nita felt for Charlie.

"I'm just so hurt right now, I don't really know what I feel."

"You need to get some counseling, Nita. Both of you. And you need to have Charlie move out of your home until you can get it."

"I've been thinking about that all day," Nita said miserably. "He's never been this bad before, but I'm not so blind that I don't realize what it means. We've got some serious problems, and sooner or later, we've got to deal with them."

"You've got it, Nita. And I'm sorry if somehow Evan is connected to all of this."

Nita avoided her gaze.

"I believe the Galbraith agency is at least part of the problem." Joanna tried to gauge Nita's reaction. "I'm right, aren't I?"

Again, Nita sipped her wine, and Joanna reached for the gold-labeled bottle and filled the mug to the rim again.

"Yeah. You're right."

"You've got to tell someone. It's going to come out sooner or later."

"I know." Her voice was barely a whisper. "I told him... Charlie," she explained, "that we wouldn't find them. Even if we tore this place apart, which we did. Every file and document for the past two weeks! I told him," she said, her voice rising, "that Evan was too smart to leave records like that just laying around." She tipped the mug and took a long swallow, and Joanna couldn't help thinking that for someone who had never made a habit of drinking in the middle of the day, Nita was having a good go of it.

"It was me taking those files home that made you suspicious, wasn't it? I figured one of you would catch on."

"Nita," she said, "back up, will you? I'm not following you. What kind of records did Evan have that Charlie thought he could find?" And did the places that the Lanskys searched include her bedroom? she wondered. Had it been Charlie Lansky in her bathroom yesterday, pretending to be Drew?

"You really don't know? He didn't tell you?"

"Know what? Come on, Nita. Tell me what's going on."

Before she answered, Nita drained the wine from her mug and licked her lips. Joanna ignored her when she eyed the bottle again. Already Nita's speech was beginning to slur. "Well, it all started when Charlie decided to bid on the development. Vista Grande."

"Which he won," Joanna put in.

"Yes. But which he *wouldn't* have won had Evan not showed him the other bids."

"He did what? But that's illegal!"

"Yeah, but you know Evan... a little thing like the law never stopped your husband from getting what he wanted." Nita's tone had become so hard and matter-of-fact that Joanna was beginning to feel like a fool. "Anyway, we won the bid. But not without paying."

"Who'd you pay?" Her stomach was churning with the answer she sensed was coming.

"Evan, of course."

Joanna felt as though she was walking blindfolded through a mine field. "How much did Charlie pay him, Nita?"

The tipsy secretary rolled her eyes. "A lot!"

"Fifty thousand dollars?" She held her breath, almost afraid to hear the truth.

Nita blinked. "Yeah. Hey, I thought you said Evan never told you."

The breath whooshed out of her in a gasp. Poor Nita. She was married to a man capable of blackening his wife's eye, a man who didn't think twice about breaking and entering and making death threats. Gathering the wits Nita's half-drunken confession had scattered, Joanna pushed on. "Go on, Nita. Tell me everything."

"Well, you can imagine what a mess we found ourselves in after Evan disappeared. We've never had that kind of money, and with the development going belly-up, we had no way to replace it."

"Replace it? Where had the money come from? A loan?"

Nita dropped her eyes, obviously too ashamed to meet Joanna's stare. "Charlie stole it from his company. He managed to cover it up so that his partners wouldn't be suspicious, figuring he could replace it as soon as he got paid for Vista Grande. He said that even if the partners eventually figured out what he'd done, they'd be so tickled by the money they'd made off Vista Grande, they'd never press the issue." She groaned and put her head in her hands. "You gotta spend it to make it, Charlie always said."

But it helped if it wasn't stolen money you spent, Joanna thought.

"Anyway," Nita continued, "now there's no Vista Grande and Charlie has no way of replacing that money. He's sure Evan made a tape or some kind of file telling all about the arrangements of their crooked deal—you know how he could be so efficient." Nita's eyes had dulled, and for a minute, Joanna thought she saw a spark of something close to affection in Nita's eyes.

"Nita, did you and my husband . . . that is, did you and he—"

Her head jerked up and she blinked several times before Joanna's meaning sunk in. "An affair? Are you asking me if Evan and I had an affair?" Nita reached for the bottle, not waiting for Joanna's invitation this time. "No." She answered her own question with such flat resignation that Joanna had to believe her. "Not that we hadn't considered it."

Joanna didn't gasp. She didn't even blink, and for once, she didn't even feel like throwing up. It seemed the more she learned about Evan from other people, the less it shocked her and the thicker her skin was becoming. Now what concerned her most was finding Evan and stopping him from hurting and cheating more innocent people. Finding him alive she hoped. Yes, she wanted him to be found unharmed, she realized. Even with all the anger, hurt and humiliation, she couldn't wish her baby's father dead.

Nita sighed, pulling Joanna back to the situation at hand. "Evan could be quite a charmer," Nita said almost wistfully. "But then, you know that. At times I think I would have left Charlie and the kids if he'd asked me to go. Then Jake called that day, and all Evan could think about was the Diamond C...oh, and you, of course." A flood of color stained her cheeks.

"But what about the checks?" Joanna asked, as eager to get to the bottom of the forgery as she was to distract Nita from a discussion of her life with Evan. "What did Evan offer you to sign them?"

The mug was midway to her lips, but she slowly set it down, shoving back a lock of hair that had flopped over one eye before she answered. "Checks? What checks? I don't know anything about any checks."

Joanna wondered why Nita would decide to stop now after confessing to so much already. "The checks Evan asked you to sign my name to."

"What!" Nita stood up so quickly her chair tipped over. "Hey, I don't know what you're trying to pull, Joanna. I've been straight with you today. I've told you things that could...well, that could put my husband behind bars. But to call me a forger!" Her eyes darted around the room. "Look, I don't know what kind of other crooked deals Evan was involved in. Lord knows, it could have been anything," she said. "But I never signed your name. Never!" She started across the room toward the door, and Joanna went after her.

"Stop, Nita. Where are you going?"

"I—I gotta get out of here. I'm calling a lawyer. I don't know what you're trying to do to me, Joanna!" She was crying, a soppy, drunken cry.

Joanna followed her. "Wait, Nita. Please. If you'll just listen to me for a minute. I'm not trying to do anything to you. I just want the truth."

But the distraught woman was having none of Joanna's reassurances, and when she reached the door and Joanna stepped in front of her, she raised her hand. "Get out of my way, Jo, or I swear, I'll hurt you."

Just then, Joanna was propelled toward Nita and they almost fell together onto the floor as the door was pushed from behind. Scrambling to keep from falling, Nita grabbed Joanna by the shoulders and pushed her back, into a pair of waiting arms.

DREW OPENED THE DOOR to find Joanna flying backward into his arms. Instinctively, he caught her and pulled her against him to keep her from falling. "What the—"

"Nita, wait! Please!" She pulled out of his arms and ran a few steps after the woman who'd charged past Drew and was now halfway down the block at a dead run.

"Joanna? What's wrong? Do you want me to go after her?"

Joanna shoulders sagged, and she turned and walked inside and closed the door. "No," she muttered. "I've already made a big enough mess of things. No sense scaring her even more."

"What happened? Did she admit to signing the checks?" He put his hand at the middle of her back and ushered her toward a chair. "And why does it smell like a cocktail lounge in here?"

Despite the situation, Joanna had to laugh, a weary laugh that didn't contain much mirth. "Sit down, Drew," she said. "This may take a while to explain."

Half an hour later, after she'd finished filling him in on the details of Charlie Lansky's and Evan's crimes, she leaned forward in the chair and pushed her hair back with both hands. "I feel as though I've just finished having tea with the Mad Hatter. It seems everyone around me has been cheating, lying or stealing from each other."

He put his hand on her shoulder. "I think Bryan Miller is experiencing the same feeling this evening." He told her about the conclusions he and Bryan had come to concerning Harley's involvement in the situation.

"What did Harley have to say about all of this?"

"I don't know yet. I think Bryan was calling him when I left."

"I suppose we have to call Bryan with the information Nita gave me about Charlie."

Drew nodded, but his main concern was not for Charlie Lansky or even Harley Platt, it was for Joanna. She seemed pale, tired and depressed, and he hated seeing her this way.

"Come on," he said. "Neither of us has had more than a cup of coffee all day. I'm taking you to dinner."

"But what about Nita? And won't Bryan want to talk to us after he questions Harley?"

"Probably. But with the size of the knot he's trying to untangle, a couple of hours for dinner won't make any difference." He could sense her starting to relent. "Come on, Joanna. Let me buy you dinner."

"Well . . . I guess."

"How about the Bon Ton in Ouray? Is it still the best restaurant west of the Mississippi?"

Joanna smiled, and he wondered if she was remembering their weekends in Ouray, soaking in the hot springs and exploring on horseback the high mountain trails outside the small mountain town dubbed America's Switzerland.

"As far as I know, it's still wonderful. Do you remember the minestrone soup they served? It's been a long time, but my mouth is already watering just thinking about it."

He rose and reached for her hand. "Then it's settled. Let's go."

"It's quite a drive. Are you sure you want to go all that way for dinner?"

"I'm sure." To put the roses back in her lovely cheeks, he would have driven to Italy and made the soup himself.

THE SUN HAD SET by the time they pulled up against the curb on Main Street in front of the St. Elmo, the historic Ouray hotel that housed the restaurant in its basement. For Joanna, the drive had done wonders. The conclusion to her encounter with Nita had left her feeling drained and depressed, but on the road to Ouray, Drew had put the top down on his sports car, and with the fresh air whipping against her face and the wind in her hair, she felt as though time had rolled back and it was just the two of them again.

Two lovers on their way to their favorite mountain hideaway for a romantic weekend. There was no denying it was a foolish fantasy, under any circumstances. But with Drew's eyes occasionally lingering too long on her mouth, the fantasy had been easily conjured.

"Give them our name, will you?" Drew asked when they were inside. "I'm going to go wash up."

When she gave her name, the hostess repeated, "Caldwell?" and Joanna nodded. "Are you any relation to Jake?" the older woman asked.

"Why, yes," Joanna said, studying the woman's face, trying to remember if they'd ever met. "He was my grandfather. Did you know him?" The woman's smile was so warm, Joanna knew the answer already. Jake had that effect on people.

"Oh, yes. I'm Stella Kent. I grew up just south of the Diamond C, on the old Quatro place. Do you know it?"

"Sure I do."

"Then you must be Joanna. But you wouldn't remember me. After you moved in with your grandpa, he didn't get up to Ouray so much. But when we were younger, Jake and I used to see. . . quite a bit of each other. He was quite a dancer, that grandpa of yours! We used to go to all the country dances—a bunch of us, usually. But sometimes just Jake and I. Anyway, we go way back. He was quite a man." In her eyes, Joanna saw a wistful longing. For the next several minutes, she engaged the woman in more conversation about Jake and their common acquaintances in the valley. As Stella talked, Joanna couldn't help wondering if at one time there had been a romantic link between her grandfather and the still attractive woman. Had he given up his personal life because of his devotion to raising her? Would she have the strength to do the same for her own child?

"It should only be a couple minutes before your table's ready," Stella told her. "For Jake's girl, I want it to be a good one." The woman gave Joanna another smile when Drew joined her.

Drew took her arm, and they stepped aside to wait for their table. "What was that all about?"

Joanna grinned with a feeling of genuine happiness she hadn't experienced since the day Dr. Lorring confirmed her pregnancy. "Coming here was a good idea, Drew," she said and impulsively kissed him on the cheek. "Thank you."

His hand was still on her arm, and he gave her a gentle squeeze. "It's good to see you smile."

"Caldwell," a waitress called from the hostess podium.

"Joanna," Stella corrected with a smile.

"Caldwell Joanna," the waitress called, misunderstanding Stella's meaning.

But Stella and the waitress and everything else faded to the back of Joanna's mind. Something came to her just as they reached their table. Her hands flew to her mouth, and she gasped.

"Joanna, are you all right?"

"Drew, did you hear what they said just now, the waitress and then Stella?"

His look was one of utter confusion. "I heard them call your name. Was there something I missed?"

"Yes," she said excitedly. "Something we've both been missing all along. Listen. Caldwell Joanna."

He sat staring at her as if she'd lost her mind.

"Caldwell Joanna!" The realization of Evan's latest betrayal stung like a slap. "Don't you get it, Drew? Caldwell Joanna. All those checks made out to that company. *Calder Johannsen. Caldwell Joanna.* Don't you see? It was all a ruse. A horrible play on my own name!" The depth of Evan's deception stunned and sickened her at the same time. To think he'd used her to get to Jake, to set up an elaborate plot to exploit and ruin the Diamond C for his own benefit, to cheat Lincoln Nesbitt, to steal from the Lanskys. And, finally, in a twist that proved he could never have felt anything for her—a perverse distortion of her own name to create a company into which he'd funneled his ill-gotten gain.

Drew's eyes were on her as she pushed her chair back and rushed out of the dining room.

A moment later, Joanna heard a soft tapping on the ladies' room door, followed by the kind voice of Jake's old friend. "Your gentleman asked me to check on you, Joanna. Are you all right?"

Joanna mumbled that she was fine, but the rolling in her stomach continued as she rinsed her mouth and bathed her face in cold water. A few minutes later, feeling better, but realizing that dinner was now out of the question, she walked into the restaurant. Stella intercepted her before she made it to the table.

"Are you all right, honey? Is there anything I can do for you?"

Joanna offered her the best smile she could muster. "Maybe a little tea. Thanks."

"But is there something else...anything at all I can do for you?" The worry hung heavily on the woman's kindly face.

"No. Thank you, Stella." Joanna couldn't imagine anything more important than what Stella had already done for her.

Chapter Fifteen

"I'm sorry you didn't get your soup," Drew said when they were walking to his car.

"Don't be. And please, if you care for me, don't mention minestrone soup again this evening. Besides, the tea and crackers hit the spot. I think I needed to get away, even if I didn't get my dinner. We can always go back."

Despite telling himself she'd made the comment offhandedly, he decided to pin her down to that promise. "I plan on holding you to that rain check."

She tilted her chin as if about to challenge him, but to his surprise, she merely said, "All right," in a soft, almost seductive voice that sent a thrill down his spine.

It was almost nine-thirty and the air was so cool and clear it felt like autumn, despite the fact that it was mid-July. Joanna took a deep, even breath. "Actually, physically I feel better than I have all day, but I'd be lying if I said it didn't hurt to know how many different ways Evan has deceived me."

Drew merely nodded, unsure of how to console her without sounding self-serving, without reminding her that if she gave him a chance, she'd never have to worry about being deceived by a man again.

Now, however, was not the time. First, Evan Galbraith had to be found. Then the legal and financial dilemma surrounding Vista Grande had to be sorted out. Then there was the matter of death threats, forgeries and anonymous callers. Once all those elements had been addressed, there would be time for rekindling old love.

And this time there *would* be time, he told himself. He'd learned the hard way the error of his thinking. He knew now that it had been ambition and youth that had tricked him into thinking life had to be a now-or-never proposition.

He had no way of knowing how long it would take to heal the emotional scars Evan had inflicted upon Joanna. She'd been badly hurt, and even though he felt sure she'd never loved Evan Galbraith the way she'd loved him, she still had deep concerns to face.

With an inner resolution stronger than any he'd ever experienced, he vowed to be there for her, no matter how long it took or how many changes he had to make in his own situation. As far as he was concerned, only one thing could keep them apart. And that obstacle was the lady herself.

Tonight, his concerns were more immediate, beginning with the hunch he'd been toying with all evening. Because the night was so cool and would probably get even cooler by the time they got back to Telluride, he put the car top up and gave Joanna a lightweight jacket he found in the trunk.

Once they were headed toward Ridgeway, where they'd make the turn to Telluride, he handed Joanna the extra key to the glove box and asked her to call on the cell phone to see if Bryan Miller had left a message on her answering machine at the ranch.

After searching through the glove box, Joanna turned a questioning expression to him. "It isn't in here, Drew. Are you sure you didn't take it out at the ranch?"

"No. I remember seeing it this afternoon."

She uttered a little groan. "When I was searching for a tissue for your cut?"

"Right."

"Oh, Drew, I'm sorry. I remember setting it on the floor while I was searching, but I don't remember putting it back. If it was still on the floor while we were in the restaurant, it wouldn't have been difficult for anyone passing by to reach in and steal it."

"That sounds likely," he said. "See what a great investigator you're turning into?"

"Yeah. Just great," she muttered. "But at the cost of an expensive phone, I'm not sure it's a bargain."

"No problem. As a matter of fact, Cole will thank you. The last time he paid the bills for the agency, he complained loud and long about my phone bill." Wait till he got hold of this month's, Drew thought.

"If you still want to call, we could stop in Ridgeway," she suggested.

"Good idea. We'll stop at the convenience store on the highway and talk to the clerk to see if his memory has improved since the deputy talked to him about that so-called anonymous lady caller."

Ten minutes later, Drew guided the convertible into an angled space in front of the twenty-four-hour gas station and convenience store. A group of teenagers was gathered around the pay phone, and he decided to take advantage of the wait by questioning the clerk.

The young man behind the counter had the same indifferent look as Michael Lansky. But as soon as Drew identified himself as a private investigator, the kid's whole demeanor brightened. "Yeah. I was on duty that night. But the cops already talked to me about it. I don't remember no lady. But then, it was raining so hard, there could have been a gorilla on the phone out there and I wouldn't have been able to see him." He laughed and Drew smiled.

"It did rain that night, didn't it? Pretty hard, I heard." He remembered Nita Lansky saying her husband's construction crew had been forced to delay working because of the conditions. And something else nagged at the back of his mind, but for the life of him, he couldn't pin down what it was.

"A real downpour," the kid confirmed.

Joanna tugged on his sleeve. "The phone's free."

After thanking the clerk, he joined Joanna at the phone. While she was punching in the numbers and waiting for her answering machine to engage, he asked her, "Joanna, what do you remember about the night of the anonymous call? I know there's a piece of the puzzle I'm missing, but for the life of me, I can't seem to find it."

"Well, let's see... oh, hold on. Yes, there is a message from Bryan. He says he's going home for the day and that he tried to question Harley, but that he couldn't track him down. Says he left word with the officer on command tonight to keep trying to locate him." A line of worry creased her face on each side of her mouth, and he longed more than anything to soothe it away with a kiss.

Refraining from that impulse, he asked, "What else? Does he say anything about Charlie or Nita Lansky?"

She shook her head and hung up the phone. "Only that he'd be in touch tomorrow. He did leave his home phone number, however, if we want to call him when we get back."

"That might be a good idea," Drew said. If he was going to get an early start tomorrow, it would be good to get an update from Bryan tonight.

As they walked to the car, a San Miguel sheriff's car zoomed past.

"Hey!" Joanna blurted. "Wasn't that Harley?"

"Get in," Drew shouted, and in a few minutes they were speeding along the two-lane highway headed to Telluride, trying to catch up with the cruiser.

"Are you sure it was Harley?" Drew asked, pushing the small, gutsy convertible into a tight turn.

"Pretty sure. Harley's a big guy. Hard to miss even in the dark. Besides, when he made the turn onto the highway, the street lamps lit up the whole car." She nodded emphatically. "Yes. I'm sure it was him."

She'd no sooner spoken the words than the flashing lights of a patrol car illuminated the night behind them. "What is it?" she asked. "State patrol?"

"No. Damn it!" Drew muttered, staring into the rearview mirror. "It's a sheriff's car." And every instinct said the man behind the wheel was none other than the mysterious Harley Platt.

JOANNA READ the barely contained anger on Drew's face as he pulled the convertible to the side of the highway and got out of the car before Harley even opened his door. Joanna started to get out of the car, thinking that her presence might prevent the confrontation she could feel brewing between the two men.

Her hand was on the door when she happened to glance in the rearview mirror in time to see Harley grab his shotgun on the way out of his cruiser.

"Drew!" she screamed. "Look out!"

Before she dove across the seat, she saw Drew drop to the pavement. The blast shattered the calm, reverberating through the night air like a cannon blast or fireworks.

She heard another shot, this time a sharp crack, and she knew Drew was firing back, though how he'd managed to grab his handgun from beneath the seat without her seeing him, she didn't know.

Dismissing the puzzle, she dared a peek over the back of her seat to peer into the darkness. Harley had shut off his lights, and the night closed around them in an ominous, black velvet curtain. Stark fear sent goose bumps prickling up her arms.

Her fervent prayer was that Drew had not been injured in the exchange of gunfire, and that he was somehow, even at this moment, making his way to the car. Sitting alone in the silence was even more terrifying than the sound of bullets flying.

A flash of light signaled the approach of another car on the highway. To Joanna, the arrival of the passerby came as a mixed blessing. The lights that might afford them assistance would also reveal Drew to the deranged deputy with the shotgun.

Again, she found the suspense too much to bear and she raised up from her crouched position in the seat to chance a peek at the cruiser. When her gaze lifted over the back of the seat, the lights from the on-coming car illuminated the nightmare about to engulf her. Harley was at the driver's side door, jerking it open.

Even as the door swung open and his bulky figure loomed, an inner voice screamed at her stupidity for leaving it unlocked, for thinking she mustn't chance locking it in case Drew had to get in.

"Drew!" she screamed with such force her ribs hurt.

"You're boyfriend's out of commission, Joanna," Harley sneered. "Now it's just you and me. The way it always should have been. Evan's gone. Drew's gone. Just you and me." He shifted the shotgun so he could bend into the small car.

Fear triggered instinct, and almost without realizing what she was doing, Joanna drew her legs up in front of her. When he moved forward to slip behind the wheel, she kicked with all her might, catching the deputy off guard and sending him sprawling backward into the road.

There was no squeal of brakes, as she'd expected. No screech of tires against pavement or even the blast of a horn. There was only a sickening thud, a dull sound that even in its subtlety Joanna knew would remain in her memory forever, as the oncoming car rolled over Harley without the driver even slowing, or probably even knowing what he'd done.

In the darkness, she heard a pathetic groan. She quickly turned on the headlights and scrambled from the car in time to see Drew emerging from the ditch, looking dazed and unsteady, with a gash on his forehead oozing blood. "Drew," she cried and ran to him. "Here, let me help you. Lean on me."

"I'm all right. What happened?"

"Get on the radio in the cruiser," she ordered him as she ran to help Harley. "Call an ambulance and get the dispatcher to put you through to Bryan. Hurry, Drew. Harley may be dying."

He mumbled something, but she didn't hear as she dropped to the pavement, leaned down and pressed her head to Harley's chest, desperate to hear a heartbeat.

Her heart soared when she heard it. Faint, unsteady, but it was there. "Okay, Harley," she said. "Don't you die on me, you son of a gun. You owe me that much. Don't die, Harley," she warned him. "Hold on. Help is on the way."

Whether he heard her or not, she couldn't tell, but just saying the words made her feel better. At the thought that she might be responsible for taking a life, her awareness of the precious life growing inside her had never been more keen.

"Hold on, Harley," she whispered to him, running her hands over his body to see if she could determine the extent of his injuries. Oddly, the only blood came from his shoulder, where the gunshot wound had obviously torn open again. His injuries had to be internal, she thought with grim certainty. "Hang on, Harley," she said again.

The next thing she knew, Drew was setting out warning flares he'd obviously found in Harley's cruiser. "Are you all right?" she called to him.

"I'm okay. How's he doing?"

"Not so good."

"An ambulance is on the way," he said, as he dropped down beside her. "And so is Bryan."

A gurgling sound sent a chill of pure dread straight to her heart. "He's stopped breathing," she shouted, but before she could act, Drew was leaning over Harley, bestowing on the deputy the gift of life that only moments ago Harley had tried to take away from Drew.

Drew continued mouth-to-mouth, and Joanna began the rhythmic CPR procedure to keep Harley alive until the ambulance arrived. As they worked together in perfect tandem, fighting to save Harley Platt's life, the deep emotions she felt for the first love of her life was reborn a thousand times over.

AFTER THE emergency room nurse patched up Drew's head, he joined Joanna and Bryan in the surgical waiting room. In deference to the head wound Drew had received at the end of Harley's shotgun, Joanna had driven his car behind the ambulance to the Grand Junction hospital, where Harley was in surgery.

"The doctors seem hopeful," she told Drew when he sat down, sipping a cup of vending machine coffee Bryan handed him.

Drew shook his head. "If it was anyone else, they'd have been crushed under the wheels, but not that big oaf."

Joanna suppressed a shudder at the thought that the driver of the car might not even realize what he'd done.

"I'd say it was a good possibility," Bryan said. "Maybe they just bumped him and thought it was a rut in the road."

"Or maybe seeing the two vehicles parked that way, with no lights and no sign of life, the driver was too afraid to stop."

"Either way, we'll try to locate the car and notify the driver. It doesn't seem likely there would be any charges. It was a fluke accident. No one is to blame, except for Harley himself."

Regardless of what they said, however, Joanna couldn't help feeling responsible. Knowing she couldn't help what had happened, she could only pray for Harley's survival.

In a few moments, it seemed Joanna's prayers were answered. The double door swung open and two surgeons, still dressed in their blue scrubs, came out to report that Harley would recover fully.

"Just in time to face charges," Bryan said when the doctors had gone.

But Joanna didn't care. As long as she hadn't killed the man, she could live with herself. Her conscience was clear, and the surge of relief made her feel weak.

She glanced at Drew and worried about the lack of color in his face.

Bryan's eyes followed hers. "Are you going to be all right, Drew? You're not looking so great."

"I must admit, I've had better nights."

Bryan's gaze swept both of them. "Neither of you looks roadworthy. How about I arrange for you both to spend the night here. At least you might be able to get some rest."

Drew gave a dry, humorless laugh.

"I'm serious," Bryan said. "I could arrange it, if you think it's necessary."

Drew draped his arm around Joanna's shoulders. "Thanks for the offer, Bryan. But that won't be necessary. We'll be staying in Grand Junction tonight, and we'll call you in the morning. Maybe not first thing," he added. "I have a feeling we'll both be sleeping in. Right, Doc?"

Joanna nodded. Suddenly she felt more tired than she'd ever dreamed possible.

Half an hour later, they checked into a hotel near the hospital. Their room was clean and warm, and Joanna thought she'd never seen a more welcome sight than the two king-size beds, each with snowy white linens turned down, waiting to receive a couple of battered and exhausted bodies.

"You can have first crack at the shower," Drew said as he sank down on the bed.

Joanna didn't argue, and a few minutes later, the warm water was sluicing over her tired body in wondrously therapeutic waves. However, thinking of Drew and how sore his body must feel, she didn't linger, much as she'd have liked to.

Pushing into one of the thick terry robes hanging on the back of the door, Joanna walked back into the bedroom to see Drew stretched out on the far bed, fast asleep. Not wanting to wake him, she turned out the lights, and by the glow of the night-light in the outlet beside the dresser, she padded to her own bed.

She sat for a few minutes on the edge of the bed. Before she crawled between the sheets and gave herself up to much-needed sleep, she indulged herself in a long gaze into the face of the sleeping man across from her.

"Good night, Drew," she whispered and leaned over to feather a kiss across his cheek. He stirred and smiled and sent a stab of pure love straight through to her heart.

Sometime later, she awakened from a dark nightmare of gunshots and screams to find herself drenched in fear. She sat up quickly, alerted by the sound of her own whimpering. The room was dark except for the soft glow of the night-light.

Drew had undressed and crawled beneath the covers. His bare chest showed above the sheets. Suddenly the remnants of the nightmare and the longing to be close to him overpowered her good judgment, and she swung her legs over the side of the bed, crept to his bed and slid in beside him. Slowly, slowly, holding her breath, she edged against him, telling herself that the effects of the long night, including what they'd been told was a mild concussion, would have pushed him so deeply into slumber by now that he wouldn't even notice she was there.

But the male instinct proved stronger than any trauma, at least momentarily. When he felt her body curling up next to his, he turned on his side and drew her into the cradle of his arms.

"Drew," she murmured. "Please. Just hold me."

"Joanna," he whispered into her hair and kissed her head, before he promptly fell back into a deep sleep.

Chapter Sixteen

Lincoln Nesbitt sat with his head in his hands, and Bryan Miller thought he'd never seen such a quiet, gentle man. "Based on insufficient evidence at this time," Bryan said, "we can't hold you any longer, Lincoln. I'd appreciate it if you'd hang around. I'm sorry about all you've been through. Myself, I don't know what to think. But Drew Spencer has gone to bat for you from the beginning and the things he keeps pointing out are beginning to make sense."

The older man nodded and rose from the chair in the middle of the room where he'd been questioned almost continually, it seemed, since the day Evan Galbraith disappeared. "And what about Joanna?" he asked. "Has she changed her opinion of my guilt?"

Bryan hesitated, wondering why it would matter. "I guess I wouldn't really know about that, Lincoln." Even if he could speculate. Joanna wasn't a law officer, and to hazard a guess as to what she thought or felt would be completely unprofessional.

Drew, on the other hand, was different. As an investigator, his actions and opinions were open for discussion.

Lincoln's hand was on the door when Bryan asked him one more question. It was a question he'd been wanting to ask for a month, and in an odd way, he didn't think Lincoln would mind answering. "I just have to know," he said.

"Why did you go along with Evan in the first place? Lord knows, I'm no businessman, but from the beginning, that deal seemed pretty lopsided in his favor. Even if the development took off as expected, you probably wouldn't have realized the kind of profits I've got a hunch you're used to making. Seems like a pretty poor business deal to me, if you don't mind me saying so."

Lincoln smiled. "Not at all. I guess a good deal, as you put it, is all in the eye of the beholder, isn't it, Sheriff? And if this deal goes the way I suspect it will, I stand to gain a whole lot more than money." He touched his forehead in a mock salute and walked out the door, leaving Bryan shaking his head and remembering that it really did take all kinds. Like Lincoln Nesbitt, for example, Bryan thought. The man had lost a million bucks, but by the way he acted, you'd have thought he just struck gold.

JOANNA WOKE in the gray light of predawn with the warmth of Drew's body against hers. What a strange set of circumstances that had brought her to this, she thought. They'd somehow come full circle, and here she was, back in his arms.

She reveled a few minutes longer in the delicious familiarity of his embrace before she started to edge carefully out of his arms and his bed. "Don't go," came the groggy request from behind her, and at the same time his arms drew her closer against him.

She yielded to his loving pressure, lost in the delicious memories of other mornings and other awakenings that his sleepy voice and warmth evoked. His hand cupped her breast through the terry-cloth fabric of the robe she'd slept in.

"Drew, please."

His hand stilled.

"We shouldn't," she whispered.

"Then we won't," he replied. "Not if you don't want to."

"It isn't a matter of wanting."

"I know." His hand slid away from her breast and came to rest on the curve of her hip.

"I just want to hold you a little longer."

"I know." If only this moment, this uncomplicated moment of sheer joy and perfect trust, could last forever. She snuggled deeper into his arms and felt a thrill when he nestled his face in her hair.

"Go back to sleep," he murmured. "We've got another long day ahead of us, and I'm not ready to let go of you. Not yet."

With her heart racing, she would have thought it impossible to sleep, but the next thing she knew, he was sitting across from her, on the edge of the other bed, sipping coffee.

"Morning. I ordered breakfast. Thought you might be hungry."

"Thanks," she murmured, scooting to a sitting position, suddenly self-conscious that she'd crawled into his bed last night. But if Drew was self-conscious about anything—indeed, if he was thinking about anything but where to go next to find Evan—he didn't give a hint. Instead, as she nibbled on the toast he'd ordered from room service and sipped the tea, he launched into a running monologue of the plans he'd made for their day.

"First we check in with Bryan. And then, before we leave, I think you should call Valerie Wallace."

"Valerie?" she asked, reaching for another triangle of toast from the tray at the foot of his bed. "Why?"

He rose and pushed the curtains aside. "What do you see?" he asked.

"Ugh. Rain."

"Right. And what did the kid say about the night the call was made from Ridgeway?"

"Oh, Drew. Please. It's too early for twenty questions."

He smiled and sat down on the edge of the bed. "He said it was raining."

"Okay. I remember. So what?"

"And where were we the night the anonymous call came in?"

"Well, we started out for Nita's, but we ended up at Valerie's. Again, so what?"

"And it wasn't raining in Telluride."

"Drew! Please! Are you deliberately trying to drive me crazy?"

"Okay. Okay. It wasn't raining in Telluride, but it was raining in Ridgeway. Raining hard. Hard enough to cancel Charlie Lansky's construction crew for two days. And hard enough to get an umbrella really soaked if someone was standing out in the rain talking on a pay phone. Wet enough that it would still need to be dried out by the time that someone got back to Telluride."

Charlie. Nita. Umbrella. Anonymous caller. *Umbrella!*

"Umbrella!" she shouted, jumping up from the bed. "Drew! The umbrella at Valerie's was still wet, wasn't it? But it hadn't rained in Telluride! So why was her umbrella wet?"

"Exactly."

"But the luggage. She said she'd just gotten in."

"All right, now I'll take your line. So what?"

"So...she could have just come from the airport in Montrose, and it might have been raining there."

"It might have been, but how wet could she have gotten between the terminal and the car? I've flown into that airport countless times, and it's small. How wet could she have gotten?"

"I don't know. It doesn't matter. What we have to find out now is why? If Valerie *is* our anonymous caller, why?"

"That's a good question. One I'd love to ask her, though I doubt she'd be very forthcoming."

"But you must have a theory."

"I do. By casting a strong suspicion of murder on Lincoln Nesbitt—a man with a motive and the means—the fact that no body had been found would eventually almost become nothing more than a technicality."

"But proving murder without a body is almost impossible, isn't it?" Joanna asked.

"But that's just it. Whoever wanted the police to believe Evan was dead didn't have to worry about proving anything. So long as everyone assumed Lincoln Nesbitt had killed Evan, eventually everyone would stop looking for him. The search, which had already been cut way back, would be truly suspended. The police might never have been able to bring Lincoln to trial, but why keep looking for a dead man, or hunting for evidence, when you believe you've already identified the killer, even if you can't convict him? The only thing missing would be that conviction, but Evan—and his accomplice—didn't need it to accomplish what they'd set out to do."

"Namely, convincing everyone he was dead," she put in. "And if Lincoln Nesbitt is ruined in the meantime, if the Diamond C is lost and my life is destroyed in the process, so be it. It's just the cost of a good scam." She despised Evan at that moment, but she hated even more the fresh tears gathering in her eyes.

"I'm sorry, Jo," Drew said, sinking down on the bed beside her and gathering her in his arms. "I wish I could figure it any other way. God help me, I'd rather it had turned out he was dead."

He felt her stiffen in his arms. "Please, Drew. Don't say that. You don't know what you're saying."

Her response surprised him. Was it possible she still loved Evan? Even after all the man had done to betray her? It was a possibility he couldn't ignore.

"I'll check in with Bryan while you dress," he said, and reached for the phone.

THE WARMTH of their earlier intimacy, the predawn cuddling and the whispered promises had cooled measurably, and Joanna felt the emptiness in the pit of her stomach when she emerged from the bathroom, dressed and reluctant to face the day.

Drew was just hanging up the phone, and when he heard her, he turned and said, "Bryan says Harley hasn't regained consciousness, but his vital signs are strong and they have no reason to doubt a full recovery."

Joanna felt another flood of gratitude that she hadn't killed Harley.

"He also said that Nita Lansky called him from a woman's shelter. She's prepared to give her statement, but she wants time to get some counseling from a social worker and an attorney."

"What about Charlie?"

"No one's seen him."

"Those poor kids," Joanna said, walking over to look out the window at the rain and the gray skies, which seemed a perfect match for her mood.

"I bounced my theory about Valerie off Bryan, but without more to go on than that, he isn't asking for any warrants."

"But the hair and the blood on the hammer. Didn't you explain all that to him?"

"They're still just theories, Jo. Even I'm not sure I'm right. The only way we'll know for sure is when we find Evan."

For several minutes, neither of them spoke. Joanna stood with her back to him, staring out at the rain.

Drew watched her, his heart and his mind aching for a way to reach her. When she turned to face him, he detected a familiar look in her eye, one he'd seen before—in the show ring when the competition was tight, in college when the hours were long and the course load was unbearable, in the chapel that day when she'd given her vow to the wrong man. It was a look of raw determination.

"Then let's go find him, Drew. Damn it, let's go find Evan."

TOGETHER THEY agreed before leaving the hotel that going back to Telluride would be a waste of time. First they visited the hospital to see if Harley Platt had come around yet. Drew had several questions waiting for the deputy, the first and most important one being who else was involved in trying to frame Lincoln Nesbitt? Disappointed to discover that the deputy was still semicomatose, they found a diner with a couple of pay phones.

"I'll try to get hold of Valerie," he said.

"And I'll call the bank."

"The last one to finish pays for the coffee," he teased and was relieved to see her smile.

In a few minutes, they met at their table. Only Joanna had results to report. "We were right in our guess. The stamp on the back of the Calder Johannsen checks is an affiliated bank in Nevada. There's an account number on the back, but no name of any individual. The officer at the bank said that wasn't unusual for a commercial account. He said we could try to get a name, but he doubted the Nevada bank would release any personal information about the individuals associated with the corporation over the phone. Some corporation," she muttered. "A bogus rip-off of my own name! In Nevada, no less!"

"Wait a minute, Jo. Don't you see? All roads lead to Nevada. Remember what we said about following the money?"

"Right. And the money leads to Nevada, doesn't it?"

"It sure seems that way." He paid the bill and they walked out of the diner into the drizzling rain.

"What now?" she asked.

"The phone booth."

"But we just—" She gave up and followed him to the pay phones, but instead of picking up the receiver, he picked up the phone book.

"Yes!" he shouted, loud enough to garner a few curious looks from a couple going into the diner.

And the next thing she knew, Joanna was in his convertible and headed for Nevada.

"I knew the area code seven-oh-two was a western state, but I had to be sure."

"Drew, tell me what's going on. Somewhere between paying for coffee and checking out the phone book, you lost me."

"Remember yesterday when you tried to call the Diamond C by hitting redial on the office phone?"

The picture was coming together in her mind. "Yes," she said slowly. "But it was a long-distance number Valerie had been calling. A long-distance number with the area code seven-oh-two—Nevada!"

"Right. And if I'm correct in my guess, I'd say the number belongs to one Tony Winston, recently deceased motel owner in Goldstrike, Nevada."

She groaned. "Just when I think I'm getting this, you pull the rug out from under me again. Okay, Spencer, explain."

"All right, but I'll warn you, this may sound like a stretch in the beginning. If you stay with me, I think you'll see that it all fits perfectly. Okay. First, Evan and Valerie take this so-called business trip to Nevada. While they're there, they set up a phony corporation—Calder Johannsen Inc." Joanna couldn't help wincing again at the distortion of her name. "Anyway, they set up the phony account, but while they're there, they have to make sure they cover their tracks by actually looking at Mr. Winston's property. This gives them a name to use when Evan contacts Valerie in Telluride. Nita and you, if you happen to answer the phone, are familiar with Mr. Winston, and you wouldn't question him calling to make a counteroffer, go lower on his price or whatever."

"But they turned Winston down, didn't they? In no uncertain terms, probably so that he wouldn't call."

"But even if he did, he would ask for either Valerie or Evan, so no one would know the difference between the real Tony Winston or the pretender—Evan! The name was their code, a way for Valerie to know it was Evan calling her."

Joanna felt the stress pressing on her rib cage. She rolled down the window to get a breath of fresh air and found that the closer they got to the state line, the warmer the air. By the time they entered Utah a few minutes later, Drew had switched on the air conditioner.

"They buy the grubby little motel, lay low for a few months or even a year. The money they embezzle draws a tidy sum of interest in the local bank, and when they feel the police have completely bought into Lincoln Nesbitt's guilt and stopped looking for a live Evan Galbraith, Calder Johannsen and his lady fly the coop. Probably to Mexico, or some other country with lax immigration laws. Practically the perfect crime."

"Practically?"

"Yes. But not perfect. A couple of very crucial elements tripped them up. First, Harley muddied the waters with the hair sample. I'm sure they thought the blood on the hammer was good enough. I'm sure Harley acted on his own to convince you Evan was dead so you'd turn to him. Also, they had no idea you'd hire me to investigate the case. With me, you'd have the advantage of getting the kind of answers the police can't pursue—"

"Like this road trip to Nevada, for example?" she asked with a wry smile.

"Exactly. Do you have any idea the amount of evidence it would take to get a government entity moving in this direction?"

"And it would have to be federal, wouldn't it? The local authorities wouldn't have jurisdiction in another state."

"Right. And, although reciprocity between states exists, it's a complicated, time-consuming ordeal."

Joanna sighed. "And by the time we convinced all the agencies involved, Evan and Valerie would be enjoying their golden years on a beach somewhere."

"That's one of the reasons Cole and I went into private investigation. Often we can help people in a way law enforcement can't."

She felt proud of him, proud to know him, to be his friend, to still love him in that deep and meaningful way she could never deny.

"What will we do when we get there, Drew? I don't suppose Evan will hop in the back seat willingly and let you take him to Telluride to face embezzlement and fraud charges."

"To tell you the truth, I hadn't gotten that far. I'd hoped you would have some ideas on that subject."

"Gee, thanks." She thought a minute. "I'll give you a quarter if you stop at the next gas station with a rest room."

He laughed. "All that tea, huh?"

"Hmm. Something like that. Anyway, in the meantime, I'll be working on the problem of how to approach Evan. And I'll let you know the minute I have a solution."

AS IT TURNED OUT, neither Drew nor Joanna was completely responsible for the formulation of the plan to apprehend Evan. The solution took form after a discussion they had as they drove across the barren landscape of the Utah desert. By the time they reached the southwest corner of the state and pulled into a small café in St. George for a late supper, the plan was mostly mapped out.

And by the time they'd finished their BLTs, it was decided. Drew would call Bryan and ask him to begin the process of notifying the Nevada authorities. It would take a degree of trust on the sheriff's part, but Joanna was betting that Drew could convince Bryan to give him a chance.

She went into the ladies' room while Drew made the call. Her stomach was in full rebellion now, and she didn't know if it was due to her condition or the fact that in a matter of just a few hours she'd be face-to-face with Evan. Either way, she couldn't wait for it all to be over.

As it turned out, she didn't have long to wait.

THE DRIVE into Goldstrike was nerve-wracking, made even more so by the fact that they'd decided to wait until dark so they'd have less chance of tipping Evan off. But the side streets were poorly lit, and Drew made a number of wrong turns trying to find the obscure Vagabond motel.

Bryan had been reluctant, but in the end willing to go along with their scheme. He'd instructed them to contact him when they reached the state line. By then, he hoped to have the kinks ironed out with the Nevada authorities.

Joanna waited in the car while Drew made the call. Her heart had been beating in what seemed like double time ever since they left the café in St. George, and the gathering darkness wasn't helping the fear that pushed that beat even faster.

Drew jogged to the car and slid behind the wheel. "Valerie has skipped town. Bryan pulled some strings and got a search warrant. She wasn't at her condo when the authorities arrived, so they let themselves in. The place was deserted. Just a lot of black-and-white furniture, but not one scrap of Valerie's personal belongings."

"That black-and-white luggage must be bulging," Joanna mused.

He nodded, started the engine and pulled onto the highway. "Bryan said he was still trying to arrange things on this end."

A ripple of anxiety slithered through her. "What's the holdup?"

"Seems state law enforcement isn't crazy about taking orders from other states, especially when the authority is a county sheriff instead of a state entity. Then there's the problem of municipalities and townships.... Do you really want to hear this, Jo? Believe me, it only gets more muddled."

"Just cut to the chase. Will we have any backup, or not?"

"No. Yes. Well, maybe." He gave her a weak grin.

The man could be positively maddening sometimes. "Damn it, Drew. Tell me!"

"Okay. But you're not going to like it."

He was right. She didn't. The best Bryan could do wasn't much.

"Since no formal charges had been brought against Evan yet, no Nevada agency will touch him—and, for that matter, until Bryan can arrange a conversation between Lincoln, the D.A. and the bank—neither will any Colorado authorities. Charges of fraud and embezzlement are pending, but those things take time, judges, D.A.s and a whole lot of red tape. As it stands now, Evan is still merely a missing person."

"And a missing person, as long as he's not a minor, isn't breaking any laws, right?"

"I'm afraid that's right. I'm sorry, Jo. But the law can be very cumbersome at times." Joanna felt like screaming. "So what can we do?"

"Ah, now there's where it gets good. We can do lots of things. We're just average citizens."

"Look out, Drew," she warned. "Don't miss the exit. That sign back there said a half a mile to Goldstrike." Goldstrike, she thought ruefully. What an appropriate name for her situation. Somehow she felt the chances of finding Evan and straightening out the mess her life had become were about as good as winning the lottery.

IT DIDN'T TAKE LONG to drive up and down the dozen or so paved streets of the small, shabby town of Goldstrike, Nevada—population two thousand, if you believed the sign.

After ten minutes, Joanna finally spotted the faltering red neon sign that read Vagabond—with the *b* missing. She pointed, and neither of them spoke as Drew guided his car past the run-down motel.

Joanna's throat felt as dry as the desert they'd crossed and unbearably tight, with tension like a clenched fist pushing up from her chest.

It wasn't until Drew drove around the block again that Joanna spotted Evan's car parked along the side of the small unit with the battered sign that read Manager hanging over the door.

"That's it," she said, her voice weak and her heart racing. "I know that's his car."

Drew circled the block once more before parking the convertible a couple of blocks away, in front of a small church surrounded by shrubbery.

"Well, this is it," he said, turning to her in the darkness. "Wish me luck."

"*You?* Don't you mean *us?*"

He shook his head. "You're not going with me, Jo. One glance out the window, he recognizes you and he's gone. I have no intention of getting involved in some bizarre chase through this little burg. I have a feeling the local constabulary, if they have one, wouldn't take kindly to an out-of-towner trying to abduct one of its citizens."

"But he knows you, too."

"Not really. The man has only laid eyes on me twice. Once at your wedding, when I was merely a face among a host of other guests—" not to me, she wanted to tell him "—and then again at Jake's funeral. I really don't think he'll remember me."

"But what if he does? Oh, Drew, I just don't think we can take the chance. He's desperate! You know that. Just look at the lengths he's gone to so far." People had been known to kill for a lot less money, she told herself with a shudder.

"Please, Drew. Let me go with you. I might be able to reason with him." If worse came to worst, she'd shock Evan by playing her trump card—springing the news of the baby on him. Not that it would have much effect, she told herself grimly. They'd only discussed children once, and Evan had been less than enthusiastic, always putting her off, using the development and the time commitment it would require as an excuse. She felt sure the child she was carrying now would not be welcomed by its father.

In fact, the baby would never have been conceived had they not attended a social function where they'd both had a bit too much to drink. Joanna remembered the night with deep resentment and a generous portion of guilt. *It doesn't matter,* she thought, hoping somehow to communicate her feelings to her unborn child. *It doesn't matter how you began. All that matters is that you're there now. And I couldn't be happier. Believe me. You are wanted, so very wanted! And already so loved.*

"Jo," Drew said quietly. "I've got to get going."

A rush of panic squeezed Joanna's heart. She'd come close to losing him last night. She couldn't take the risk again. "Forget it!"

"What?" His face expressed his complete shock.

"I said forget it. It doesn't matter. I don't care if you find him. It doesn't matter if I never see him again. It's over. The whole marriage was a sham, anyway."

"Jo, you don't know what you're saying."

But she did. And she couldn't say it fast enough. "Please. Let's just go. I'll find a way to get a divorce, an annulment, whatever. Please. Don't do this, Drew. I can't bear the thought of something happening to you. Let the authorities deal with him. Let him go to Mexico or Timbuktu. Anywhere. But let's just leave now. Please." The emotion that clogged her throat made her hoarse, but she hardly noticed the tears until he brushed them away.

"You know we can't just walk away. He's hurt people. He's hurt you. He's got to be made to come back and face the crimes he's committed. I'm going to find your husband, Jo," he said softly. "That's why you hired me, remember? This thing has to come to an end. We can't just walk away, never knowing."

She caught his hand and held the palm against her cheek. Of course he was right, but the thought of losing him terrified her and made everything else irrelevant.

"I'll give you a quarter to change your mind," she said.

"Sweet Jo," he said with a sigh.

The look in his eyes and the love she saw there broke her heart.

"I've got to go. I can't wait any longer."

"But why? He has no idea we're on to him. The element of surprise is still in our favor, isn't it?"

He shrugged. "That's the problem. We don't know that, and there's a dozen reasons not to take the chance. Evan is smart, and so is Valerie."

New fear seized her heart when she remembered that Valerie had fled Telluride.

"If Valerie is still in the area, she's bound to pick up on the rumors about what happened last night to Harley. If she's tried to reach you, if she's contacted Nita or Nita has called her... Who knows, she might have even managed to see Harley, and if he's regained consciousness, there's no telling what she knows. The woman is cunning, and if she smells even a whiff of trouble she'll alert Evan and he'll be gone."

She knew he was right, of course. But that didn't make risking him any easier.

Chapter Seventeen

"Stay here and keep your eyes open. If I'm not back in fifteen minutes, drive to that gas station we passed when we got off the highway and call 911. Just tell them there's a fire and give them the address."

He kissed her quickly on the cheek and then moved toward the door, only to turn back, reach for her, and pull her against him and kiss her again. Hard this time. A rough, hungry kiss, one she wouldn't forget if she lived to be a hundred. A kiss that felt so much like goodbye, it caused a lump to form in her throat.

He stole her breath when he dragged his lips from hers and reached for the door, and opened it this time. She slid into driver's seat but couldn't resist a final warning through the open window. "Be careful, Drew," she whispered.

"Always."

She memorized his smile for the millionth time as he walked away.

"Please come back safe," she whispered to herself, and somehow, as if her message had reached him, he turned, jogged back to her, leaned down and kissed her again.

A quick, hot kiss, one that said he had every intention of coming back to her.

AT THE SIDE of the motel, Drew shined a penlight on the license plate of Evan's car, and it came as no surprise to him that the green-and-white Colorado plates had already been replaced with Nevada plates.

Nice job, he thought, noticing how dirt and grime had been intentionally smudged over the numbers.

When he banged on the side door of the motel office, he heard a dog barking. A big dog, if one believed the sound. But in his experience as an investigator, Drew had learned to detect the difference between the bark of a real dog and the cassette tape variety. And like everything else about the man, Evan Galbraith's dog was a phony, too.

"We're full up. No vacancies," came the voice from the other side of the door.

Drew thought fast. "Express delivery," he called as he pulled a piece of silver duct tape off the roll in his jacket pocket and settled it, sticky side out, in his palm.

"What the—"

"Express letter for a . . . Mr. Tony Winston. Can you tell me what unit he's in?"

"Put it under the door," came Evan's quick reply.

"Can't do that sir. Sorry. Got to get a signature."

The door opened a crack, and that was Evan's mistake. He flew backward across the room with the force of Drew's shove, and just as quickly as the door was forced open, Drew closed it with not much more than a click.

Drew quickly dragged Joanna's husband to his feet and held him by the collar, fighting the urge to ram his fist into Evan's face.

"Who the hell are you?" Evan managed to ask, though with his collar bunched so tightly around his throat, Drew wondered how he'd managed it.

"The more appropriate question, I believe, is who the hell are you, Mr. Winston, aka Evan Galbraith? Are those your only aliases, you son of . . . or are there others in your crummy little past?"

Evan's eyes filled with naked panic. "Look, I don't know who you are, or who sent you, but I can explain. I've got money. I can pay—"

"Oh, you'll pay, all right," Drew promised. "You'll pay your debt in money and in time, I would imagine."

Evan, obviously realizing that Drew couldn't or wouldn't be bought began to struggle against Drew's grip. He was thin, but wiry, and his strength and the amount of effort it took Drew to cuff and gag him was surprising.

There was surprise in Evan's eyes when he found himself so quickly subdued and bound. But surprise quickly changed to rage and his brown eyes turned black as Drew shoved him toward the back door and into the deserted parking lot.

Moving as quickly and as quietly as he could, with his squirming, muttering prisoner fighting him every step of the way, Drew realized he would make it to the car with time to spare in the fifteen-minute limit he'd given Jo.

A half a block away, however, it struck him what a shock it would be for Joanna to see her husband this way. If he had it his way, he'd knock Evan out with one punch, throw him in the trunk and drive him straight back to Telluride without stopping. It was better treatment than Evan deserved for what he'd put Joanna through.

But for her sake, there had to be a more civilized way. With perverse pleasure, he ripped the duct tape off Evan's mouth, quickly replacing it with his hand to stifle the inevitable shriek.

Grabbing Evan with his other hand, he dragged him into the bushes that crowded the sidewalk and pressed his revolver against his captive's temple. Evan's eyes bulged.

"Now listen, you worthless jerk. If I had my way, you wouldn't even be mobile right now. But the fact is, I'm giving you a break. For the moment, anyway. But if you make one sound, utter so much as a sneeze, I'll make you wish you'd never been born. Have you got that?"

Drew felt Evan trembling, and he wondered if the man was going to faint before he could get him to the car. With his hands still cuffed, Evan stumbled along in front of Drew with the nose of Drew's revolver pressed against his back.

At the car, he grabbed Evan by the handcuffed wrists and bent down, intending to give Joanna a bit of warning before shoving her husband into the back seat.

But, as it turned out, when he saw what was waiting for him, Drew decided he was the one who should have had the warning.

"WELL, HELLO THERE, Mr. Spencer. Good to see you again." The sight of the gun pressed to the back of Joanna's head caused Drew's blood to turn to ice.

"Val!" Evan cried. "Oh, Val. I knew I could count on you."

"Shut up, you idiot," Valerie said angrily as she opened the door, forced Joanna out of the car and pushed her into the shadows of the thick shrubbery in front of the church. "Thanks to you and your stupid phone calls, and that even more ridiculous deputy I was nearly arrested." She focused her attention on Drew. "Let him go, Spencer. And hand me your gun."

Drew hesitated. His gun was still drawn, but with Valerie's gun at Joanna's head, his weapon was rendered useless. It was an advantage Valerie clearly understood.

"Don't try to bluff me," Valerie warned. "I'd kill her in a minute. A million dollars is a lot of money, isn't it, Mr. Spencer? At most it would mean a change of plans to kill you both, but even with that hitch, Evan and I could be out of the country before midnight, and you know it."

He knew it, and so did Joanna, judging by the fear in her pretty brown eyes.

Drew shoved Evan forward and walked slowly toward where Valerie was holding Jo hostage.

"Joanna, I—I—" Evan began stammering when he saw his wife.

"I thought she told you to shut up!" Joanna snapped.

Valerie's laugh was bitter. "Come now. No domestic squabbles, you two. This way, Spencer," she said. "Hand me the gun, nice and easy. Okay, now uncuff him."

When Valerie had both guns, Evan's confidence seemed to return full force. "Come on, Valerie. Get them back to the motel. Quick, before someone sees us."

"You heard him," Valerie said. The fact that she was still holding both guns struck Drew as odd, but he hadn't figured out the dynamics of the Valerie-Evan situation until they were inside Evan's seedy apartment. And by then it was too late.

"Evan, shut off those lights," she ordered him, indicating with a wave of the gun the outside motel lights.

Evan hurried to do her bidding, and again Drew wondered how Valerie had managed to so completely gain the upper hand over her embezzling partner.

"Now, get over here and tie them up."

She shoved Joanna down hard in a metal kitchen chair and pushed Drew toward one behind it, so that when they were tied, Joanna and Drew were sitting back to back.

Evan disappeared into a small bedroom and came back with a length of nylon rope. "What are you going to do with them?" he asked, his eyes filled with very real, very nervous concern.

"Just tie them up, you sniveling coward. If you'd done what you needed to do at the time, it wouldn't have come to this."

"Evan, don't do it," Joanna said, her voice so surprisingly firm Drew felt a rush of pride surge through him. "You've stolen and you've committed fraud, but as of yet no one's really been hurt. No charges have been filed against you."

"Shut up," Valerie ordered.

"There's nothing to keep you from going back home," Joanna persisted. "We can work this out. We can. Trust me, Evan."

He'd already tied their hands and was working on their feet, but the look on his face told Drew he was considering what Joanna had offered. "I'm pregnant, Evan."

Her confession hit Drew with physical force. Pregnant! For a moment, he could only brace himself against the word reverberating through his brain. Gradually, the events of the past few days started making sense. The nausea. The fainting. Of course. What an idiot he'd been not to know, or at least suspect. Pregnant. Joanna was pregnant with her husband's child.

He wanted to touch her, to assure her that it didn't matter. He wanted to, but he couldn't, not with his hands and feet bound and a gun aimed at his head. And not with his mind reeling in a dozen different directions.

"Don't believe her, Evan," Valerie yelled, her voice shrill and cutting. "She's desperate, can't you see that? She'd say anything."

The dangerous uncertainty in Evan's eyes forced Drew out of his own deep shock. "It's true, Evan," he said. "Everything she said. No charges have been filed against you." His fingers worked the cords. "Call Bryan Miller. He'll confirm everything."

He sensed the battle raging inside Joanna's husband.

"Call him, Evan," he urged. "Do it now."

Valerie shoved her gun, a small thirty-eight equipped with a silencer, harder against Drew's temple. "Shut up, Spencer, or I swear I'll kill you and then I'll kill her." Drew saw her cold blue-eyed gaze shift to Evan and he realized in a chilling flash of insight how deadly dangerous the woman was. "Don't be a fool, Evan. You and I both know it's not that easy. They're just trying to rattle you."

Again, Drew was struck by the power Valerie held over Joanna's husband. "Tell them, Evan," Val said. "Tell them before we go why you can't go back. Why you can't ever go back."

Evan shook his head, his eyes wild, the eyes of a cornered animal fighting for its life. "Please! For God's sake, Valerie. There's no reason to say any more. No reason she has to know. She's pregnant, for heaven's sake. If we're going to leave, let's just go. We got the money. All of it right there in your stupid black-and-white suitcases." He took a couple of steps toward her. "We have nothing holding us now. Please, let's just go. Now." His voice and eyes pleaded with her.

"You're right about one thing, Evan," Valerie said. "We don't have anything holding us. Not here, anyway. Not since you closed out the last Calder Johannsen account. But if you think Bryan Miller or these two will ever give up hunting us, you're only fooling yourself. They're like that old man. They won't let go. They'll fight us every step. Always complicating things."

"Old man?" Drew asked. "What old man?"

Joanna could feel him working the cords around his wrists, and she wondered if his question had been meant as a diversion to give him time to work himself free.

"What old man?" she echoed, hoping to assist Drew in whatever scheme he was hatching. A brush of his fingertips against her back through the slats of the chair told her she'd read his signal correctly.

"Tell them, Evan," Valerie demanded. "Tell them why you can't go back and work things out. Tell them before I turn on the gas and we get out of this rattrap."

She edged over to the filthy two-burner stove and leaned down to blow the pilot light out. Immediately, Joanna could smell the deadly gas escaping.

"No. No, I won't." Evan's voice rattled with panic. "Please, there's no need for this. You can't just kill them. You don't mean it, Val."

"Oh, I mean it, all right. Just like I meant it the day that old man wouldn't sign the agreement that would have given us Lincoln Nesbitt's money."

"Valerie," Evan begged. "Please. Don't say any more."

Joanna felt a chilling premonition of the horror to come.

"Shut up, you sniveling coward. I'll say what I please," Val told him and then she walked around to face Joanna. "Your grandfather was nearly as stubborn and unreasonable as you are, wasn't he? But your gutless husband here couldn't bring himself to force the old man out of the deal."

Evan released a moan as if he was suddenly in pain.

"But I came to your rescue, didn't I, Evan? Just as I'm rescuing you now."

"You killed Jake?" Joanna gasped. "Evan? Tell me. I've got to know. Say it isn't true, that you didn't kill Jake?"

"Joanna," he cried. "Please...you've got to understand. It wasn't me. I didn't want it to end that way. It was a simple scam. Tell them, Val." But before his partner in crime could explain, he went on. "Just like the deal we pulled in Seattle. It worked the same way there and nobody got hurt."

"You killed... Jake," Joanna said, her voice racked by pain that couldn't compare with the deep grief that lodged in her heart.

"I didn't," Evan cried. "You must believe me. It was Val. I could never have done that to you, to Jake—"

Joanna had never heard a gun with a silencer fired before, but she knew instinctively that the muffled pop had killed her husband when he crumpled to the floor. The rage inside her magnified, and she struggled against the cord that bit into her wrists and cut off the circulation to her ankles.

She felt the rope around her wrist give at the same time Drew sprang up from his chair and lunged at Valerie. The sound of the second pop accompanied the sound of Drew crashing back against his chair. Joanna felt her own heart shatter.

"Valerie, please," Joanna begged, "Please, for your own sake, just go. I think Evan might still be alive." At some level, she knew she was lying, but nothing mattered now, nothing but trying to save Drew's life and the life of her child. "Please let me help him. You can go. Please. Go. I promise I won't follow you. I won't tell the police anything you've told me. Just please don't this."

Valerie's face, which Joanna had once thought pretty, had turned into an ugly mask of desperation and madness. "It's over, Joanna. Don't beg. Don't you see? It's so much easier this way." She lowered the gun and took careful aim at Joanna's head. "Just one more shot and it will all be over—"

"No! Wait! Can't you smell that gas? It's getting thicker. If you fire that gun, but you'll be signing your own death warrant. The flash of the powder—any spark at all—will blow this place to hell, and you and me with it!"

The flash of doubt in Valerie's cold eyes told Joanna she'd gotten through to her tormentor, at last. But what a bittersweet victory it was! Valerie was leaving her here to die of asphyxiation, with her husband and her lover dead at her feet.

"You're right, Joanna," Valerie said, backing slowly toward the door. "Sorry. But I can't return the favor. It's nearly a million dollars, Jo!" her eyes sparkled. "A million. A million dollars is just too much money to resist." She reached behind her to open the door, while still aiming the gun carefully at Joanna.

With one last all-out effort, Joanna jerked hard against the cords, and the last knot broke free. Her hands flew in the air, startling Valerie and catching her off guard.

Out of nowhere, a hand snaked out and grabbed Valerie's ankle, and she crashed to the floor at the same time

Joanna tipped the chair over on top of her and grabbed for the gun.

Valerie shrieked and tried to shove Joanna and the chair off her, but by then Drew had untied Joanna's feet and she scrambled clear of the hysterical woman beneath her. The hand that had grabbed Valerie's ankle—Drew's hand—now held one gun and Joanna held the other.

"Open the door, Jo!" Drew yelled before he broke into a coughing spasm.

Joanna felt light-headed as she stumbled over Evan's body to get to the door and precious air.

Behind her, she heard Valerie whimpering over Evan's body, but ahead of her lay life, and the sight of Drew Spencer walking toward her, his arms outstretched and his eyes full of love.

SINKING DOWN onto the porch swing, Joanna inhaled deeply, drinking in the fresh cool morning air. She needed to leave in a few minutes in order to make her appointment with the loan officers at the real estate office at nine. Yesterday, the district attorney had finally finished gathering the documents needed to support the many charges brought against Valerie and Charlie Lansky. Today, Joanna and the bankers and Lincoln Nesbitt would begin the task of untangling the rest of Evan's financial knots. Somehow, the complicated process that lay ahead seemed less daunting than Joanna might have imagined just a few short days ago.

Thanks to Drew, her baby's life had been spared, she reminded herself, placing a gentle hand to her still-flat stomach, and with that tiny miracle safe, every other obstacle in her life could be surmounted, if not easily, at least eventually.

Just as eventually even her bouts of morning sickness would cease, Joanna told herself, heartened by the milder nausea she'd experienced earlier. But she knew it would take more than time to rid herself of the ache that had settled around her heart these past few days. In fact, the longing for Drew that had caused that deep ache might never end, she told herself.

Since the night of their harrowing escape in Nevada, they'd been separated by the stark business of clearing up the details of what had transpired inside the seedy motel where Evan had been murdered and Drew and Joanna had nearly lost their own lives.

Drew's hospital stay had been brief, following minor surgery to repair the damage Valerie's bullet had done to his left forearm. Even though she'd visited him every day during his confinement, they hadn't been afforded any real time alone. Someone else always seemed to be there—the authorities, Bess, and other well-wishers and friends of the Spencer family. With never more than a few moments alone to talk, she and Drew hadn't seemed capable of covering the emotional distance the truth had placed between them.

Now, Joanna was beginning to wonder if they ever would. Obviously, the fact that she was pregnant had dashed whatever future they'd imagined they might share. She couldn't hate him for no longer wanting her; accepting this situation would be a lot to ask of any man. Even a man as special as Drew.

She fought the wave of sadness that threatened to overwhelm her. Even the joy of the life growing inside her couldn't quell her grieving the prospect of her future without Drew Spencer. She only wished she'd had the chance to explain why she felt she couldn't confide in him sooner.

But, now, she'd probably never have that chance.

Immediately upon his release from the hospital three days ago, Drew had been called back to Denver to testify in an important trial that involved one of his clients. She hadn't heard from him since. Bess called yesterday to see how Joanna was feeling, but she hadn't mentioned her nephew, and Joanna hadn't had the courage to ask if or when Drew planned to return to Telluride.

With a sigh, she rose and headed for the house to get her car keys. Her hand was on the screen door when the sound of a car drew her attention to the ranch road. At the sight of the little red sports car kicking up a trail of dust behind it, her heart turned over.

Still standing, nearly transfixed, she watched Drew get out of the car and stride across the yard.

"Joanna," he said, as he moved up onto the porch.

"Drew." Her voice sounded shaky and she clasped her hands in front of her to stop them from trembling.

"How are you feeling?" he asked and she sensed he'd had to fight to keep his eyes from moving to her stomach.

"Better. Thanks." God, how much longer could she endure this small talk without screaming? "How's the arm?" She wanted more than anything to touch him.

"Not too bad," he said absently, his gaze searching her face so intently she felt physically touched.

"Drew," she blurted out at the same time he said, "Jo."

They laughed, nervously.

"Go ahead," he said. "You first."

She took a deep breath for courage. "Let's sit down."

He nodded and followed her to the porch swing. For a moment, Joanna gazed passed him to the mountains, where the sun spilled a flood of golden light, making all of nature appear ripe with the promise of a new day. If there was to be a new day for them, she told herself, they had to put the past to rest.

"When I came to you in Denver, I only suspected. I didn't know for sure until a few days later. But by then, everything was in such turmoil—"

"I didn't know for sure either," he said.

"What? You mean you suspected?"

His mouth curled into a smile she'd remember for the rest of her life. "Of course. Didn't you know?"

"Well . . . no, I mean, I guess I did wonder . . ."

He reached for her hand and her breath hitched in her throat at his touch. "I didn't leave much room for guessing, did I?"

"You?"

"Yes. By the things I said and the way I acted, you had to have known almost from the first day."

She drew her hand out of his and sat back, gazing at him from a little distance. "Drew. What are we talking about?"

"Love."

"Love? But that's not the issue here, is it?"

It was his turn to stare at her. "As far as I'm concerned, it's the only issue, although I didn't think I had the right to tell you while you were a married woman. But that's all changed now," he said quietly. "I love you, Joanna. I've known from that day in Denver when you walked back into my life that I'd always loved you. That I always would."

"But what . . . about . . ." This time she was the one who couldn't look at her stomach.

"The baby?"

"Yes. The baby." The breath rushed out of her, relieved to finally have the subject out in the open. "We can't just ignore the fact that I'm pregnant, that I'm carrying Evan's child."

"No one's ignoring that," he said, as he reached over to put a protective, gentle palm on her stomach. "Although I must admit, it came as quite a shock finding out the way I did."

"I—I'm sorry—" she began, only to have him interrupt her with a gentle finger to her lips.

"And I'm sorry for taking so long to come back to you. I had to think it all through, Jo, to be sure I could be the kind of husband and father you both deserve. I could never allow you to be hurt again. When I came back to you, it had to be forever this time. And, well . . . here I am, Jo. I want to be here for you and for the baby, for the rest of your lives, if you'll have me."

"Oh, Drew." She threw her arms around his neck and pressed her face against his neck. "I've never wanted anything or anyone more."

Epilogue

"Did you ever think one hospital room could hold so many people?" Drew said, smiling as he watched his wife's gaze move from one happy face to the next.

Bess and Stella stood by the window, chatting happily with Cole and Anne and passing little nine-month-old Andy from one set of loving arms to the next. Bryan stood, looking a bit uncomfortable in his uniform, at the foot of Joanna's bed, watching his wife, Helen, arrange a bouquet of roses—a gift from the Jessups. Doc Anderson and his wife Sheila were admiring the menagerie of stuffed animals piled in a chair in the corner, while Pete and Seth, the hired men from the Spencer ranch, edged inside the room, holding a large potted plant and looking a bit sheepish until Bess called out to them, "Might as well come in, boys, everyone else is here."

"Do you mind, honey?" Drew asked. "I can run them all out if you want me to."

She shook her head and reached for his hand. "Don't you dare. I'm glad they're here. Every one of them."

And everyone, it seemed, *was* there, all their closest friends and family, including the most surprising addition to their extended family: Lincoln Nesbitt. The father Joanna had never known existed.

She smiled at Lincoln across the room. "Happy Easter, Joanna." He said, coming over to the bedside and kissing her on the cheek. "How are you feeling?"

"Never better, Linc. With our family all here together. What more could I want?"

"I know Jake would have been pleased."

She nodded and squeezed Drew's hand tighter. "I still can't believe he found you after all those years."

"We'd been in correspondence for some time when he suggested I meet with Evan. It seemed a good way to let you get a look at me and decide if you liked me before I barged into your life."

Joanna smiled at her father. "I'll never forget the look on your face the night Drew and I came back from Goldstrike. Poor Drew, his arm in a temporary cast. Me, exhausted, still fighting morning sickness—"

"Make that morning, noon and night sickness," Drew put in, laughing.

"And you, standing there holding your picture, the picture like the one in Jake's bible."

"I only wish I could have come to you sooner. If only I'd known where you were, or that you even existed—" Lincoln shook his head, still regretting the lost years.

"But you're here now and that is all that matters. My Christmas came in July—a father!"

"And it isn't every daughter who recovers her father's fortune, is it, Linc?" Drew asked.

"I have to admit, that black-and-white luggage filled with cash was a nice bonus, but honestly, just seeing the two of you home safe was all I ever wanted."

"Hey, Linc," Cole said, "Drew tells me you've moved to Telluride permanently."

Lincoln nodded. "I've been separated from my family long enough."

"And besides," Bryan put in, "I think he wants to be the first to tee off on the new Vista Grande course when it opens next week."

"Well, I must admit, the greens do look inviting." When Lincoln moved over to talk to Cole and Bryan about their respective golf scores, Joanna said in a low voice, "You never stopped believing in him, did you, honey? Somehow you knew what kind of man he was. You took a chance and believed in him and risked your life to bring us all together. How can I ever thank you?"

He lifted her hand and touched the gold band around her finger. "You already have, Mrs. Spencer. You've given me everything I want—" Despite the fact that the ordeal she'd been through just eight hours earlier still showed in her tired eyes, Joanna looked as beautiful to him as she had the day she'd stood beside him at the altar and promised to be his wife.

"All right, everyone," a stern-looking nurse called from the doorway. "Make room for the guest of honor. And I do mean make room. Everyone out. Someone's hungry and this diner is well over capacity."

One by one, Joanna's loved ones gave Drew and her their best and filed quickly out of the room.

"One hour," the nurse told them. "Then it's three at a time, and no more! You know, Mr. Spencer, I tried to be understanding about your wife needing a bodyguard, but honestly, this is just too much!"

Drew caught Cole's eye at the door and the two men laughed.

"Happy Easter, darling," Drew murmured, turning his full attention back to his wife.

"You've given me the perfect Easter present." Bending down, he bestowed an exquisitely tender kiss on her cheek before pushing the soft strands of dark hair away from her face.

She saw the tears shining in his deep blue eyes and she wondered how she could love him more. "It was you who gave the perfect gift," she whispered, her voice raspy with emotion. "The night, you saved my baby's life."

"Our baby," he corrected lovingly. "Our little girl. I couldn't be prouder, Jo. Of you. Of her. She's the most beautiful baby in the world."

"Now you wouldn't be a little prejudiced, would you, Papa?"

"Not at all. See for yourself." He turned and accepted the fragile bundle the smiling nurse handed him, thinking his heart might burst with the joy that filled it.

HARLEQUIN®

INTRIGUE®

In steamy New Orleans, three women witnessed the same crime, testified against the same man and were then swept into the Witness Protection Program. But now, there's new evidence. These three women are about to come out of hiding—and find both danger and desire....

eye WITNESS

Start your new year right with all the books in the exciting EYEWITNESS miniseries:

#399 A CHRISTMAS KISS
by Caroline Burnes (December)

#402 A NEW YEAR'S CONVICTION
by Cassie Miles (January)

#406 A VALENTINE HOSTAGE
by Dawn Stewardson (February)

Don't miss these three books—or miss out on all the passion and drama of the crime of the century!

Look us up on-line at: http://www.romance.net EYE1